QUEST FOR A QUEEN
The Lark

QUEST FOR A QUEEN
The Lark

Frances Mary Hendry
illustrated by Lorraine Gilmour

CANONGATE KELPIES

First published in Great Britain in 1992
by Canongate Kelpies

The publishers acknowledge subsidy of the
Scottish Arts Council towards the publication
of this volume.

British Library Cataloguing-in-Publication Data
A catalogue record for this book is available on request from
the British Library

ISBN 0 86241 380 X

Typeset by The Electronic Book Factory Ltd, Fife, Scotland
Printed and bound in Great Britain by
Cox & Wyman Ltd, Reading, Berkshire

CANONGATE PRESS
14 FREDERICK STREET, EDINBURGH

Contents

Relations of MARY, QUEEN OF SCOTS

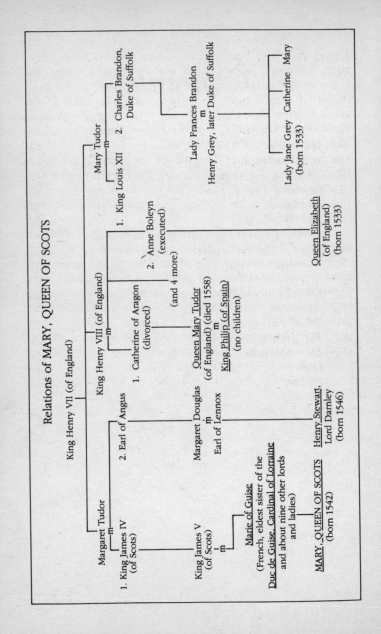

Author's Note

I have done my best to weave fact and fiction together here, as usual. John Russell and his family, Pierre and Guy, are imaginary; but all the other people in the story did exist. The Count de Lorges definitely killed Henri II as I have described, but the title is given to both Gabriel Montgomery and his father, James, Count of Montgomery, at about this time, in the records of the Garde Ecossaise. For the sake of my story, I decided to make it Gabriel who jousted with the king, though it was more likely in fact to have been his father. I invented the masque of the castle, at Mary's wedding feast. The others were performed.

The atmosphere and incidents of the French court are as accurate as I could make them. Dr Rosalind K. Marshall, of the Scottish National Portrait Gallery, has again been kind enough to check my historical accuracy, and I must also thank Max Diamond, of the British Jousting Centre, Chilham Castle, Canterbury, for information about jousting and tournaments.

I hope you enjoy reading this story as much as I've enjoyed writing it.

The Interview

'Would you like strawberry jam or raspberry?'

'Yes.'

Maman didn't turn, nor lower the hand she held raised to take a jar from the shelf. Her voice was thoughtful. 'I know a boy not a hundred miles from here who's going to get such a wallop . . .'

My little sister Lark giggled, grinning over the sandy rag she was polishing dad's helmet with.

'Who's that, maman?' I asked innocently, and she swung round and dived at me in a whirl of yellow linen. I dodged. Lark tripped me slyly, and she and maman pounced, tickling mercilessly. Maman's terrier Youpi leaped from his basket in the corner to seize my dropped sausage. Laughing, we rolled around the floor, Lark squealing with glee, maman crowing like a cock, me yelling and kicking. Dad's helmet fell with a clang to the tiles.

'Careful, Jean! You'll have the table over!' maman called.

'It was you lot started it!' I should have kept quiet. They just tickled harder, fiendishly driving their hands in under my armpits and down my neck, till I yelled, 'Yield! I yield!'

Maman knelt back, adjusting the lace frill of her cap, panting, sniffing scornfully. 'What a hero! My brother wouldn't have given in so easily, and there were six of us girls.'

I tried to recover some dignity — difficult with a little sister bouncing on your stomach. 'Well, I've to be in school in half an hour, and I'd rather not be whipped again.'

'Again?' Maman's voice was stern.

I quickly changed the subject. 'And a man can't use all his strength against mere women.'

'Man! Mere women!' Lark was small for twelve, but wiry and energetic.

'Unh! Stop that! You'll burst my points! Stop laughing, you — you whale! Get off!' I heaved over, and found myself nose-to-nose with a white suede shoe. I jumped back as if it had been a snake, dislodging Lark. She squeaked as she bumped down, looked up and gasped. Lieutenant Montgomery, second in command of the Garde! Here, in our house! And father behind him, back from duty at not eight o'clock!

Youpi yapped as if at strangers, and then in embarrassment wriggled on his belly across the floor, his stumpy tail a black-and-white blur, to apologise for not knowing his master. We all scrambled hastily to our feet. Lark pinned on the engaging smile that always charmed her out of trouble, especially with elderly gentlemen of over twenty. I wasn't charming; I turned furious crimson, painfully gripping the sagging gap at my stomach where the laces at the waist of my trunk hose had snapped.

Maman rose, flashing a 'Now see what you've done!' glare at Lark and me — as if we'd known! She took time to smoothe the long panels of her skirt and brush a speck of imaginary dust from her apron, to calm her annoyance before she turned to face them and dipped a brief, cold curtsey, her spine straight as a pikestaff. 'Good day, sir?' she said icily.

The lieutenant swept his plumed hat in a bow. 'Madame! Your servant!'

'Politeness would knock, sir, and wait until invited to enter.'

'Indeed, madame. But I did knock, and no-one answered me.'

With the carry-on we'd been having ... Flushing again, maman bowed slightly, admitting the possibility. 'Well, sir, how can I help you?'

We all knew Lieutenant Montgomery, of course; eldest son of the Count of Montgomery, First Captain of France, Commander of the Garde Ecossaise, King Henri the Second's Guard of Scottish Archers, the premier regiment of the French army. The lieutenant was in charge of the elite twenty-four men of the king's personal bodyguard. He was, as always, polished and perfect in the white uniform with its silver braid. His bow was stylish. His fair, trimly pointed beard was perfumed. A gold earring glinted in his left ear. But he was an energetic, experienced soldier. I'd be like him, some day!

For a moment he just stood in the centre of the kitchen looking round. Table, stools, stove, cupboard; green shutters, whitewashed plaster, red tiled floor; a simple cottage just outside the Paris city wall — what more, on dad's pay as a sergeant-instructor, even in the Garde — but bright and cheerful, and spotlessly clean. Just as maman started getting annoyed all over again, he smiled almost as charmingly as Lark. 'Sergeant Russell! Introduce me to your beautiful lady wife, and I'll explain why we're here, instead of on the parade ground shouting at the recruits in sackbut drill.'

'Hackbut!' Dad sounded brusque as usual, but the lieutenant just grinned. 'You will have your jest, sir! Dear God, it's soldiers we've to turn them into, not trumpeters. Not but what those big sapsies would be as much use with the one as the other!'

The lieutenant coughed delicately. Dad broke off. 'Lieutenant Montgomery, Martine. My wife, sir, Madame Martine Russell. And my children. John, and Alice.' Under father's eye, I did my best bow, Lark curtseyed.

'Martine,' dad said, 'we're in a hurry.'

'So?' she nodded. 'Excuse me one moment only. Jean!' Beckoning me, she reached for her needlecase. 'I'll put a stitch in those laces. Alice, get your brother's doublet and book. Run, or he'll be late.'

I was aching to find out what was going on. I'd never heard of an officer of the Garde visiting a sergeant's home. But I couldn't disgrace dad by arguing, or dawdling like a half-trained recruit. Lark winked over mother's head. 'Tell you after!' she mouthed, her back to the visitor.

Then dad said the finest words I'd ever heard. 'No, Martine, he's not going to school today!' Lark gasped in surprise. So did I.

Montgomery was smiling; it wasn't trouble. What did he want here? Was it dad's promotion to the Archers, at last? A special mission? What?

Rising, Maman was too polite to show her curiosity. 'Would the lieutenant care for a glass of wine?' At her glance, I jumped to set a stool for him, while Lark turned to the cupboard where the cups were kept.

Dad cleared his throat. 'No, Martine, we've no time —'

The lieutenant raised a finely gloved hand. 'We have time, Russell. An honour, madame. But I pray you let your son John serve it.'

Father, tugging at his moustache, nodded to me. I pulled myself together. While Lieutenant Montgomery ushered maman to a stool, and seated himself, I got out the pewter cups and the good wine; this was definitely a special occasion. I opened the flask without spilling any, and was about to lift a cup to fill it when Lark's eyes flickered, warning me; something on the sideboard . . . ? A tray — it should be served on a tray. I put the cups on the best carved cherry-wood one, poured them nearly full, set the bottle down, picked up the tray. No accidents so far. Then I hesitated.

The lieutenant's dark eyes were alert. 'What's wrong, John?'

He that spares to speak spares to speed, dad always said. I bit my lip. 'Sir, I'm not sure whether I should serve you first, because you're an officer and our guest, or my mother, because she's a lady.'

My parents tensed, but relaxed as the lieutenant smiled agreeably. 'The guest first, Jean,' maman said. I bowed gratefully, and held the tray for Montgomery to take his cup, trying to control the gentle rattle. Behind the lieutenant, dad nodded; I'd done well. I hid a sigh of relief.

'To fortune!' The lieutenant gave the toast. My parents' glances met as they joined him. Lark fairly radiated curiosity, bright-eyed as any real lark by the window; I stood like a scarecrow, wondering what was going on.

Lieutenant Montgomery beckoned to me. 'Come, stand here in front of me, John. Let me see your hands. M'hm. You're fourteen? What do you plan to do? Join the Garde, like your father? Good. I hear your teacher is a famous hand — or maybe I should say arm — with a birch rod. Have you felt it?' He grinned as I confessed nervously. 'What for? Hah, I played truant also. But it doesn't bother you much? Good!'

What languages did I have? English, of course. A little Latin. Spanish, Italian? Enough to swear with? Ah. How well did I ride? Dance? Use a quarter-staff, crossbow, sword? Pistol and arquebus? 'No? Really?' Well he might doubt it. Of course dad had taught me. I was a fair shot, too, but it was against regulations, and I knew fine I mustn't admit to it.

13

The questions snapped out fast, most in French, some in English. Had I ever been ill? When maman was sick last year, did I help nurse her? Youpi snapped at a fly; what tricks had I taught him? Did I play an instrument? No? Sing? 'Show me.' My throat was dry. After ten notes, 'God's wounds! Enough!' Lark giggled. What pastimes did I enjoy? Riding, skating, bowls? Backgammon, cards. Chess? 'You make friends easily? Good.'

I felt turned inside-out and spring-cleaned when at last it was Lark's turn. My wee sister was charmed to have the lieutenant's attention on her at last, but to her annoyance the questions were still about me, not her. 'How does John get on with your friends, Alice? Do they like him? Why?'

'Well . . .' She considered. 'He doesn't tease them, sir. Not much, anyway. He makes them toys and whistles. And he tells them jokes.'

'Jokes? He is amusing, your brother? Good.' Smiling, he turned to maman. 'Now, madame, pray you tell me about yourself. I know about your husband. Younger brother of Sir John Russell of Alyth, here in the service of King Henri to make his fortune. It comes slowly, eh?'

'No, sir,' dad disagreed. 'I've already won all the fortune I need.' As maman met his eyes, she blushed at the unexpected public compliment.

The lieutenant bowed on his stool, also delighted. 'My mistake, Russell! Your pardon! But tell me, madame, who are your family?'

Maman took a deep breath. 'My mother was youngest child of the Marquis de Brion, sir. My father was Sieur de l'Enduse, a small manor near Rennes.'

'I do not believe I know your parents, madame.'

'You would not, sir. My mother's father was displeased that she married beneath her. They never invited us to Court.' And then a small estate could give little dowry for a fifth daughter of six; maman had been lucky not to have to go into a convent, we all knew. A Scots

Guard of good birth was a fair match, even if he was only in the lower-ranked Company of Men-at-arms. But if great-grandfather had taken any interest, dad could have been promoted to the senior Company of Archers long ago.

The lieutenant tossed off his wine, and eyed me thoughtfully. Lark fidgeted; I bit my lip; dad stood tense; maman controlled herself nobly. At last Montgomery nodded. 'I think he'll do.' Do?

As maman opened her mouth he held up his hands in defence before him. 'No, no, madame! I can tell you nothing. Nor can Robert here, for he knows nothing. I regret, madame, but blame my orders!' He slapped dad's shoulder. 'I'll off and report to my father, Russell. John, I'll be back for you in an hour, to take you for another interview.' He smiled dazzlingly to maman, and kissed her hand in farewell. 'His best clothes, madame, but his own, I insist, not borrowed ones! He must be himself.'

He bowed himself out, dad escorting him out to his horse, while maman sat suddenly down again, gasping. Lark jumped round me, squealing. I just stood, grinning. What test had I passed?

Then maman leaped to action. 'Lark, put water on to boil and set the iron on the stove while I get Jean's Sunday clothes out of the chest. Strip, Jean! Oh, your hair! Get the scissors.' I was scared she'd snip an ear in her fluster. 'Jacques Munro has a new doublet, but the lieutenant said . . .' Dad came back. She swooped on him. 'Robert, I demand —'

'Demand away, Martine, I don't know any more than you! You heard him!'

'Ah! Men! Always making mysteries . . . There's a stain on his doublet! My God, the hose! Lark, run to the hosier for new stockings, red or black.'

Father picked her right up, fluttering, and held her close. 'Stop! Stop it, wife! You'll have the lad all upset!' I was excited, not scared; yet. 'Now, calm

15

down! John'll go in his own clothes, as Montgomery said —'

She broke away, puffing in exasperation. 'Pah! You cold-blooded Scots! Robert, it is not for any small matter that the second-in-command of the Garde comes here! Maybe his father wants a new pageboy! What a chance! New hose — it is little enough, and how can the boy be at ease, knowing that he has a darn in his knee? Are you still here, child? Go, go!'

When Montgomery came back, I'd been standing for twenty minutes, washed, trimmed, sponged, pressed, brushed and polished, in my best doublet and shirt, new hose, the feather ripped from dad's Sunday hat to replace the one on my cap that had got broken last week when we'd used it as a football. I hardly dared to twitch while maman and Lark circled me hunting for specks of dust. It was a relief to be rescued.

There was a pony waiting with the lieutenant's horse at the garden gate, and a couple of guards, friends of mine, who grinned behind his back while I held his stirrup politely for him before mounting myself. As I did so, the pony shied, jerking the reins from the guard holding them, and I had some trouble getting settled in the saddle and controlling it.

'What's wrong, lad?' the lieutenant asked. 'Can you not manage him?'

In scarlet confusion, going round for the second time, I answered honestly. 'Never that, sir, but he's got the mouth and manners of a hog!' He laughed. I suddenly realised it was another test. What was going on?

The two guards opened us a path through the crowds, into Paris by the gate beside the Bastille fortress, and along the narrow, packed streets which were stinking already, even at the start of May. 'Who have I to see, sir? Can you not tell me?' I asked.

'No, lad,' Montgomery said firmly. 'I've orders not to say.' He leaned over and put a hand on my shoulder.

16

'John, a word in your ear. I don't know how your parents have told you to behave.' I didn't either, though they'd not stopped talking for more than ten seconds. 'Don't ape court speech or behaviour. You're not trained to it, and you'd just look a fool. Your strength is your simplicity. Your straightforwardness. Do your best. Admit what you don't know, like with the wine — that's most important. We can teach you anything you need to know, but not if you play silly games. You've a great fortune offered you, lad. A chance any French boy would give his hope of heaven for. Just —' he shrugged, with a wry grin — 'just be yourself. Relax.' Relax? He laughed at my expression. 'As far as you can! You look grand. You'll do fine.' That helped. 'Don't panic.' That didn't.

'Is it not polite to use folk's titles, sir?' That might draw him . . .

He just smiled. 'You'll not go far astray if you call every lady madame, and every man my lord. They'll put you right if it matters. Here we are. Stay close by me in the crowd.' We turned into a great courtyard and dismounted. It was the royal Palace des Tournelles. I was petrified. Who was I to see, then?

Montgomery strolled in, sucking me in his wake like a rowing boat behind a galleon, and with practised ease snared a passing page from the bustle. 'Boy! Take in this note. We are expected!' Impressed by his uniform, his manner and a silver coin, the youth bowed himself away. I looked after his satin-clad back in mingled admiration and resentment. I was nothing like so fine. But if my doublet was coarser, my Scotch blood was equal to any Frenchman's. I held my head high, and wished that in her flurry maman had thought to give me another slice of sausage.

A steward bowed us into the first antechamber, packed with people hoping to present a plea or petition. Some waited for weeks, Montgomery told me. But we were led straight through into an inner room, with only

17

about thirty people there, those who had a fair hope of seeing someone soon. We waited half an hour or so, sweating and stifling in the crowd. I was growing more nervous by the minute. Every few minutes there was a surge towards the far door as a chamberlain entered and called a name.

At last it was our turn. We were ushered past resigned or jealous stares, through a passage hung with tapestries and into a shadowy little room. A small window with panes of real glass looked onto a bright garden where a fountain splashed among flowers. At a lectern by the window a man in a scholar's gown was pointing out something on a large sheet of paper to a plump lady in blue who was no more than a dark silhouette against the light behind her. In the corner a very pretty young lady sat quietly watching.

I sighed with relief at the cool quiet. The young lady and Montgomery exchanged smiles. At last the man lifted the paper and moved away. Pearls in the cap of the lady by the window gleamed as she nodded to Montgomery. He bowed, with a glorious flourish of his plumed hat. I tried to copy him. I swept off my cap, lost my grip on it as I swung it back to bow, turned still bent to snatch after it, bumped into the lieutenant, staggered, tripped over my feet and knocked the lectern crashing.

There went my fortune! I could feel Montgomery's sigh.

After their first startled gasps the ladies sat quietly as we hastily set the desk upright again. The one in blue was studying me. 'So, lieutenant. I have your note. Tell me about this boy. He has been told nothing?' Her voice was firm with authority, and a slight foreign accent.

The lieutenant bowed again. 'Nothing, er — madame.' She nodded again. 'Jean de Rouxelle, madame. His family is of minor nobility on both sides. He is well-mannered as far as his training goes, discreet —' he must have noticed father tensing at the question about the hackbut — 'and takes a hint readily.' He'd seen Lark's warning about the tray. 'He cannot sing.' What! 'His horsemanship is quite competent. He is neat in his movements.' He glanced at the lectern. 'Usually. He makes friends readily, and enjoys playing the fool. He is good at outdoor sports, knows something of indoor ones, and is kindly and at ease with children or the sick. As you see, he is not handsome, but he is sensible, sturdy and quick-witted, and has an amusing honesty which could be effective. He cares little for the cane, though his teacher is known for his ferocity. As a result, the boy's education is barely adequate, which I feel must be a point in his favour.'

Quite competent horsemanship! Not handsome! Barely adequate education! Amusing honesty! I didn't know whether to swear or spit. I did neither.

'You recommend him?'

He took a deep breath. 'I do, madame. The others, more polished, more courtly, more educated, have all failed. This boy is very different. He might succeed.' At what? I was nearly bursting.

The lady nodded slowly. 'So. Very well, lieutenant. You may leave him with me now.' He bowed again, and winked to encourage me as he left.

Strange, how the room had turned hot, rather than cool. Or was that just nerves? I wished I could see the lady's face clearly. She must be a royal lady-in-waiting. The girl still and silent in the corner, seemed to be her attendant. But although the lady's deep blue gown was silk, it had a narrower skirt and less embroidery than maman's. She liked pearls. She had them stitched round the brim of her cap, and a double rope of huge ones round her neck, far too big to be anything but fish-scale imitations.

I looked at her; she looked at me. My stomach rumbled.

I felt embarrassed. Make the best of it. I shrugged,

rubbed my belly and smiled cheerfully. 'Excuse me, madame. It's my belly asking if my throat's been cut! I'm empty. I had nearly no breakfast. I'll not die a while yet, though.'

'Ah, you have been waiting long?' I could just see her teeth glinting in a pleasant enough smile. She pointed to a stool beside her.

Glad of a seat, I sank with a puff of relief to the tapestried cushion. 'Thank you. No, madame, not very long, but that room back there, with all the crowd — it would smother you. It's better here.' My stomach rumbled again. I bit my lip to stifle a sudden urge to giggle. 'I'm sorry, madame. I can't help it.'

There was a sideboard along one wall, with a flask and glasses, and a silver bowl of fruit. I sighed in longing, and the lady chuckled. 'Boys! I know how boys' minds work! So! Would you care for some juice of oranges? And maybe fruit, or a biscuit, to quiet your internal workings?'

She didn't need to ask twice. I was over by the flask in two steps, grinning my gratitude. 'May I pour you some, madame?' I asked, just remembering my manners in time. I served her as I'd done the lieutenant, and then the other lady and gentleman, who smiled their thanks.

'Madame,' I ventured, 'who have I to see, do you know? Is it your mistress? Have you to take me to her?'

The other two exchanged a glance. Should I not have asked? But then they all smiled. 'It is the queen herself who wishes to see you.'

I was half delighted, half appalled. 'Queen Catherine de Medici! What does she want with me?' Now I could place the slight accent. This must be one of the queen's Italian friends. Thank goodness I'd been polite!

'You have no idea? So. She will no doubt tell you

20

herself, when she feels the time is right.' She chuckled. 'Would you like some more fruit?'

This time, when I offered her the dish, she took a strawberry with me. 'It seems strange to get a strawberry so early in May,' I said.

'Not all the king's gardeners work for Madame de Poitiers.'

That was the king's mistress, Diane. He spent all his time with her, not with the queen. No wonder the lady's tone was chilly. Change the subject, fast. 'My little sister rubs them on her lips to redden them.'

'Maybe La Belle Diane does, too. She is growing old, after all. Nearly sixty.' Her teeth glinted as she smiled, but she didn't sound amused.

Get away from this . . . 'My father says you should never mention a lady's age. She's as old as her tongue and a little older than her teeth.' Both ladies laughed out loud. I felt much happier.

We talked for quite a while. I did most of the talking, but still managed to polish off half a dozen delicious little biscuits and another glass of juice. The lady in blue chuckled at my stories about school and home, and when I told her how embarrassed I'd been when Montgomery had caught me rolling about the floor with Lark, she laughed again.

'Lark?' she asked. 'Why do you call your sister that?'

'Her real name's Alice, madame, but dad always called her Alouette.' I was quite at ease now. We'd finished the strawberries. Well, I'd finished the strawberries. 'And Alouette means a lark. And she's small, and sort of bright and chirpy, and she sings very well. Though I can't say so, of course, or she'd get big-headed!' She nodded her understanding. 'Maybe you could hear her some day? Maman would be honoured by your visit.'

'I doubt if that will be possible,' she said pleasantly. 'I shall be leaving Paris soon. So.' She lifted a finger,

21

and the scholar approached the window. 'Well, Signior Nostradamus?'

My jaw dropped. I scrambled to my feet. Nostradamus! The queen's own fortune-teller! The tales they told of him!

He didn't seem very awesome, apart from the sharpness of his black eyes. 'When were you born, boy? September 27th.' He nodded thoughtfully. 'Libra, madame. I told you some days ago that a Libran would be entering your service, and would bring balance where it is sorely needed. This may well be the person. And in person, if I may say so, he seems an excellent choice.' His laugh was dry, and nearly silent.

She considered, and nodded slowly. 'I agree.' She rose, and pointed to the door. 'Be so good as to open for me, Jean de Rouxelle. Come along. It is time you met the queen.'

My stomach crawled with new apprehension. The others followed us into the next room. It was long and narrow. Bright tapestries hung between tall windows. Round a lady playing a set of virginals in the middle, a group of richly dressed people, jewelled and perfumed, stopped singing, turned and bowed or curtseyed deeply. I looked up. For the first time I saw in full light the face of the lady I'd been talking to, so easy and relaxed. Those huge pearls! They were famous! I should have known!

The queen gestured to the lady to go on playing, and walked quietly to a high chair at the side, where a servant brought her wine. Her shallow, dark eyes studied me. 'So, boy? What are you thinking?'

I gulped. 'Madame, what can you want of me? You have pages —'

'More than enough,' she nodded, and considered before answering me. 'My eldest son, Francois, the Dauphin of France. He is betrothed to your own young Queen of Scots, Marie. Rather older than he is, and vigorous. Athletic, almost. And he loves and admires her, and wishes to be in all things her equal. You will see when you meet him.' Meet him?

She sighed, looking at something away beyond the tapestries. 'My son is high-spirited. Rashly so. He is — he was sickly, but is growing stronger. Stronger every day,' she repeated, as if to convince herself. 'But he is too courageous for his own good. He forces himself too hard, and takes long to recover. And yet, if anyone tries to restrain him, he is insulted, and drives himself even harder.' I could almost see the boy as she spoke of him, and felt sorry for the lad.

Suddenly she gripped my arm fiercely. 'You will take care of him for me, Jean. You will be his friend. You will help him become the man he wishes so desperately to be, but little by little. You will distract him from foolish over-exertion, but help him to grow up. That is what I told Lieutenant Montgomery to find me. A boy who is strong but kind, who will be a true servant to my son, to help and support him. To that boy the future King of France will give his friendship. Honour, money, rank, power, anything is possible for the right boy.' Maybe I'd get into the Garde? As an Archer, even? 'And I think that Montgomery may have chosen well. You will be a good friend to my son, Jean de Rouxelle. And I shall be a good friend to you.' She smiled. The shallow eyes stared steadily into mine.

My grin of joy faded at a sudden chilliness. What if I failed her . . . ?

She was waiting for an answer. What could I say? 'I promise I'll do my best, Your Majesty. But —' I had to ask — 'why me? Surely some of the sons of the nobles of France would be better friends for the dauphin than me? More suitable? Will they not be angry? Jealous?' I trickled to a stop.

She was laughing again. 'Jean de Rouxelle, I think

23

there is not one of the young men who serve my son who will be jealous of you. For I am sending you to him not as a companion, although I trust you will become his friend. You are going to join my son's household as his whipping-boy.'

Introductions

The glitter in maman's eye matched the proud gleam in
dad's. 'The dauphin's service! Marvellous!' She danced
dad round the room, laughing excitedly. 'Good fortune
at last! A bottle of wine in celebration, Robert! Two!'

'Your turn next, lass!' dad joked to Lark as I poured
liberally for us all. 'You'll sing for the king! We'll get a
singing teacher for you!'

Hugging Youpi to stop him joining in and tripping
them, Lark was puzzled. 'But why does the dauphin
need a whipping-boy?'

I laughed, but dad answered her seriously. 'He'll be
king, anointed by God! How can any common man
be let say, 'I whipped the king when he was a boy'?
So they pick one of his friends, and it's him who's
punished when the dauphin does wrong. So that —'
he interrupted her opening mouth — 'the dauphin'll
behave so that his pal won't be hurt. That's why the
lieutenant asked if you make friends easy, John. You
must make the prince like you.'

'That's it,' Montgomery smiled at me over his wine.
'He's a strange lad, the Dauphin Francois. He takes

against every boy after a while, and misbehaves on purpose to get them whipped.' What?

Maman's smile faded, and Lark was quite upset. 'That's not right, sir, for Johnnie to be hurt just because the prince is horrible and cruel!'

Montgomery reached to pat her hand. 'No, it's not exactly that, lass. It's my idea the boy's not the fool they think, John. I think he's seen that the charming crawlers he had before were only faking friendship, and got them punished for their lies. But an honest, friendly lad — maybe he'll be that lad's honest friend in return. I was told to seek among the sons of the Garde, and of all the boys I've seen, I think you've the best chance. I'll wager my reputation on it. I am wagering my reputation on it!'

'Aye,' dad put in, 'and don't you dare let the lieutenant down! Or me, and the Garde. Or your country!' I promised, gulping at the responsibility.

'Right, John,' Montgomery said. 'Tomorrow dawn, you'll come to the royal stables behind the Louvre palace, and we'll start your training.'

'Training?' I was surprised.

'Yes, of course! You must learn etiquette —'

'What's etiquette?' Lark demanded. 'It sounds tickly.'

'How deep I've to bow when I take the dauphin's shoes off, and — er —'

'You'll not get near his shoes, my lad! It's dukes' sons take them off! But first we'll polish up your riding. It's the only exercise the dauphin enjoys, and you must do it well. I've a fine little mare picked out for you. A beauty, not the hard-mouthed nag you had this morning!'

'I can ride, sir!' I protested in the big round riding-hall next day. 'This is why I skipped school. With six thousand horses to see to, the grooms are glad of an extra lad to help exercise them. And it's the young lads get the half-broken ones. I can hang on like a monkey.'

'So I saw yesterday! But you're not a monkey. Not all

26

the time, anyway. You'll ride like a gentleman. Or I'll know the reason why!'

For ten days he worked me like a slave. Star, the little mare, was all he'd said. I'll swear she moved under me to stop me falling. 'Mount — jump, don't scramble, she's not a wall! Off, and do it again. Again. Head up, hands and heels down. Don't drag at her head! She's a lady with a soft mouth and better manners than yours. Trot. Use your legs. I didn't say kick her! Heels down. Elbows in. Canter. Over the jump, lean forward — don't drop the reins — God's wounds! Catch her for him. Remount. Smoothly!' Hour after hour, the guards off duty were hanging over the rails to comment till my shirt was full of sawdust and I learned the word for 'idiot' in nine languages. My friends played truant to watch enviously. It was wonderful.

Whenever I was too sore to go on riding, there were lessons on behaviour at court; how to stand, bow, serve wine on bended knee; how to speak to the dauphin, the attendant lords, the servants, the king himself.

At the fittings for my uniform, Montgomery had words with the master tailor. 'He can't breathe. Get the whalebone out.'

'It's the fashion, even for a Scots barbarian! The whalebone stays!'

'You want your successor to use your rib-bones for the next one?'

At home, I peacocked in the high-necked blue doublet of fine wool, tight even without the whalebone, embroidered with the H and linked D's that was the king's monogram; the fine lawn shirt, the blue breeches puffed over blue hose, the blue leather shoes, and the fashionable flat blue cap with its curled white feather. Maman was in raptures, but Lark poked fun at me. 'You'll never keep it clean! It'll be black in a week!'

'That's all you know! I'll have a servant of my own,

27

Montgomery says. And I'll be paid more than father! If the dauphin accepts me.'

'Of course he will!' maman encouraged me. 'How should he not?' Well . . .

By the time I was judged presentable, the Court was about to move from Fontainebleau. I had to go on my own, since Montgomery was away on duty. Maman's eye-watering pride, dad's over-heartiness, Lark's giggles, Youpi's loving tongue on my cheek — I thought of them all the way down the thirty miles of farmland and forest, with my stomach sinking ever further into my new riding boots. I couldn't be homesick already, surely?

I travelled with a royal baggage-master, taking two hundred big mules to help with the removal of the Court. One of them scarcely noticed the weight of my little box. We arrived late that evening in the courtyard of the château, amid a million servants, pushing and panicking, hauling chests and furniture on and off carts, carrying crates, bumping bundles. 'Name of a name!' the man swore as he dismounted. 'We move every few weeks — you'd think by now —' A surge of mules swept us apart.

I looked round in dismay. My sweet-tempered Star was tired, unhappy in the crush, her eyes rolling, starting to sidle and rear. What should I do?

Suddenly a hand grasped the reins. 'I'll take her for you, sir!' a stable boy was shouting up to me in the din. 'Your name, sir?' I gaped. The lad explained briskly but politely, as if to a rather slow child, 'So that when you call for her, we know which mount to saddle.'

'I'm John Russell!' I yelled, sliding down stiffly, my legs aching.

'The new whipping-boy? Best of luck, sir!' He stood grinning, looking expectant. 'Thank you, sir?' Embarrassed, I hastily found him a couple of sous. 'Thank you, sir!' He pointed helpfully. 'In that door, sir!'

I pushed the tall door open and escaped from the chaos

into the cool, high halls inside. How had he known? Lord, my box! Oh, get it later . . .

I asked hurrying passers-by for directions to the governor of the dauphin's household. 'Monsieur d'Urfe, if you please?' Along here, turn right, first on the left . . . Across the hall, up another stair, can't miss it, carved door . . . No, no, back down there, right to the end . . .

Limping down a stair, I came on a group of children carrying bundles. A solid little boy in a lemon-yellow doublet with black fringes was prancing on a crunching pile of striped cloth and wood. Huge yellow ostrich feathers in his hat jiggled as he jumped about, his back to me. 'Real gold leaf!' he was squawking. 'In splinters! Handless cow!'

The girl facing him, who had presumably dropped the bundle, was crying already, but he started to hit her with a broken strap of wood while the rest laughed. Her green dress had huge flowers stuck on all over it, and he was buzzing about with his hideous yellow-and-black striped suit like an outsize wasp. The thought made me chuckle, in spite of my weariness, or maybe because of it. I felt sorry for the girl. I reached forward to catch the swinging baton. 'Come on, son —'

The boy jerked, hard. Tugged off balance, I fell down the last steps on top of him. He swore harshly. I was surprised by his voice, his vocabulary, and his strength as he slung me off. I grabbed at his beard —

Beard?

In the moment of shock the dwarf punched me in the belly. I fell coughing among his cheering friends. He cracked the wood down over my arm, and drew himself up to his full nearly three feet of height, his face and voice raging. 'You dare lay hands on me? Do you know who I am?'

I cleared my throat, and spoke with some difficulty

as I rose. 'I apologise. I had no right to interfere —
I regret —'

'You called me son? You thought me a child? Me?'
The dwarf raised the broken spar again with his stumpy,
powerful arm.

Blast him, he wasn't my master! If he hit me again,
I didn't care who he was, I'd shove the wood down
his throat!

Maybe he saw it in my eyes. Anyway, he controlled
his temper, smiling tightly, smoothing his beard. He was
about as old as dad, I saw now. 'A common mistake.
Most common.' Like you, his tone said. 'You find my
appearance comical? I am delighted.' He didn't sound
it. 'To play the fool, it is our trade.' It's natural for you,
his voice hinted. He waved a surprisingly small hand.
'Toto, tell this — gentleman — who I am.'

One of the others announced in a resonant, deep
voice; 'This, young sir, is the prince of puns, master
of merriment, joker of genius, wizard of wit, Chicot,
Jester-in-chief to His Royal Highness Francois, Prince
Dauphin of France.' The little man's bow was an
elaborate mockery.

I swallowed. This was a fairly important man, then.
'John Russell, sir.' I'd not say I was at his service. My
weary legs trembled as I bowed, as if I was afraid of
him, blast it!

'Ah. The latest of the whipping-boys. The Scot. France
must be running short of noblemen's sons.' He implied I
wasn't of good birth! But he hadn't actually said a single
word I could object to. He was like poisoned cream.

'You are pleased to take an interest in our affairs.
This clumsy fool —' he waved a hand at the sniffing
girl — 'this rubbish has just ruined a highly-crafted
miniature theatre — suitable, you say? Ha, ha.' His
laughter grated. 'A puppet theatre, then, a moment ago
worth some four gold ecus, now worth — nothing. I
seldom allow myself to be enraged, but this is —' He

swung on the girl. 'Peasant! You're dismissed from the troupe. I wish never to see your ugly face again.'

The girl — the dwarf, I could see now — began to cry again. 'But where will I go, sir?' she sobbed. Some of the rest were smiling, some frowning.

'To hell, for all I care!' Chicot snapped. 'Out of my sight. Out of my life. Go!' He turned back to me, his voice changing again to a purr. 'You seek Monsieur d'Urfe? I am happy to direct you. Descend the stair at the far end of the passage there, turn right, and it is the third door along. Walk straight in. It is somewhat stiff. You must push hard.'

'Thank you, Monsieur de — Monsieur Chicot.' I bowed respectfully. He and his friends flourished bows and curtseys round me.

But as the dwarf pointed out my route, the girl's head had moved just a fraction, and the others' faces had lit up with half-hidden grins. The directions were false; they led to some kind of trouble. As soon as I was out of sight on the spiral of the far stair I stopped to listen.

Over smothered laughter I heard a whisper, 'Pepi, Riard, run down this stair and be ready to shove him in!' Giggles and feet pattering away. The sound of more blows. 'Drop that, Nicola! Did you not hear me, block? Go! I shall no longer suffer you in my troupe. If you starve, what's that to me? The world is well rid of you.' The shrill voices laughed again, and faded.

I walked back. The girl was sitting on the steps, rubbing a red weal on her cheek. Silently I lent her my handkerchief. 'Are you all right, girl? What will you do now?'

She nodded, tears already dry. 'Yes, sir, thank you. Oh, he'll take me back. I need only beg hard enough to please him, as usual.'

'What? Beg? In public, you mean? That's disgusting! Hateful!'

She shrugged. 'That's the way he is. Full of hatred. Or

31

envy, maybe, because he's not tall. That's why he was so angry when you called him 'son'. And why he's such a good jester. There's always a spice of it in his jokes, to keep them sharp and keen. Like those directions — that door's to the cess-pit. And with the lads waiting to push you in . . .' I shuddered in disgust and relief. 'He can think of more tricks than any of us. But he needs me. I'm the pretty one.' It wasn't vanity; she seemed to stand back and talk about herself as if about a stranger. 'And what else am I to do? Who'd wed a freak like me? It's service, or a convent, or begging, and the dauphin's service is almost the finest there is.'

I saw what she meant; but her resignation worried me. 'I'll get a servant, Montgomery said, if the dauphin likes me. I'll take you on!'

She just smiled patiently. She was older than I'd thought; maybe five years older than me. 'It wouldn't do, young sir. You're truly kind, but you need a manservant, not me. Besides, Chicot's an ill man to cross. He'd have the dwarfs mock you till they drove you from the Court. They've done it before. I thank you, sir, indeed, but it'd not be safe for either of us.'

She wouldn't be shifted. At last, I had to agree, 'Well, all right. But I owe you a favour, er — Nicola, wasn't it?'

She nodded. 'I'm called Nicola la Jardinière.' One small hand gestured to the gaudy silk flowers sewn on all over her dress.

'Well, Nicola the Gardener, do something more for me, please. Show me the right way to the governor's rooms, before my feet fall off!'

Quite willing to delay her return to her master, Nicola led me through a maze of halls and passages to the right door at last. Just as I raised a hand to knock, the door whipped open and a tall thin man rushed out, followed by two secretaries. 'No, no, no, there's no time, not when we're moving tomorrow. What are you doing under my feet, boy? The new whipping boy? De Rouxelle, isn't it? Sweet Jesus, what a time to arrive, what a time! Well, you'll have to wait, the dauphin's on his way to bed — no, well, maybe . . . Who's that? Nicola? Good, you know the palace, take him to the chamberlain and tell him to find him a servant right away, good, good, that's something I don't have to see to, thank God. Be back here in half an hour, de Rouxelle, not a moment more, and tell your man to brush your clothes, you look as though you'd been riding all day.' I opened my mouth to say that I had, but he was already stalking away.

'Is he always like that?' I asked. Nicola nodded, grinning, whisked me off to the steward of the chambers, and vanished before I could thank her.

Within minutes a small man, red-haired and sharp-faced as a fox, was brushing briskly at my doublet. 'Page! Hot water, right away! Legs stiff, young sir? I'll rub them. Eaten lately? No? Page! Roll and cheese, and a mug of beer. Run! Here's the lad with your box, sir. Ah, good, fresh hose! Page! Where's that hot water? Feel better, sir?'

'Yes, thank you,' I mumbled rather dazedly, chewing as he combed my hair. 'You've done wonders! What's your name?'

'Thank you, young sir. Pierre Legrand, sir. Happy to be your man if you're accepted. Come along, this way, eat up, only two minutes!'

Monsieur d'Urfe whisked me off along corridors till I was lost again. 'It's not a formal coucher, that's a ceremony of going to bed, you know? No, no, not formal, not when we're moving. Of all the times to arrive . . . In here. Kneel. Stand up again. Wait here.' I tried not to pant too loudly.

At the far end of the high yellow room a small boy was being undressed beside an enormous blue-canopied bed. As in a ritual, attendant lords knelt twice as they advanced to ease off his gorgeous doublet and ruffled

33

silk shirt. Bowing servants took the used clothes and presented a lace-trimmed nightgown. The lords knelt before slipping it over the lad's head; knelt to ease off his slippers, trunks, embroidered garters and hose; knelt to hold a basin of warm, scented water for him to rinse his face and hands, and a warm towel to pat him dry. And this was an informal coucher! If my stomach rumbled here, I'd probably be executed.

As the lords respectfully folded down the gold-embroidered coverlet, the dauphin turned yawning and scratching grumpily towards the close-stool, its seat padded in white velvet, and his eye fell on me. The young prince hitched up his nightshirt, sat down and beckoned.

He was small, plump and pale. His fair hair hung lank over his puffy eyes and slack, sulky mouth. His nose was running and raw with wiping.

Liking the dauphin would be difficult.

I bowed, but the prince's eye had wandered past me to a suit his valet was displaying for him. 'Oh, no, de Mars, not that tent again tomorrow!'

His governor tut-tutted. 'Your Royal Highness must be warmly dressed for the journey. And the silver braid on the crimson is so — so striking!'

'It's so — so scratchy!' he mimicked rudely. 'And baggy! Is this my new whipping-boy at last? All right, call up the whipper, because I'll not wear it! And how do you like that, eh, my friend?' He was sneering at me.

Nasty wee rat. Suddenly I wasn't overwhelmed with awe any more. 'I don't like it at all, Your Royal Highness. But I suppose I'll just have to put up with it.' I shrugged, looking innocent. Amusing honesty, Montgomery had said. Well . . . It was hard, but I grinned.

The prince lost his smirk in surprise. 'Put up with it? You can't be that stupid. You mean you won't cry when you're beaten? You don't care?'

I made a face. 'Well, it's not my hobby. But I'm a Scot.

I'm tough. It doesn't bother me much.' I shrugged again. 'If you want to be bad-mannered, go right ahead. Don't mind about me.'

A silent gasp exploded round me. Monsieur d'Urfe turned bright pink.

The dauphin's jaw dropped. Then a kind of glee lit his pasty little face. 'Let's see! D'Urfe, call in the whipper! Call him in! Now!'

The governor drew himself up. 'Sire, this is not a proper way for a prince to behave!'

'So whip my whipping-boy!' the little prince crowed cheekily. 'That's what he's here for, isn't it? Go on! I wish it!' He jumped off the stool, scarcely waiting to have his bottom wiped before clambering unceremoniously up the steps onto his high bed and gesturing for his valet to pile up the lace-trimmed pillows behind his back. The waiting lords tucked the sheets round his legs, exchanging doubtful, carefully blank glances.

I stood still. Me and my big mouth . . .

At last a thick-set man strode in, a bundle of springy-looking rods in his hand. 'Georges!' the dauphin squeaked, bouncing happily. 'Georges, the new whipping-boy says he's a Scot, so a beating doesn't worry him!'

The whipper smiled confidently. 'Indeed, Your Royal Highness?'

'He says he won't cry! Whip him till he yells!'

Dear God, what had I let myself in for here? The wee maniac! A spurt of anger rose in me. Folk here were far too quick with their beatings! As the man chose one of the sticks, whistling it fearsomely through the air, I quietly started taking off my doublet.

'What are you doing?' the dauphin asked, puzzled. 'It'll protect you.'

'It's the best I've ever had, sire. I don't want it to get spoiled. Besides, it's your father's, not mine.' His jaw dropped. Before he could order the pages to hold me still,

I took a good grip on one of the bedposts, and braced myself. This man couldn't be as bad as old Fraser . . .

He wasn't. Not quite. His energy didn't make up for the old teacher's years of practice. But it was bad enough. The dauphin counted. 'One! Two! . . . Nine! Ten! Eleven!'

Blood started trickling under my shirt as the cane cut through raised weals. From anger, and pride, and sheer bloody-mindedness, I'd not let a whimper out of me. At every blow, I thought, 'I'll show you! I'll show you! I'll show you!' My jaw was clenched till it ached. My back was on fire; I couldn't breathe; I must yell . . . 'No! I'll show you! I'll show you!'

'. . . Fourteen! Fifteen!' The rod snapped. A rest, for a few seconds. Worse, after . . . 'I'll show you!' '. . . Twenty! Twenty —'

'Stop!' The dauphin hurled himself down the bed, between me and the rod. The whipper just managed to stop his arm in time, yelping himself in fright at his near escape from hitting the prince.

'You are brave, boy! Are you all right?' He waved to the servants around. 'See to him, you fools! Get bandages! Ointment! A clean shirt!' He chattered in admiration as I slowly unclasped my hands from the bedpost, straightened degree by degree, and felt myself led to a stool and my back attended to. 'None of the others could have done that! They all cried! Cry-babies! Marie was right, she said that a Scot would be better! You know the Queen of Scots? We'll be married when I'm fourteen. She said Scots were different. And she was right. She's always right! Do you know her?'

'Not personally, Your Royal Highness,' I managed through my teeth.

The dauphin gaped, and then screeched with glee. 'Not personally! Not personally!' All the attendants smiled and laughed as he grinned round to share the joke with them. 'Oh, I like you, boy! What's your name?'

'John Russell, Your Royal Highness. Jean de Rouxelle.'

'Jean! I like you, Jean! Do you like me?'

I took a deep breath. It was nearly possible to move without my spine breaking. 'Well, not this instant spotted minute.' There was another silent gasp, and the dauphin's mouth fell open. I was irritated. 'What d'you expect? You've just had me whipped for nothing.' The boy looked as if he was about to cry, with shock and frustration. I forced a smile. 'But in time, well, I like most people. Why not you?'

There was a short hush, as we waited to see how the dauphin would take this. Amusing honesty, eh? He could be furious. But he smiled brilliantly. 'Yes, Jean, yes! You will like me! I'll not get you whipped again! And you'll like Marie as well. But not all the rest. You'll be my friend, mine, not theirs!' He nodded firmly, my future quite decided.

Eyes shifted all round the room. The new whipping-boy, it seemed, was acceptable. Monsieur d'Urfe exchanged a glance of relief with the Steward of the Bedchamber. The whipper sensibly picked up his rods and melted away.

Suddenly the door burst open. A mob of chest-high savages capered in, wrapped in checked cloth and goatskin rugs, pheasant feathers bristling in their hats. Screeching, the dwarves pranced round the room. 'Hooch aye! Where's the Scot, then? We've come to give him a good Scotch welcome!'

Chicot, wrapped in the brightest check of all, saw me sitting in my new shirt. 'Sitting before the dauphin? Scotch manners! Here, my fine Highlandman!' he shrieked, brandishing a raw black pudding in one hand and a length of tartan in the other. 'Here's your kilties, and your supper!'

He held one end of the cloth while one of the other dwarves ran round and round me with the other end till I was wrapped in it and couldn't move my arms.

Meanwhile, Chicot slid the black pudding down under the tartan wrap, produced it again from underneath, and started to poke it at my mouth, smearing my face. 'Don't you like it? You can't be a real Scot!'

The other dwarves' hilarity had faded before the stiff faces all round. Chicot at length noticed that his backing was missing, that his rudest gestures with the black pudding weren't drawing the howls of mockery he had expected. He hesitated, looked round, saw the dauphin's expression. His own grin froze; laughing desperately to cover up, he pranced towards the door.

'Stand!' For the first time, the dauphin looked like a prince. He slid out of the bed, the lords leaping to support him, and stalked forward in his nightshirt to face the dwarf, nose to nose. 'How dare you? This is my friend! How dare you insult him and his country! The country of which I shall soon be king!' Chicot swallowed. His mouth twitched, trying to smile. The dauphin snapped his fingers. 'Take him away and beat him!'

Ach, enough was enough! Chicot had hurt me less than this malicious brat had; I felt annoyed at the dauphin, and sorry for the wee man. 'Heavens above,' I asked plaintively, struggling to get free of the cloth, 'have we not had a month's ration of beatings already this day?'

The dauphin turned, frowning; then smiled, and laughed as Nicola held the end of the tartan and I spun myself out of it. 'All right, Jean!' he exclaimed. 'What will we do with him? It's you he's insulted. You say!'

Again I could feel the eyes meeting round the room. Chicot was purple. Behind him, Nicola had a hand over her mouth to hide a grin.

I wiped off a lump of black pudding from my chin. 'Oh, leave him be. It was just a joke. And not a very good one.' I bent down, painfully, and lifted the edge of Chicot's cloth wrap. 'Look! He doesn't know anything about the real Highlanders! He's wearing his trunks under his kilt!'

The dauphin gaped, and understood the implication, and howled with mirth. 'He's funnier than you are, Chicot!' He slung an arm round my shoulders, forgetting how he'd just treated me. I yelped. 'Oh, Jean, have I hurt you?' He was horrified. 'De Mars, bring a bed for Jean. He'll sleep here, in my bedroom. I wish it! The rest of you go away! Now!'

The attendants and the dwarfs bowed themselves out. As he passed us, I saw black hatred in the look Chicot cast up at me.

He's funnier than you are! I'd made a bad mistake, making a jest of the jester.

The Boating Trip

From then on I was the best friend of the Dauphin Francois.

I had a couch at the foot of his bed; I didn't realise at first how great a favour this was. The first morning he tugged apart the heavy brocade curtains round his bed and called doubtfully, 'Jean? Jean?'

I was awake, lying on my front. 'Yes, Your Royal Highness, I'm here!'

'I was afraid I'd dreamed you,' he said, leaning back with a sigh. 'I have lots of dreams. Dreadful ones, sometimes!' With a discreet tap at the door where he'd been listening, his valet, de Mars, brought in a soft roll and a cup of warm milk, and Pierre helped me put on my hose and shirt while the dauphin was propped up with pillows as plump as his cheeks. 'Your back! It's all bruised!' he said, sipping his milk and frowning. 'Is it sore?'

Was he daft? 'What do you think?' I demanded. 'No, Your Royal Highness, it's not sore. It's just the pain makes me think that.'

De Mars' face stiffened in apprehension, but the dauphin snorted with laughter. Little brat . . . Then he frowned again. 'No, Jean. Don't call me Royal Highness, or sire. You're my friend. Call me Francois.'

'I can't do that! You're a prince,' I protested. He started to look sulky. 'Can you just see your father's face if he heard me?'

He giggled. 'Well ... When there are other people about, you can say sire. But when we're quite, quite alone, call me Francois.' I was still doubtful. He grew excited. 'I wish it!' His lower lip pouted. 'Nobody calls me Francois now that I've left the nursery. Except Marie, of course!'

Nobody to call him by his name ... Poor lad.

Pierre shoved my pallet away under the bed. De Mars combed his master's hair and lifted the tray. I licked my lips, suddenly hungry, and the dauphin noticed. 'In future, bring some for Jean too!' he ordered. The valet blinked before he bowed himself out, smiling at me approvingly.

It was time for the ceremony of the dauphin's rising, his levée. There was a solemn knocking at the door, and the attendant lords and servants knelt and bowed their way in, ignoring me. I finished dressing in a corner out of the way. 'This isn't my ruff!' I whispered.

'Sh! You'll be needing a lot of new things, sir!' Pierre breathed in my ear. 'I'll see to everything. Don't you worry.' He faded like a shadow.

All through breakfast the dauphin was bouncing and chirpy. 'We're moving today!' he kept telling me. 'We take everything, you know! Even the beds, and the windows! It's better than lessons!'

He insisted I ride beside him. His horse Fontaine, a big, lively grey, looked far too spirited and powerful for such a puny boy, but his hands were astonishingly strong. Before we were well out of the forest of Fontainebleau, he grew tired of the gentle pace his governor set. 'That big oak, Jean!' he called suddenly. 'I'll race you there!' I spurred Star after him, through a clump of briars, leaping a ditch, across a meadow scattering geese everywhere, but he reached the tree well ahead of me, and set Fontaine rearing in triumph. 'I beat you, I beat you!'

'Well, I should hope so!' I was irked by his bad manners.

'What?' He stopped crowing and gaped unattractively.

'I'd be surprised if you hadn't, sire. Star's a good little mare, but no match for your beauty there, and you ride lighter and better than me.'

A delighted grin spread over his face again. 'Yes, Fontaine is a fine horse! And I am a good rider, no? Better than you.' He exaggerated bumping about in the saddle. My face must have shown my annoyance because he stopped his nonsense, slightly taken aback. Experienced courtiers hid their feelings, laughed with their masters. 'But you ride very well, too!' he reassured me. I couldn't stay angry with him, he looked so anxious.

He couldn't apologise out loud, of course. Suddenly his face lit up. He had an idea. Lord, what was it this time? 'Do you only have one horse?'

'I don't have any, sire,' I told him. 'This is the king's.'

He giggled. 'We can't have that, Jean! You're my friend! And say Francois!' By this time the rest had cantered up to us. 'D'Urfe!' he called. 'I want Jean to have another horse. No, two. He's my friend, and friends of princes should have good horses. Besides, we're going to race, and it won't be fair if he hasn't a good horse! The best in the stables, except my own!'

The tall man bowed approval. 'Noble generosity, your Royal Highness!'

Chirpy with pleasure at the praise, the dauphin called up his Master of Horses to discuss with him the points of every mount he owned. There were over a hundred, and he knew each one. At last he made up his mind; and I owned two horses. Monsieur d'Urfe smiled, well pleased with me. We'd had two solid hours of peace. I was keeping everybody happy. So far.

Francois, his mother, his father, his bride-to-be, and the Royal Nursery each had their own household, and lived and travelled separately, moving on from château to château as the game was hunted out, the food was eaten and the cesspits filled. By July we'd stayed in seven. We'd explored from creepy, stinking, spidery dungeons, which the dauphin enjoyed, to high turrets, where he forced himself to hide his fear. When we raced our horses, he usually beat me, but I'd managed to win once or twice, risking his sulks, so that he'd not despise me — and truthfully, it wasn't easy.

We went hunting at least twice a week. Francois insisted it was always the chase, not game driven in front of a stand to be shot at. The risks he took in a kind of crazy excitement would turn your hair white, but scurrying among trees and rocks after him did wonders for my own riding. He sometimes collapsed after the hunt, and was in bed for days, moaning about his head, his ears . . . In spite of what his mother had said, he wasn't well.

In Blois, after four days' sickness he was bored and fretful, and delighted when he heard that the Queen of Scots would arrive next day. 'You'll get to know her personally now, Jean! Marie's the most beautiful princess in the world! And I'm going to marry her!'

'What will we do, Francois?' I asked. 'To welcome her. Go hunting?' His eyes lit up. But I was supposed to calm him down, specially when he wasn't well. 'Or will Her Majesty be tired, in the heat, and want a rest?'

Thinking about someone else's preferences and welfare was still a novelty. He struggled with it for a second or two, and found a compromise. 'No. She'll not be tired. She's strong! But we'll not go hunting tomorrow. I want to talk to her. I haven't seen her for ages and ages and ages! Not since May! We'll do something quieter. What can we do?'

'A picnic, maybe? A boat trip on the river?'

'Good! Good! We'll do that! That's a good idea! Arrange it, Jean!'

That was easy, of course. I just told Pierre.

The dauphin fidgeted through his lessons next morning, worse even than usual. His tight-lipped tutor abandoned the history of Italy with relief at the clatter of horses in the courtyard. We ran out to the new spiral stair built half in the wall, half out open to the court. Francois leaned out and waved wildly. Under our hands, the stonework carved like lace was hot enough to bake a cake. 'Whew! It's burning!' the dauphin gasped.

'No, no, sire, it's just the heat makes it seem that way.' He squeaked with laughter. He was finally starting to appreciate the old family jokes.

Pages racing after us like an avalanche, we leapt down the steps and across the cobbles to the shade of the arches by the great doors. A tall girl, elegant in golden damask, stooped to greet him with a friendly kiss on the cheek.

Queen Marie was pretty enough, but her nose was long; and though she moved gracefully she was far too tall to be beautiful. Not that my opinion mattered, of course. She beckoned. I rose from my knee, advanced and knelt again to kiss her hand; a real courtier nowadays! Pierre had got me a fine new suit just that week, of cream satin. I was all ready to meet my queen.

'Jean de Rouxelle? I'm glad, Jean, that you are Francois' friend.' Her brown eyes were direct, and her hand was firm, for a girl.

'He's very funny, Marie,' the dauphin broke in eagerly, 'and clever. Look, he made me a whistle yesterday!' He still had it in the breast of his doublet. With all his gold chains and jewelled brooches, a simple willow whistle had charmed him, because he had watched me make it for him alone.

'Oh?' She was kind to his enthusiasm. 'Maybe he'll make me one too?'

'A pleasure, Your Grace. As well as an honour,' I bowed.

The dauphin's nose was running as usual. As usual he was going to wipe it on his sleeve, but I had my orders, and a dozen handkerchiefs ready. I grabbed his arm, and gave him one. He looked annoyed. He hated being babied, specially in front of her. 'Sire, will you please use the kerchief, or Monsieur d'Urfe will explode. And think of the mess he'd make! We'd have to move again, and Her Majesty just arrived!' That should make him laugh.

'Oh, all right, Jean!' Giggling, he turned back to his betrothed with the lace still flapping at his nose, holding out the whistle to her. 'Isn't it beautiful, Marie? Try it!'

She peeped it, to please him, and smiled down at him, a young lady of fourteen to his puny, very childish twelve. 'It was a good idea of mine, then, to get a Scottish youth for your whipping-boy, Francois?'

'Oh, yes, Marie! He's my good friend. You like me, don't you, Jean?'

'Yes, sire.' Rather to my surprise, it was true.

I think she realised it. She gave me a dazzling smile. 'Thank you, Jean, for serving His Royal Highness so well for me.' I suddenly felt happy at her praise, but the dauphin was already tugging her off with him towards her maids. 'We're going boating! Come on, Marie! We're going on the river!'

The boating party was a great success. We had five boats. The dauphin and Queen Marie went in the first one, with me and one of the four Scots girls, all named Marie, who were the young queen's friends. The other Maries and some lordlings were in the second boat, and two Archers and a dozen servants followed us with the picnic hampers. Musicians played and the boatmen sang as they rowed us up the cool, wide stream, till we found a shady beach and deep oak groves to explore. The picnic was perfect; linen cloths, cushions, little birds baked in spicy pastry, tiny crunchy pies, honey and almond cakes, bright fruit jellies in silver dishes. I made a fire, to the dauphin's amazed admiration, and we sat singing and talking till near sunset.

I was pleased to find that few of them knew my old jokes. 'Was Madame de Lavallière's baby a boy or a girl?' the queen asked once.

'I expect so, Your Grace,' I said innocently.

Even the young lords laughed. They were neither jealous nor toadying, but there was no warmth either; just a rather off-hand politeness. That afternoon I'd heard one say, 'How long will he stay in love with his Scot? Four months is the longest so far, isn't it?' Clearly, I was just a passing fancy. A nasty sinking feeling. But then the other answered, 'This one's not too bad, is he? Maybe he'll last.' I'd last, see if I didn't!

We all enjoyed ourselves. As I gently shepherded the dauphin back towards the river, one of the Archers winked to me. 'Doing grand, son! Keep it up!' he murmured. I was pleased with myself as we boarded the little skiffs and the boatmen pushed off the bank.

A wasp flew by. Not the first, of course, that day; but the last.

Queen Marie flinched as it hummed round her red hair, but she sat still. Her maid didn't. She started to flap at it. 'Sit still, Fleming!' the queen told her, smiling. 'You'll upset the boat!'

She was right.

The foolish girl stood up, swinging her arms wildly. The dauphin was laughing. I thought of the dwarf Chicot, like a wasp, and grinned back. The boat tilted to one side. Naturally, we all hurled ourselves back to steady her. We overbalanced the other way. The Marie fell into the water.

So did the dauphin.

I was in right behind them.

I found myself in water up to my neck, on tiptoe but perfectly steady on firm sand, one hand holding the side of the boat off me and the other holding the dauphin's belt. He was spluttering and excited, not alarmed, still laughing as he wrapped his legs round me like a monkey. His parents wouldn't think it was funny, though, when they heard of it!

The Marie in the water was floundering about, splashing and squawking. She didn't seem able to find her feet. I couldn't let go of the dauphin to help her, or he'd drown, being six inches shorter than me. But I pushed him out towards her. 'Grab her, sire!' I said, and in his excitement he did just that. He gripped my shoulder with one hand, leaned out away from me, reached far out for her skirt and pulled her in to where the servants and boatmen now leaping out of the skiffs could get a hold of her.

It took about ten seconds, I suppose, from the first tilt to the moment when the others grasped the girl.

At the drag of his sopping clothes as we waded ashore, the little prince's lip started to tremble for the first time. But when the servants cried, horrified, 'Your Royal Highness is all wet!' his eyes met mine. 'No, no, it's just the water makes you say so!' he crowed, and doubled up in triumphant laughter at their uncomprehending stares.

Queen Marie took charge. 'Fleming! Stop screaming! Be silent, all of you!' There was a natural hush. 'Now. The day is still warm. No-one will come to any harm if we get you all out of those wet clothes. Who has a towel? Kindle that fire again! Find dry clothes for the dauphin at once!'

Pierre had packed towels and slippers, in case we got our feet wet, but he hadn't expected anything this drastic. However, one of the Archers stripped and in a few minutes we had the little prince dried and struggling into much rolled-down stockings and uniform, giggling as they tickled and stuck. I stayed in my ruined satin, wrung out and dried damp at the fire. The Marie had to make do with a tablecloth toga, to the dauphin's glee.

'Now.' Marie looked round us all, gathering us into a conspiracy. 'If word gets out, we'll all be stopped from doing this again.' We nodded. 'Do we want that? No? Then we must keep it secret. Not a whisper! Not a hint!'

It was her maid, Fleming, who objected. 'Your Grace, it's not right that His Royal Highness should be denied recognition of his heroism!'

'What?' Nobody knew what she meant.

'Prince Francois, Your Grace! He rescued me from the river. He pulled me back.' She smiled at him gratefully. 'He saved my life.'

I'd told him to, and held him, but I couldn't spoil it for him. I nodded. 'Yes, Your Majesty, His Royal Highness pushed away from my hand to reach her.' Not a word of a lie . . .

The queen and all the rest looked at me, and at Fleming, and at the boy flushing scarlet. Her face was bright with admiration. 'Francois! To save my friend, and say nothing! How noble! Truly princely!' He bit his lip, delighted. She clapped her hands, and we all joined her applause. The dauphin glanced up at me, but I was smiling and clapping too, letting him have all the credit. His smile fair glowed, and he wiped his running nose bashfully. On his sleeve . . . Oh, well.

In the end we crept into the castle by back streets and back stairs. Queen Marie paid the Archers and boatmen silver for their silence, and the story never came out in the Court.

Francois took no harm of his adventure. He was so happy that he had won his beloved Marie's praise, he gave me a jewelled dagger that would pay for a score of satin doublets, and not a word spoken.

I never received my pay, but I didn't need it. The dauphin loaded me with presents; money, jewels, clothes, horses, a royal falcon. He was desperate to keep my friendship, and buying it was the only way he knew.

Here, my man Pierre was a godsend. He knew the Court and its ways. Without his advice on how to behave, I'd have appeared ignorant or stupid in a Court always ready to notice and condemn awkwardness and impertinence. He helped me with the dauphin's gifts. He told me how long to display them, to be tactful; he knew the jewellers who'd pay the highest prices, and the bankers with the best rate of interest — all for a percentage, of course, but he still did much better for me than I'd have done alone.

He ordered new clothes for me; far more, and finer, than I'd have dreamed of, but I found I needed all of them. I've no doubt he made a commission off them, too, but I was too grateful to care. We disagreed on only one thing; he said every young man in the Court dressed as richly as he could, and ran up debts to do it; I insisted he pay my bills at once, even if it meant keeping a plainer style. Besides, I said, it was silly for me to pretend to be one of the nobles, when everybody knew I wasn't. Why waste money? He muttered balefully. But the dauphin was so generous I dressed as fine as I should, finer really than I was happy in — though I got used to it fairly quickly, I must admit — and was still well on the way to being rich.

Another source of income was the flow of bribes I was offered, to help people kiss the dauphin's hand, or supply his household with mousetraps, or get their children into his service. When I told him about these 'presents' the prince was astonished; not that it happened, but that I'd mentioned it. 'Take the money, Jean, and don't bother me with the requests.' Typical.

Sometimes people begged for a letter to release a relative held in prison under a private warrant, a lettre de cachet. If the warrant hadn't been issued by one of the really great lords, a Bourbon or Guise, I'd mention it to Francois, and occasionally it tickled his fancy to graciously grant the plea. If I misjudged his mood he'd snap at me pettishly, 'Don't give yourself airs! It's I am the prince, not you!', but his anger never lasted long, for I just turned it off with a joke and in laughter he'd lose his annoyance.

He liked me, for the moment; but I remembered the first day. And I saw what happened to his pages — floggings, brandings, ears cut off, instant dismissal or imprisonment for tiny or even imagined offences.

What with the dauphin's uncertain temper, and the constant worry about what his mother would think of the way things were going, my fingers, eyes and toes were constantly crossed.

And still, I only knew the half of it.

See-Saw

Occasionally the dauphin gave me the evening off. It wasn't a regular thing, but every three or four weeks he'd grow edgy over a day or two, and would say to me, 'Jean, I don't want you tonight. Go away.' I'd sleep in the pages' room, and in the morning he'd wake late, but fresher, calmer-tempered. I thought he must ask his physician for a sleeping draught.

One of those nights, in October, I came back to get gloves I'd left behind. The guard at the door stopped me, to my surprise. 'Master Russell,' he said, 'Were you no sent off the night? Are you meant to be here, sir?'

'Of course I am, Forster!' I grinned. 'Don't you know me by now?'

He frowned, but stood aside. 'I didn't think you were like that,' I heard him muttering while I pushed open the heavy door. Like what?

The dauphin's voice shrieked at me as I entered. 'Shut the door, you fool! They'll get out!' He was crouched down with his back to me. Several of his young attendants were there too, laughing at something squeaking

51

on the floor. I leaned sideways to see what it was that was so amusing.

They had a basket there, full of sparrows. The dauphin was plucking them. Alive. Just one wing, and letting them go, to try to fly. And he and his friends had rackets, to play tennis with the little birds . . .

I'd seen worse in Paris. Public executions in the Place de Grève. Cats and dogs and heretics burned alive in the Easter celebrations; pigs flogged to death to make the meat softer. I quite enjoyed bull and bear baiting, and ratting, and I loved the bright valour and excitement of cocking. But that child crouched greedily over the tiny flutterings — I groped behind me for the door and slid out again, my throat full of bile.

The man-at-arms shook his head as I rubbed my mouth in disgust. 'Aye, sir,' he said quietly. 'I thought that wasn't your taste. He gets the stable lads to bring him in the birds, or kittens maybe, every so often.' He was an elderly man, and left his post to pat my shoulder like a father.

'Why does he — ?' I heard myself asking. But it was a silly question. He did it because he enjoyed it. He'd had me whipped for nothing.

The guard took it another way. 'Hide it from you, you mean? Well, lad, I'm thinkin' it's a compliment to you. He knows you'd dislike it, so he tries no to let you see that side o' him. An' I'll tell you this,' he went on warmly, 'you've made a fair change in him! It's no half as often he does it now. Maybe you'll wean him off it entirely, in time, the same as you've improved his manners.'

'What?' I couldn't believe it. From what I'd seen of how he behaved . . .

'Man, you've no idea! Before you came, if he was ill-tempered he'd stab any man with his wee sword for just bein' there. He'd drink red wine an' sick it up off a balcony on top o' the guards below. Aye, quite deliberate. For fun. The sergeants gave us hell for the stains. He ruined a horse near every week with his crazy ridin'. But he's far, far better now. His tutors, even, they say he's startin' to listen to them. You've no been whipped once, have you? Since that first time? See? He's improvin'.'

Well! That heartened me. 'But what do I do now?'

'H'm.' He considered. 'Did he see you, in there?'

'I don't think so. I don't think anyone did. They were all looking at — looking down. And it was darker where I was, by the door.'

'That's fine. Just say nothin'. Accept it, for you'll no stop him. No by speakin' out. You'd just turn him against you. He can't bear to be crossed. He'd turn wilder than ever. Just go on as you are, lad.'

It was good advice. I went up to the pages' room and played knucklebones, and tried to forget the side of my master that I could do nothing about. At least he didn't expect me to join in. If he knew I knew, and I sometimes thought he did, he said nothing either. And as the man-at-arms had said, I was sent off for the night less and less often.

When the Court returned to Fontainebleau in November the dauphin reluctantly let me go home for a few days' visit. Youpi went half crazy with delight. Lark was pleased to see me, but she flatly refused to sing for me. All summer I'd sent home money for singing lessons, and Maman said the old Italian musician who taught her praised her to the skies, but I thought maybe Lark herself knew she wasn't as good as he said. Maman exclaimed how thin I was, and how stylishly dressed! She showed me off proudly round all the neighbours, and dad took me in to the Garde barracks to meet Lieutenant Montgomery again, and display me to his friends. We talked and talked. It was such a relief to relax! I couldn't tell them, of course, about that night. If word of it spread, we'd all be in trouble.

At the New Year, there were always great celebrations.

One day King Henri and Queen Catherine came to dine with their son, with half the Court. After the banquet, the dwarves put on a special entertainment.

The jester Chicot had been working hard to win back into the dauphin's favour. He had apologised to me, crawling till my stomach crawled too, and gushed my praises to everyone. But though the dwarves often entertained us, Nicola seemed to be avoiding me. I was rather hurt.

That night, with the help of some acrobats, they acted an uproarious play about a princess, named Marie, of course, kidnapped by the ogre Calvin Cowsbelly — a dig at the Reformed Religion that made us all laugh — and rescued by a gallant knight, naturally named Francois, played by Chicot. Nicola acted 'Marie'; in the hands of the dwarves' servant, a huge, grossly fat man who played the giant, she was a tiny doll. We all cheered her on as she wriggled from the giant's clutch, dodged between his legs, climbed up him like a tree, twisted her legs round his neck, dragged his orange wig down over his face, thumped his head with a balloon and yelled for help.

'Francois' and his friends charged to the rescue. The fight with the giant was ear-splitting, breath-taking and achingly funny, with a glittering fountain of dwarves tossed high, tumbling shrieking through the bright candlelight to land in the arms of their friends and race back to the battle. At last, to cheers and applause from everyone, the giant sank under a final swarm of small people. The dwarves pranced all over him, the heroine tied a pink ribbon round his neck, and they led him up to Queen Marie to kneel and beg for pardon.

Chicot was praised for his gallantry, skill and wit, and Marie motioned to an attendant to give him a purse. Amid his bows of thanks, he gave me a special smile and bow where I stood behind the dauphin's chair.

The tables were removed and the musicians struck up

a gavotte. Francois wiped his nose — on a kerchief, I was pleased to see — and led his bride-to-be out to lead the dance. They made an odd couple, the tall, elegant girl, bright in carnation silk edged with silver, and the small, podgy dauphin, treading the intricate measures of the dance. Purple and gold didn't suit him. But he adored her and she liked him, maybe for that very reason; everyone smiled on them.

I wasn't of a rank to take part, and was glad not to, for I danced as if I had two left feet. The dauphin insisted I join in his own lessons, and I was improving, but his dancing master still winced at the sight of me. I stood watching, not yet bored by the pageantry, the brilliant clothes and jewels. King Henri was taking the polite duty dance, which he never omitted, with his wife, both watching their six-year-old son Charles dance with Diane de Poitiers, who somehow made every woman in bright colours look merely a gaudy frame for her severe black velvet. The dwarves scattered among the gorgeous crowd, grinning, joking, hoping for tips.

Behind me, there was the sound of a slap, and a gasp of pain. 'The half is mine!' a harsh voice whispered. 'Remember it in future!'

I swung round. A short yellow figure was slipping away between the chairs. Nicola was standing there holding a hand to her face, cursing under her breath. 'Nicola?' I said. 'Was that Chicot? Are you all right?'

She drew a breath and tried to smile up at me. 'Yes, sir, thank you!' But as she lowered her hand, I saw the mark of fingers on her cheek. I lifted her a glass of wine from a passing pageboy's tray and stood where I'd shelter her from curious eyes. 'I'm grateful, sir.' She didn't drink it; she dipped a corner of her handkerchief in the wine to cool her face without lifting her make-up. 'Bastard! We call him the Wasp, you know, sir, for his yellow suits and his temper.' She glanced up at me. 'Watch out, de Rouxelle, or he'll sting you.'

I was taken aback. 'Me? Are you sure? Why?'

'He hates you.' I could scarcely believe it. Hate? Real hate? For me? 'Yes, sir, indeed. You made him look a fool. Playing the fool's our trade, but that was different. We're used to being laughed at.' She shrugged with a wry face. 'We have to be. But it maddens him. And it's you who's the dauphin's friend now, not him. Oh, yes, he hates you.' She looked up doubtfully. 'That's why I've stayed away from you, sir. I was sorry to do it, but if he knew I was your friend, he'd hurt me just for that.'

'You are my friend?'

She bit her lip. 'If you don't mind, sir?'

'Mind?' I saw she was afraid I'd feel insulted that a dwarf dared claim friendship with me, and tried to reassure her. 'How silly! I'm glad, Nicola! But why? And you warned me on that very first day. Why?'

She shrugged uneasily. 'I don't know. You're — kind. You remind me of home. Before father died.' She sighed. 'I didn't choose to come here, you know. My mother sold me to the Bishop of Bourges to train as a jester, and he gave me to Madame de Poitiers. I liked her, but . . . she sent me here.'

'Aren't you happy?' I felt sorry for her, in her expensive gown, cut down from some fine lady's cast-off, and her fake jewels and her rouge.

'Happy?' Her soft voice and pretty face were bitter. 'But what else can I do?' She sniffed, braced her shoulders and set her cap straight. 'Ah, it's not so bad, if you don't weaken . . . There's the dance ending. You'll be looked for. Take care, now!' She slipped away cautiously, to appear smiling and bouncy at the other side of the room.

As the court settled back in their seats, a musician came forward with a lute. He sat on a stool below the king's chair, and a slight figure in blue stepped demurely out to stand beside him. At first, thinking about Nicola and Chicot, I paid scant heed to the new-fangled Italian madrigals. But as a lovely clear voice soared in a delicate cascade of notes to fill the hall and hush the murmurous gossip, I turned and stared. It couldn't be . . . But it was! It was my little sister, Lark!

It was the first time the Court had heard Lark. Charmed by the clear voice, they applauded, demanding more. She blushed, and sang again.

At Queen Catherine's lifted finger, I came to kneel by her. 'Well, de Rouxelle?' she smiled. 'She does indeed sing like a lark. Are you pleased?'

'I can't believe it, Your Majesty!'

'And will you still be unable to tell her how well she sings?' There was a sly twinkle in the shallow eyes.

'Well — scarcely. Not now, Your Majesty,' I had to admit.

As she laughed, from her other side a deep voice said, 'De Rouxelle? Come here.' It was King Henri, his long dark chin jutting above his gold-lace ruff. Though I'd stood by the dauphin in his presence before, this was the first time he'd paid attention to me personally. I knelt, to rise at his nod and stand nervously waiting. He looked me up and down silently for what seemed an age. 'I hear good things of you, my boy.'

Diane de Poitiers on his left fanned herself gently, the scented white egret feathers dazzling against her gown. She might be over fifty, but she was still the most beautiful woman there. A widow, she never wore any other colour but black and white. Her friends and supporters wore them also, in tribute. The king was in white satin tonight; the queen, cherry-red brocatelle. Then I forgot all the rest. Madame de Poitiers turned her great violet eyes on me, and for that moment I was the most important person in the world because the full attention of La Belle Diane was on me alone.

'The dauphin praises you highly, young man.' Her voice was sweet and soft. 'As does Monsieur d'Urfe. You have done well.' I gasped for breath, overcome by her beauty, her smile, her presence even more than the king's.

King Henri nodded jovially. 'Well, indeed! As we hear that your sister does, also!' He beckoned Lark forward. She knelt beside me, and rose at his genial nod to cast one glance at me, bright with glee and triumph. 'A lark indeed, and a surprise for you, I am told! A gift for the New Year!'

I stammered my thanks, but he raised a hand. 'We have another gift for you, at the instance — at the insistence of our son.' I tried not to make a fool of myself by gaping as he gestured to a pageboy to hand me a scroll.

'Open it, Jean!' The dauphin was grinning by his father's knee. Slowly, nervously, I broke the seal and spread the stiff parchment. It was the title deed for an estate. Loyes, not far from Calais.

'Well, Sieur de Loyes? Does it please you?'

I stammered in amazement. The king laughed again, and reached to draw his son into the embrace of his long arm. 'My son Francois is well pleased with you, Jean de Rouxelle, Sieur de Loyes. And therefore so am I.' Queen Catherine, Madame de Poitiers, everybody was smiling. Lark was glowing with delight for me. The dauphin was squeaking with mirth at my face.

'It's far too much, Your Royal Highness!' I protested.

'No, no, Jean!' he grinned, pleased and proud of his generosity. Then his mouth twisted, suddenly cynical. 'Take it while it's offered!' There was a sudden silence between us, till the truth we never admitted to, that some day his humour would change, was quickly covered by my thanks.

Lark and I spent a happy afternoon together while the entertainments went on in the great hall. She told me about the visitor who had sat in the corner of her singing teacher's room one day, the summons to sing before the queen's musicians, the joy of being accepted for training. But she had persuaded our parents to say nothing, because she wanted to surprise me.

'You did indeed, lass! Your voice is wonderful!'

'Oh, it's nowhere near finished yet,' Lark said. 'I'm learning the new bel canto style, and I've a long way to go. Tonight was just a joke on you. It was Queen Catherine who suggested it. She likes playing jokes. My tutor and I, we just picked a dozen songs that suit my voice, and I've practised nothing else for days. But I'll be staying in Paris for a while yet.'

I hid a stab of disappointment. 'Well, you can visit me some day on my new estate!'

She grinned. 'How big is it?'

'Lord knows! Pierre can tell us. He knows everything — or at least he knows where to find out.'

It turned out to be very small; three farms and a shabby eight-room manor-house, with an old steward and his daughter to look after it. But dad, who rode out to visit it with me that spring, was bursting with pride. 'A bit of right good luck Montgomery's eye lit on you, eh? Your mother's fair hoarse with crowin' over the neighbours! May it be the first o' many, son! But mind — you're high now, but hall seats are slippery!'

He wasn't wrong.

In May the Royal Nursery and the dauphin's household moved to opposite ends of the huge white maze of the Château de Chambord, in the best hunting country in France; but the very day we arrived, he fell ill. He was wretched, moaning pitifully, 'My ears ache! And my head!' Complaining, crying, making our lives as much of a misery as his own. With loving care Marie came several times to visit him from Blois about six miles away.

One morning he sat up, peevish but determined. 'Marie's coming today. And tomorrow she's moving to Amboise, that's thirty miles away, and I'll not see her for ages! I'll get up to greet her! I wish it!'

To my joy and surprise, that day Lark was one of

Marie's attendants, very fine in a new pale green gown. As Marie kissed the dauphin, I slipped round. 'Away, Lark, you'll never keep it clean!' I murmured in her ear.

She recognised her own words. 'No, I've my own maid!' she whispered back, as I'd told her the year before. 'What a change for us, eh? Her Majesty asked for me to join her household, for I'm half Scots, and Queen Catherine agreed. Sh! They're looking! I've to sing for them.'

The dauphin was upset at losing Marie. 'You'll join us soon, my dear,' she tried to soothe him, but he fretted, not yet well, interrupting Lark's songs to call for sweets, a fan, a drink, a cold wet cloth for a headache.

However, when Marie rose, saying she'd visit his brothers and sisters in the nursery before she left, and I was dismally anticipating another long evening of sulky, bad-tempered card games — he cheated so badly it was hard to pretend not to see him, and he still didn't win — he suddenly shook his head. 'Jean, I'm not considerate.'

'Who told you that lie, sire?' What was this leading up to?

He smiled, but persisted. 'Jean, this is the first time you've seen your sister in months, and maybe the last for as long. Marie, may Jean escort her back to Blois and stay to see her off with you tomorrow?'

His bride smiled. 'How thoughtful, Francois! Of course he may come!'

'On you go, then, Jean!' the dauphin said. 'Don't hurry back, now! Oh, and send for the jesters as you go, to amuse me in my room.' Surprised and grateful, I sent a page off to call Chicot and then pass word to the stables to saddle me a horse along with those of the queen's attendants.

While Queen Marie was in the nursery, I took Lark up the huge double spiral stair that ran from the ground

60

floor of the castle right up to the walkways on the roof. We strolled among the high turrets, looking out across the stables and kennels, over the village where the hunt servants lived, down the long alleys through the deep forest that was preserved all round the castle specially for the royal hunt. Lark complained that her voice was suffering; Marie's musicians were good, but not as good as Catherine's. Then she studied me, suddenly serious. 'You look tired, Jean! Is it so hard, serving the dauphin? What's wrong with him?'

'Generally, or just this time? He's got a sickness somewhere inside his head, that his mother and the doctors won't admit exists. Maybe it's that. Or maybe he's got a cold. Or the water disagrees with him. Who knows? Who cares?' I leaned wearily back against the warm stone. 'Lord, Lark, I'm not tired. I'm worn out. I wish I was back with old Fraser flogging me.'

Lark might be better dressed, but otherwise she'd changed little. She still had a charming grin. 'It must be bad!' But her tone held sympathy. 'His mother thinks the sun shines just on him, but they say he's a brat.'

'I just hope they don't tell you the half of it, wee sister.' At my side a salamander, the emblem of the dauphin's grandfather, was carved in the white stone. In the setting sun it glowed like a blood-red dragon. I stuck my hand in its mouth. 'It's like this. One wrong move, and snap, he'll have my hand off.' She looked anxious. I shouldn't be worrying her. 'Ach, never heed me. As soon as he's better, I'll be better.' I leaned to peer down into the courtyard. 'They're bringing out the horses. Come on.'

Suddenly a dwarf raced up. 'There you are at last, de Rouxelle! We've been hunting you all over! The dauphin's calling for you and your sister!'

'What is it?'

'I don't know, but you'd best run!' If I'd been less tired I might have noticed a malicious gleam in his eye. We rushed down the stair, slipping on the polished marble.

A new young guard opened the dauphin's door for us as we ran through the anterooms, and we hurried in.

There was a dreadful din of dogs yelping. Something raced squealing in front of us. It was a puppy, about eight weeks old, limping, wailing. A voice I knew well called, 'Catch it! Don't let it get away!'

God, he was at his tricks again! I must get Lark out! I reached to drag her back, but it was too late. Puzzled, she'd scooped up the pup and was walking forward with it. Then she froze, staring appalled.

The dauphin was standing by a brazier in the middle of the room, surrounded by a dozen young dogs. They were standing on their hind legs in a crazy circus act, with four of the dwarves capering round them, cracking whips. In that same instant Lark and I saw the dauphin take a wriggling pup and press its forepaws deep into the red-hot charcoal. It screamed, and cackling he tossed it down to join the rest, wailing in agony, whipped into movement, dancing desperately to keep their burned paws off the ground.

Lark leaped forward. I grabbed at her arm. I missed. She slapped him.

Their faces were equally contorted in horror.

Behind them Chicot's face grinned in the red glow of the brazier, like the carved dragon on the roof.

Striking the heir to the throne. Lark would lose her hand, at least. Torture. Flogging. Prison for life. Execution. My God!

The dauphin reached for his dagger. I flung my arms round him. Death for me, too. As he drew breath to screech for help, call the guard, have us arrested, I snapped in his ear, 'I'll tell Queen Marie!' Not his father, who would avenge the insult to a future king, whatever he said to the boy after. Not his mother; she'd forgive her son anything and us nothing. His beloved Marie, his adored bride-to-be, whose approval he valued . . .

He stopped, like Lark, as if frozen.

There was a knock at the door, and a page entered. Too well trained and experienced to raise an eyebrow at the pups, at the prince and me hugging in the middle of the floor, he stared blankly ahead. 'Your Royal Highness, Her Majesty of Scotland is about to leave, and asks are you well enough to come to bid her farewell, or will she come to you?'

We all stood still. Lark was as white as a sheet, realising what she had done. The dwarves were waiting for the signal, to attack or ignore us. If he spoke . . . or if Queen Marie came back . . .

I whispered, 'What would Marie think of you?'

Slowly the boy mastered himself. He nodded to the page. 'Tell Her Majesty I shall attend her in a moment.' He pushed aside my arms, and stepped clear. Ignoring Lark completely, he snapped his fingers at Chicot and the other dwarves. 'Not a word of this. Ever.' They bowed obedience.

He spoke to me without turning. 'Get out. I shall never see you again. Never.' Head high, more like a prince than ever before, he walked out.

Chicot bowed elaborately. 'Jean de Rouxelle, Sieur de Loyes, may I wish you a happy retirement from Court?' His voice was creamy with triumph. His friends followed him from the room, after the dauphin.

Lark collapsed on the floor, nursing a hurt puppy. 'Oh, John! I'm sorry! I'm sorry!' she whispered, tears streaming down her face.

I looked at her, and the crying puppies, and the sumptuous, wretched room, and a weight I'd scarcely known I was carrying fell from my neck. 'You know something, Lark?' I said. 'I'm not.'

I hurried her down to safety among the queen's ladies, well warned that whoever asked, she knew nothing about anything, I'd just said I couldn't come. In my room, Pierre was slashing silver buttons off a doublet to poke into a bulging saddlebag. I gaped, panting. 'How did you know?'

'Pages have big ears,' he grunted. 'All due respect, young master, your sister's well named the Lark. Bird-brained!'

I couldn't disagree. 'Horses —'

'Waiting for us in the village, or I'll gut the grooms.'

'Us? You mean you're coming with me, Pierre?'

He glared. 'If you get a move on! Suit on the chest there.'

It was dull tan linen, plain and ordinary. 'I never ordered that!'

'No. I did. Thought we might need it. Get it on, then, sir!'

'But you're the dauphin's servant really, not mine. Why take my side?'

He puffed out in irritation. 'God knows, when you're wasting time this way! Do you stir yourself, sir, or must I dress you too?'

Just as I pulled off my trunks, the door was flung open. I jumped round; it was Sir Robert Niddrie, the Archer in command of the castle, looking grim. I tensed. 'Don't stop, no, no! Packed already, man? Good, good. Better get out fast. Lose yourself in Paris.'

'We will, sir!' Pierre was strapping up the bags already. I was hauling at my mud-brown hose, too flabbergasted to speak.

'Good, good! Sorry I can't wait.' The big man put a hand briefly on my shoulder in brusque sympathy. 'A pity, lad. A great pity. Good luck!'

As he slipped stealthily out of the door, a tiny figure slid in under his arm. Pierre snorted. 'Dear God! Secret getaway? Could sell tickets!'

Nicola ran over to help me with my points. 'I tried to warn you, but I thought you'd gone to the gardens, sir! Oh, sir, I'm so sorry!'

'Sorry doesn't mend dishes!' Pierre snapped. 'Come

on! No time to hang about!' The saddlebags were heaved
to his shoulder.

'Wait! The Wasp hoped you'd be arrested. Now you're
disgraced, it may be enough, but he may send men to
attack you on your way home, like robbers. Not to kill
you, I think, in case your sister talked, but — take care!
Go roundabout!'

'Thank you, Nicola!' I hesitated, and then bent to
kiss her cheek. She blushed as scarlet as my discarded
doublet. 'I'll see you again.'

'I hope so, sir!' I flushed too as she kissed my hand.
'The passage is clear. Everyone's in the courtyard seeing
off Queen Marie. Good luck, sir!'

If there were attackers, I never saw them. Within two
days my mother was weeping over me. I have to admit —
I cried too.

Explosion

Three days later Lieutenant Montgomery marched in. 'What happened, you tomfool?' He was neither friendly nor dandified this time. His golden beard jutted dangerously. 'You realise your disgrace will affect me? Well?'

Twice a week for a year I'd faced down the dauphin in a rage, and he could do worse to me than Montgomery. 'I'm sorry, sir. I can't tell you.'

'What?' Polite but steady opposition was the last thing he'd expected. About to explode, he stopped and eyed me carefully. 'Can't, or won't?'

'Won't, sir. Not till you give me your word that you'll not tell a soul. I shouldn't even tell you. But I need advice. And help.'

'H'm.' He studied me. 'Go ahead. I'll say nothing, on my honour.' That was good enough for me . . .

When I'd finished, he was nodding. 'I've had a letter from Niddrie. He didn't know details — no-one does. Just that there was trouble. The prince has been ill since you left. Raging with fever. His parents visited him, blamed you, wanted to send to arrest you. But that threw him into a worse state, till they swore to leave you alone. He seems to think a lot of you, in spite of all.'

'I — I liked him, sir. In spite of all.'

'Could Jean not go to his estate?' maman suggested, wringing her apron to floor rags. 'He'd be out of the dauphin's way.'

Dad grunted. 'Easy to arrest him there.'

Montgomery agreed. 'Or a quiet murder, even.' Maman started to pray. 'Hush, now, madame. There's little enough risk. If you're harmed, Jean, your sister will speak out — and no-one wants that. And while you're alive, she's safe. He'll keep that jester gagged, too. I'd say you're in small danger, while you keep silent. But what do you do now, eh? H'm.' He sniffed, and looked at me shrewdly. 'What do you want to do, lad?'

'Same as aye, sir. Join the Garde. But it's impossible now. Isn't it?'

He grimaced. 'Tricky ... But I'll see what can be done.'

A week later I was summoned by his father, James, Count of Montgomery, Chevalier de l'Ordre du Roi, First Captain of France, Commander of the Garde Ecossaise. I nearly died of fright. But I'd had to trust somebody ...

The count eyed me coldly across his fine polished desk as I stood to attention on his equally polished parquet, knees trembling, throat dry. 'John Russell, you have caused a great deal of trouble. You will tell me exactly why you left the dauphin so abruptly.' His tone was stern.

I had to try twice before my voice would obey me. 'I regret, my lord. It is at His Royal Highness's own order that I remain silent.'

'You wish to join the Garde? Then I insist.' I couldn't ... I stood silent. 'You are discreet, at least. H'm.' I stood sweating while he paced round me, stroking his greying, neatly-trimmed beard. He seemed not too displeased. What was he thinking?

He stopped, facing me. 'In view of the circumstances, I thought it best to inquire what were His Majesty's own wishes.' What? I'd not realised the brown suit was so tight. I could barely breathe. 'He considered the matter with care.' He would. He perhaps knew of his son's nasty habits, suspected what had happened, and didn't want any scandal. 'He says that you did well by the dauphin while you served him.' So? Hurry up, for God's sake! 'He agreed.'

I couldn't help squeaking like a child with relief and joy.

The captain smiled thinly. 'Yes. However, His Majesty —' Lord, what now? — 'King Henri has declared that as a former friend of the dauphin, you can scarcely join the ranks as a man-at-arms. He graciously commands that you be enrolled, not, of course, into the Royal Bodyguard; but there happens to be a vacancy for one of the hundred Archers of the Garde.' He lifted a parchment from the table beside him. 'John Russell, Sieur de Loyes, here is your commission in the first and finest Company in Europe. Do you accept it?'

What a stupid question!

And so, not ten days after fleeing from the dauphin in fear of my life, I took my oath to defend the persons of Henri, King of France, his heirs and successors, which meant the dauphin, with that same life; and was enrolled as most junior member of the Royal Guard of Scots Archers.

When dad heard, he turned puce. 'I'll have to salute you, lad!' His hug nearly cracked my ribs, and his moustache fair bristled with pride.

With the money Pierre had saved for me, I was far richer than I'd ever dreamed. We bought a new house in the Marais, the area that had been the Paris ghetto and was becoming fashionable now, in the Rue où Dieu fut Bouilli; the Street where God was Boiled. There were at least twenty monasteries and convents near us, and not a few nunneries of the unholy kind too; it was a lively area.

We now had five rooms on three floors. There was a big room on the first floor to receive visitors, where my parents slept, and my own room. Above was a bedroom for guests, or for Lark and her maid whenever she was in Paris, with a smaller room beside it for Pierre and dad's new valet Louis, and the maid that maman could at last afford slept in the kitchen. I hired a groom, who slept above the stable across the yard at the back.

Lark wrote that all was well with her. No-one had pressed her too much about why I had left the dauphin. She was quite happy in Queen Marie's train, going on with her music lessons, and learning how to be a lady.

From the moment I got my first uniform, fine blue doublet and trunks and a white surcoat with the silver crescent moons, sign of the Goddess Diana, that the king had chosen to honour Diane de Poitiers, Montgomery took me under his wing. 'You're no small boy now, lad! You're a gentleman. Your honour is the honour of the Garde Royale Ecossaise, which is the king's honour. It must — must! — be upheld. Never forget that as an Archer, you outrank any French lieutenant, or any untitled landowner. A man of good blood will, we trust, treat you with due courtesy. If not, you must teach him his manners. Never demean yourself by brawling, of course. Politely request a meeting with his friends, to arrange a quiet moment when you can argue the question of precedence in the correct form, with your sword. I'll always be happy to support you.' I thanked him, rather taken aback.

'But if any common man shows less than respect, use your boot, or a whip on the impertinent scoundrel. Don't dirty your glove or sword on him! You're now an Archer. You'll live or die with honour!'

I didn't much fancy this kicking people out of my way business. Besides, I was only five foot two. But if that was what an Archer did . . .

They took me out to baptise me into the Garde. I paid. Six of us finished off twenty-three bottles of wine and brandy. Next day I couldn't lift my head without being sick. Pierre gave me a foul potion to drink and a cold wet cloth for my head, cleaned my uniform, and warned me coldly that unless and until I could handle my drink I'd better stay sober. Which was good advice and I followed it. And if I should have kicked him for impertinence, I didn't.

Every Archer needed a valet, which I had, a groom and two or three men-at-arms to support him in action, backing his lance, it was called, so that the hundred Archers actually made a fighting regiment of about four hundred men. Dad picked me three men he knew well, and I saw little of them, for they knew their business better than I did.

In addition to the Royal Archers, the Garde had three companies of men-at-arms and mounted archers. Dad was now Homme d'Armes, or Sergeant-Major, of the First Company. Montgomery set me to work with him for some weeks, to learn my drills. I didn't argue, of course, though I was sure I knew them already. I found out rapidly that there is a vast difference between repeating the forty-two orders of the hackbut drill, for instance, along with the sergeant, and actually standing out in public alone, giving the commands yourself. Your brain jams. On one dreadful occasion I watched a squad march right off the edge of the parade ground, my mind a total blank, trying frantically to remember how to turn them while the sergeant beside me commented disgustedly, 'Sir, for God's sake say something, even if it's only goodbye!'

Every day now I spent among the finest fighting men in France. I practised fencing, with rapier and dagger. I bought a fine pistol and a new arquebus, and Montgomery himself started my training in the use of a lance. He was a fine jouster, as good almost as the king himself. With his advice I bought a charger and started riding at a barrel of sand slung from a gallows, building up strength and control of my lance. I listened eagerly to tales of courage and glory in past wars and duels, and soaked up the atmosphere of high duty and honour. I was having the time of my life.

That summer the king declared war on Philip, King of Spain. Philip's wife Mary Tudor, Queen of England, sent troops to help her husband's general the Duke of Savoy attack the north of France. The Duc de Guise, our best general, was away in Italy. So the elderly Constable of France took command. With his nephews, followers of the Reformed Religion — for even some of our nobility had caught it — he tried to hold off the attack. But they failed. In August our army, including two companies of the Garde, was destroyed, and the Constable himself captured. There was absolutely nothing to stop Savoy's Swiss mercenaries marching into Paris itself.

The Court went into a panic. The treasury was carried to the crypt of the Abbey of St Denis for safe-keeping. The dauphin was sent off south to safety in Touraine, and the whole Court, dressed in penitential black, walked barefoot to the Cathedral of Notre Dame to pray for deliverance.

De Guise's brother the Cardinal of Lorraine, a tall, handsome, striking figure, preached the sermon. This defeat was God's punishment of France, for allowing our country to be befouled with vile heresy. Calvinists were servants of the devil. They damaged statues of saints, even figures of the Mother of God; they attacked priests, burned churches. How could God support a country which permitted such wickedness? To win God's favour, this evil must be rooted out; every heretic destroyed!

Queen Catherine frowned; Diane de Poitiers nodded

71

eagerly. The king, of course, agreed with Diane. And the people of France believed the cardinal. Where there had been a kind of uneasy indifference, now a frenzied hatred sprang up. Calvinists were arrested, tortured and burned, their houses looted and destroyed. Informers against them were rewarded with some of their goods, at the suggestion of Madame de Poitiers. And it brought us disaster.

Dad was busy training new men; I was working hard, enjoying life, looking forward to going to war. Lark was busy and happy with Queen Marie. But for the first time in her life maman had time on her hands.

Now that she had a maid, and her children were grown, she had little to occupy her. She was happy enough at first, arranging the new house, chattering cheerily about carvings and crockery and painted cloths for the walls. But by July she'd lost some brightness, somehow. Her mind was always somewhere else. Then there was a change in her dress. She had always liked rich colours, with plenty of embroidery. Now she bought dark grey cloth. We thought it was for Annette, the maid, but it was for maman as well.

Father objected. 'Where's your red gown, Martine?' he asked one day.

'Oh, it's in the chest,' she said with a smile. 'It's too gaudy for a plain woman to wear. A sign of worldly vanity.'

'Vanity?' His voice rose in annoyance. 'It's a sign of your position, and mine, and Jean's. I'll not have my wife dress no better than her own serving-maid. See to it you're properly gowned tomorrow, Martine, as befits your station.'

She faced him firmly. 'I am already, husband. For we are all servants of the Lord, and vanity will drag our souls to hell.'

'God!' Father stared in horror. 'You're infected! You're a heretic!'

'I've found the truth, husband. Yes, I am a member of the Reformed Religion. I'm glad it's come out at last, for it has been weighing on me.'

'It'll do more than that! It'll kill you! You'll be burned! You've seen it — you've smelt it from the Place de Grève! How can you face that?'

She smiled, a curiously exalted smile. 'If I am chosen for martyrdom, Robert, the flames will waft my soul straight to Heaven. I am not afraid.'

He groaned. 'No, Martine. I can see that. You're mad!'

We loved her. We did our best to bring her back to sanity and safety.

Dad tried first, calling on her love for us. 'You'll bring ruin on the rest of us, Martine, execution even, for sheltering you!'

'I do regret that, Robert, truly, but I can no longer live a lie.'

My turn next. 'Maman, the Pope and Church condemn all the works of Calvin, Luther, Zwingli, all the other ranters!'

She was firm; 'Ranters? They preach the Holy Bible, the true and only Word of God. Show me there any mention of Pope or Church of Rome!'

Lark tried. 'Maman, do you not fear the wrath of God?'

Maman smiled, almost pityingly; 'Should God be angry that a poor soul seeks Him through His own Word? Join me in the search for Truth!'

Dad again. 'The Church declares your soul will be damned, Martine!'

She actually laughed. 'Who in the Church is fit to decide what will best profit my soul? Cardinals or bishops, with their lands and jewels, silk doublets, palaces, aye, and lady-loves? Or should I ask the Pope? At least there's only one Pope now, instead of two — or three.' She held out her hands to him. 'Robert, my dearest, I

73

pray you come with me to our chapel,' she begged him. 'There's a pastor visiting there now, a Master Sinclair. He's a Scot like you. He can explain to you better than I can what we believe, and why.'

Dad scowled. 'A Scot, eh? I know of him,' he said. 'And his name's not Sinclair. It's Knox. A murderer and traitor!' His voice was rising. 'He and his kind have tempted you from your soul's safety, from your love and loyalty to your family and your God. Pray I don't meet him, Martine, for if I do I'll kill him!'

Weeping, maman ran up to her bedroom. Dad drew one long breath and followed her. I could hear blows, and maman crying out, 'God! God!'

Much later dad came down again. I was hugging Youpi for comfort by the parlour fire. He slumped on a bench and stared at me, white-faced, for a long time. Suddenly he sank his face down into his hands, and wept, deep, racking sobs that shook him back and fore, while tears dripped through his fingers. 'God, Johnnie! She'll burn! What can we do? What can we do?'

We loved her. We did our best to keep her safe. We took turns to guard her. She was never let out alone. We told the neighbours she was ill with a fever of the brain. In a way, it was true enough.

She forgave us, with a gentle, resigned smile, for what we were doing.

Nothing could have depressed us more. She was so sure she was right . . .

The Court moved out to St Germain for a quicker escape if the Spanish approached. Dad couldn't get away, but rather reluctantly, for she was generously worried about possible risk to her young musician, Queen Marie granted Lark leave to stay in Paris to look after maman.

And then it all blew up. Literally.

One afternoon I was going on duty at St Denis, guarding the Treasury chests of gold and jewels that were down in the crypt beside the holy relics. I was leading a squad of men-at-arms to relieve the Archer before me when, with my mind on maman, I took a wrong turning in the dark passages and got lost. In some embarrassment I headed for a faint light. Cover up my slip by demanding, 'Who's that? What's going on here?' Very official. And in the fuss, find out where I ought to be . . .

The light was a candle beside two men kneeling by a heavy iron-strapped door. As I opened my mouth, I suddenly realised the tools they had in their hands were wire picklocks. Thieves!

I used my breath 'Sergeant Boag! Arrest those men!'

Boag was fast — faster than I was. He'd already drawn his sword, shouting to the men to surrender. With execution facing them, of course they didn't. They kicked their candle over and charged at us. One stabbed the man-at-arms who was holding our torch, and shoved him to knock me aside. Somebody fell on the torch, yelling. A man passed me and darted off down the corridor. I pushed myself up, not scared, but outraged, laughing with excitement. The thief mustn't get away, after knifing one of my men!

He was dimly silhouetted against the faint glow of a wall torch down the passage. The man-at-arms on my right had his arquebus half raised. 'Fire, Hamilton!' I shouted, pointing. 'Fire!' He hastily took aim, and just as the thief reached the turn he pulled the trigger.

There was an almighty bang by my ear, and a stabbing, thudding agony. The light flared into lightning, tilted crazily and went out.

I woke dully, slowly . . . Aching . . . Bandages . . . Cool cloth on my face . . . Cloth in my mouth. I spat it out. Someone bent over me. 'Maman? Maman?' Jaw hurt. Head hurt. Gap at one side where I'd lost some teeth.

'Oh, John, thank God! Lie still! You're hurt.' I knew that, dammit . . .

'Lark? Wha' . . . happen'?' Mouth wouldn't work. Talking hurt. Everything hurt. Couldn't see properly. One eye bandaged.

'The arquebus exploded just beside you. You're lucky you're not dead. Your jaw's broken, and you're badly cut. But the physician says your skull's not cracked. Your thick head!' Trying to cheer me.

It gradually came back. '. . . Thief? An' Hamil' on?'

'The thief's caught, and — er — Hamilton's fine, Johnnie. Don't fret.'

Not right, her tone . . . 'He's . . . dead? Eh?'

After a moment, she nodded.

Pierre was there too. His hands were shaking. 'Thank God you're alive, young master! When they brought you in —' He broke off, amazingly upset.

'Maman?' I whispered. I needed her. Why wasn't she there? Lark bit her lip. I saw there was more to her worry than me. 'Where . . . ? Lark?'

'Oh, John! She's gone!' She burst into tears. Pierre looked disgusted.

My head was agony. And my mouth, and neck, and left arm . . . Left? Oh aye, I'd had it raised to point. Oh, God, maman . . . 'Gone? Ou' of house?'

'Are you well enough, sir?' I must look worse even than I felt.

I flapped a hand at him. 'Don' was'e time! She's away ou'?'

'Yes, sir. Stupid bitch Annette let her out of her room. Knew I was at the well and the young mistress at market —'

The sobbing out of sight behind me must be Annette. Things blurred, cleared, blurred. Voices boomed, faded, boomed again. Must help maman . . . Do something . . . Think . . . 'When d'she leave?'

'About an hour ago, sir. None of the neighbours have seen her. Said she was ill again, delirious, and they're all looking for her. Couldn't stop them. But if they find her, and she preaches at them, they'll know . . .'

'M'hm.' I was lying on a mattress in the kitchen. Though Lark tried to hold me back, Pierre helped me to my feet. In spite of his arm I could barely stand. Bandages all over my top half. My trunks were covered with dark red stains. Blood. Never get it out . . . Concentrate! I couldn't have been home long. I could just about manage. If I sat for a minute . . . 'Pierre. Ge' me dressed. 'N' then you an' Anne'e leave. Come back la'er, if safe.'

He glared at me, insulted. 'Run away? Pack, sir, yes, but won't —'

There was a soft rapping at the door. Annette wailed and Lark drew her breath in, hissing in fear, but I gestured at the door. 'Yes,' Pierre agreed. 'Provost's men would thump harder than that.' He opened a crack, just enough to peer out. 'Friend of mine, sir!' A whispered warning; maman was at the Protestant pastor's house in the Rue des Capucines. Not far; but they were holding a prayer meeting. And the neighbourhood knew about it.

I held my head. Only six days before, Calvinists leaving a meeting had been stoned, and many killed. Rescue her. In my state? I had to . . . But how?

Call on the Garde? No. The sergeants would delay till too late — they knew civil disturbance was a matter for the provost, not them.

Dad would have a squad ready in no time at all.

Dad was away in St Germain with the Court. Oh, my head . . .

Lark jumped at another knock.

It was Montgomery. He came in, asking quietly, 'How is he?' Then he saw me. His jaw dropped. 'What are you doing up? God's wounds, John, have you no sense? You should be in your bed! Why on earth . . . ?'

77

It was Lark who told him. I was finding it hard to stay on the stool. The room swung madly, and grew and shrank round me like a nightmare. At last I heard her say, 'Sir, will you help? We must try! We must!'

I couldn't see him. I stared round dully. 'Where . . . ? Pierre, where is he?' The door was open. I forced myself towards it. Outside, some blue uniforms were scattering at top speed in various directions.

The cold air helped clear my head. I heard Montgomery telling Lark, 'And we'll bring her back safe, lass.'

I interrupted. 'Goin' wi' you.'

'You're going to your bed,' he said flatly. 'Trust me to see to this for you, lad. A determined butterfly could beat you, the state you're in.'

'I'll go,' said Lark. 'I'm small. Nobody'll notice me. I can slip in places you and your soldiers can't.' As he argued, she grinned perkily up at him, excitement at the idea of an adventure displacing her worry for the moment. 'I've got to! It's my mother, sir! And anyway, how will you stop me? It's only three streets away.'

He sighed. 'God's wounds, you're as crazy as your brother! Well, at least put on the maid's dark clothes instead of that yellow!'

'Come on, sir,' Pierre muttered. With Annette's help he hauled me up the stairs and settled me on my bed. True, I was nearly blind, my head was splitting, I could scarcely stand. I'd only get in their way. It was still hard to let them go without me. Especially my wee sister.

A few years, or minutes, later I heard the clatter of shod hooves. Pierre, leaning out past the shutters of my room, told me what was happening. 'A score of them, young master. Mounted Archers. Sergeant's a friend of your father's. That's them off, hear them? Lord, the lieutenant's quick! Your sister's on his saddle-bow. Hear the crowd rioting? Men running to join in, and women — hear the feet?' I could barely hear his voice over a roaring. In my head, or in the street? 'Glow in the sky

— there's a house on fire. Sparks flying, high as Notre Dame towers. Set the whole city up if they're not careful. Men down there lifting the cobbles from the road.' He leaned further out. 'What's happening?' he called.

A voice yelled, 'A gang of filthy heretics trapped! The house is burning! We'll get the rats as they run! Come on, mates! We'll miss it!'

Pierre turned back into the room. 'Stone them as they try to escape,' he said bitterly. 'Your sweet lady mother, and your sister — no, sir, lie still! I'm no hero, and you're not fit. Nothing you nor I can do.'

A year, a century — maybe twenty minutes later I thought I heard hooves again. 'Pierre? Is tha' them? Safe? Tell me, for God's sake!'

'Horses, sir. Uniforms — the Garde. Just two of them. Women with them. Your sister, sir — and your mother!'

Seconds later maman was at my bedside, sobbing, apologising for leaving, demanding how I was, calling for fresh hot water. I was suddenly so happy . . . She was there, she was safe, I was safe . . . All was well . . .

Then a silence.

Montgomery carried Lark in. She was unconscious.

'Where will I lay her, madame? Here beside your son for the moment?'

Maman started up from beside me. Her hair was coming down from its neat cap. 'What's wrong with her? She came out just behind me! One of your men picked her up onto his horse, I saw him!'

He laid Lark down, and spoke reassuringly to me, ignoring maman as she sat down and anxiously rubbed Lark's hands. 'She's all right, John. I sent for the provost, but I'd no great hope he'd risk his men to save Calvinists. When we reached the house, the thatch was burning already. Some of them had tried to run, but the crowd had killed one and hurt five or six more with stones and bricks. The rest wouldn't risk it. I shouted to them that we'd protect them, but they didn't believe me. Then your sister slid down from my saddle and before I could stop her she'd darted into the house, with the burning thatch falling round her. A braver act I've never seen.' He cast a cold glance down at maman. 'If they'd come out earlier, we'd maybe have got them away with little harm done.'

'We didn't know you in the smoke!' she snapped. 'But when Lark came in, we knew God had sent her to save us!'

'It was Johnnie sent us!' His anger worried me, and I reached out a hand to maman, who clasped it gratefully. 'When they came out, the stones started flying again. The mob were wild with the fire. Two of my men were hurt, but we drove them back and closed in round the Calvinists, and lifted your mother and sister to ride off. I shouted that we were arresting the heretics, or we'd never have got them away. We had to force our way out as it was. They threw stones after us as we left. It was one of them stunned your sister. I shouted to Sergeant Forbright to take the prisoners to the provost, but he knows as well as I do that we want no trouble brought here. They'll all escape in the dark. We'll owe him, John.'

Even as he was speaking, I could feel Lark stirring beside me. She groaned, opened her eyes, tried to sit up and was sick. Maman cradled her in her arms, rocking her, crooning to her, 'You're all right, my dove!'

Montgomery sniffed. 'Yes, madame. When you boast of your sacrifices for your religion, remember your daughter near sacrificed herself for you. Look, her hair's singed! She was that close to burning for your sake! Think on that, next time you feel you must parade your holiness.'

Maman pushed herself to her feet, with a gasp of pain. She was paper-white, but her head was proud and high. 'Sir, I honour my daughter's courage as much as you do!

You wish to judge who is to blame? Then consider that we met only to worship God, and had done no harm to those outside who meant to kill us.' She turned back to Lark. 'Annette, bring me water to bathe her face.' She set a hand to the small of her back, with a grimace. 'Ah! A woman struck me as I left the house. It's been paining me — it's —' With a look of surprise, she collapsed on the floor, said, 'What — what is it?' and lost consciousness.

I rolled over painfully. I could just see the small dark stain of blood where a thin blade had stabbed her.

She died within a day.

The Wedding

I nearly died myself. I was far too ill to go to maman's funeral. Dad told the neighbours she had been killed by the Protestants, which in a way was true.

I was unconscious, thank God, through most of the daily visits of the Garde surgeon, probing for pieces of the shattered arquebus that had sprayed into me, and festered deep in my body.

I was delirious during the visit of King Henri himself.

When at last I woke to awareness, Dad was sitting at the foot of the bed, turning something over and over in his big hands. He glanced up, saw my eyes open, and stood up almost unbelieving. 'John? Are you awake? Oh, thank God! You're back in your senses. Oh, Johnnie, Johnnie!' His hands trembling, he held up above me the thing he'd been polishing. 'You see this? It's a gift. For you. From the king's own hand.' It was a matching rapier and dagger, beautiful, the gilded hilts set with pearls, the damascened blades rippling with light among the gold inlay.

I couldn't care ... I missed maman so much ... We all did.

On top of that, I had a trouble of my own. I felt guilty. If I hadn't got lost, or if I'd acted differently, Hamilton might still be alive. I'd got a fancy sword, but one of my men was dead.

Dad dismissed my worries, glad to talk shop instead of skirting round — other subjects. 'Think, lad!' he barked. 'The treasury would have been robbed, an' the Garde's honour an' reputation damaged. Hamilton was a man o' the Garde. In Omni Modo Fidelis; Faithful in Every Way. That's our motto, an' our duty, an' we'll die to do it if we must. Never fret about this. It was a flaw in the metal; no in you!' He winked. 'But mind, never admit you were lost. You saw a light an' investigated, that's what to say. Then you'll get credit for zeal, no luck!' He patted my shoulder. I winced — it had had another splinter dug out of it the day before — and he backed away out, like a big clumsy dog. He was always uneasy about sickness.

The wounds slowly healed and the stabbing aches faded. I had more sympathy for the dauphin than I had before, if he had to bear this so often. But even when the pain passed and I felt well enough, I could neither see nor hear clearly. Everything was blurred. And I simply couldn't keep my balance. As soon as I sat up, even, I felt sick. So I stayed flat on my back for another three months, irritable and impatient, rubbing Youpi's ears as he lay beside me on the bed, staring at the ceiling and snapping at my visitors, even my friends from the Archers. Lark read to me for hours; from the Bible, often. Maman's Bible, in French instead of Latin — illegal, but . . . Some of the stories were interesting, when you could understand them. That Sir Jacob was a right tricky lad!

Lark hadn't been badly hurt, physically. But she had been out in the riot, and run through fire, and been stunned; and wakened to find maman dying beside her. And maman had always said she was finer stuff than I was. She wasn't too bad in the house, but it was long before she could force herself to go out among people, even for her beloved singing lessons.

I asked her once what it was like. She looked away, her eyes going dark with horror, and started to cry silently. 'The faces! Hating and jeering and ugly! No, not the Calvinists — the Catholics!'

'Well,' I said, 'you can't blame them. Calvinists sacrifice babies, and drink their blood. Like Jews. Why else do they meet in secret?'

'Why? Because they're persecuted! Don't be silly, John. Do you think maman would do anything like that? I don't believe it.' She turned fiercely to me where I lay flat out on the bed, and for a moment I feared she'd throw herself on top of me. 'But the hatred — I believe that! The laughing, jeering faces — that was real, satanic evil!'

I was quite shocked at her. And she'd made my head ache again.

Her singing teacher, a Fleming called Arcadelt, arrived one day. 'Mademoiselle, our voice is at a delicate stage of training. It is vital that we continue. Until we are recovered, we shall sing here for one hour at noon each day. And we shall exercise for six hours, privately.'

He was ruthless with her. 'Sing through the mask of the face. No, no, no! Imagine the neck of a swan! The voice lifts and turns! A swan, not a pelican! Our voice is waddling, girl, not soaring! Think of the phrasing, girl, that third note is doubled. Make the first note ring. Use the stomach muscles! How can we control our breathing, if our belly is wobbling like a jelly?' She was always tired out when he left. Singing seemed to be as tough as riding.

She sang her exercises again and again for him, and over and over when he had gone, till we were tearing our hair. But when she practised songs, shutters opened all round us as the neighbours enjoyed the music too.

Lieutenant Montgomery called regularly. No-one, to our relief, asked why the Garde had interfered in a civil matter. We just kept quiet about it. And at Christmas he had news for me; for my 'bravery and zeal', just as dad had said, I was promoted to ensign. I felt a real fraud.

Maman would have been delighted, I thought. And suddenly at last I could weep for her, and the wretched hole in my life started to heal.

Then one day something inside my head went 'ping', like a bubble bursting, and the dullness in my ears cleared magically. When I called Lark, my voice shaking, and asked her to lift me, though I was limp as a wet thread I could raise my head, sit up, try to stand. Youpi, Lark, little Annette, even Pierre danced round me in delight.

It took a long time for me to regain my strength, but I found I'd grown two inches! I wasn't tall, and never would be; but now I was five feet four inches; quite passable for sixteen.

Meanwhile, the war turned round. The Spaniards dithered about in the north until the weather was too bad for campaigning. Their mercenaries, unpaid, went raiding all round for food, including my estate at Loyes.

But now we had a new army. Queen Catherine had gone herself to the Palais de Justice to ask the Paris Parlement for aid. She didn't order them haughtily, as King Henri would have done; dressed in black, for she'd just lost a baby daughter, she begged them to help save their country. Charmed and flattered, and knowing very well what would happen if unpaid mercenaries captured Paris, they gave her three hundred thousand francs, which raised an army for the Duc de Guise, on his return from Italy, to head north in spite of the weather, and drive the Spanish and English troops out of all the captured towns; even, in January, out of Calais itself, which had been in English hands for two hundred years.

The prayers and sacrifices had apparently worked.

The king and the dauphin rode on a ceremonial entry into Calais, and the Duc de Guise was worshipped as the saviour of France. Nobody thanked Queen Catherine. But then, nobody ever did. And the wedding was finally, formally announced between Marie, Queen of Scots, nearly sixteen, and Francois, Dauphin of France, just fourteen.

The Archers were polished to an incredible degree of brilliance. Each of us was allotted a visiting notable — an ambassador, a bishop, or maybe one of the nine Scottish delegates who came to work out the marriage contract. We had to shepherd them round, keep them happy, make sure they were in the right place at the right time. Each of us, except me.

My hair had been shaved for the fever, and was still unsightly. Scars wove a violet web all over my face and head, which ached easily even yet. I had a huge puckered scar in both cheeks, where a lump of metal had gone right through, taking some teeth with it, but fortunately not touching my tongue — I must have been yelling at the time. The sight in my right eye hadn't fully returned, and nor had my strength. I wasn't fit for any duty till March, and then was stuck at headquarters doing paperwork, well warned to keep myself in the background till I looked approximately normal. Frankly, I began to doubt if I ever would, but Lark reassured me. 'Don't worry, Johnnie, in a year or two you'll have a fine beard to hide the scars. You'll be handsome again — or maybe at last! And in the meantime, you can hire yourself out as a scarecrow!'

She herself was nearly recovered. She still liked Annette to go out with her to market, but she could stay out all day now at her lessons. Queen Marie hadn't recalled her, being occupied with planning her bridal gowns with the expert help of Diane de Poitiers.

Finally, one day, Lark came home in a glow of glory.

'John! I've been chosen! I'm to sing in the masques at the wedding feast!'

She was to sing the part of Hope in a little play where a great swarm of devils attacked a tower called Loyalty. Then Faith, Hope and Charity were to defeat the devils by the power of their singing. Typically daft.

She sang her Hope song to us. 'Well,' I said, 'the tune isn't bad, but the words! 'That joy and hope your lives entrance, O future King and Queen of France, Of Scotland and of England too, Marie, Francois, we wish for you!' Yeugh! Who wrote that rubbish?' Suddenly it struck me. 'England? But Mary Tudor's queen there, isn't she?'

'I wondered, too,' Lark said. 'But it's the king's own order.'

Dad, home on two days' leave, nodded. 'Why d'you think he'd let the heir o' France wed Marie? No just for wee Scotland's sake. Mary Tudor'll never have children, she's far too old, and who'll follow her? Not Princess Elizabeth, Henri thinks, for her father Henry the Eighth married her mother while his first wife was still alive. He had her declared illegitimate himself. It can't be her. And Henry's elder sister married James o' Scotland, young Queen Marie's grandfather. She must be the legal heir. That's what Henri's sayin' to the world. He wants to claim England. He's got as much chance as a cat has o' becomin' a cardinal, I'd say, but that's his business.' He turned to Lark, dismissing the subject. 'And what are you to wear for your big scene, lassie?'

I bit my lip to control it. When she'd told me about her costume, I'd nearly choked. 'God's wounds!' That was Montgomery's favourite oath, so of course I copied it. 'Greek, you say? A wisp of silk and a silver ribbon to tie it on one shoulder? Just down to your knees? Dad'll have a fit!'

She'd grinned at me. 'Who's going to tell him, foolish? Till it's over, and then I don't care!'

Now she smiled innocently. 'Draped blue silk, dad, and silver tissue. It's elegant!' Dad nodded approval. Lark winked at me.

Three days before the wedding, when I came in I found her trembling and nearly in tears in Annette's arms. She leaped at me, nearly hysterical. 'The dwarves! The ones at Chambord! The chief one! He's in it! He's a devil! He's a devil!' The 'devils', played by dwarves, had come to rehearsal today for the first time. Chicot was one of them. And he had recognised her. 'There was such malice in his eyes, John! I could feel it! He'll wreck it for me! The faces! Oh, God, the grinning, hating faces!'

We told her it was nonsense; why should he want to harm her, even if he had recognised her? She'd done nothing to him!

'He will! He will!' she sobbed.

When we finally got her to bed, with a rosehip tisane and Annette sitting beside her to comfort her if she woke, Pierre and I discussed it for hours. 'May be right, sir, that he wants to harm her. Nasty character, very nasty. But what can we do? Mademoiselle can't drop out at this date.'

'No,' I agreed. 'But he's bound to silence, too. It'll have to look like an accident. That cuts down the possibilities. What could he try?'

An attack on the way to or from rehearsals? Poison — something in a drink beforehand? A booby-trap, or snakes or spiders let loose inside the tower? We took precautions against everything we could imagine; but never thought of the simplest, and most devastating, attack. We should have remembered he was a jester.

The day of the wedding was fine — naturally, after all the prayers for good weather. By seven o'clock there was no-one left at the barracks but me and an old clerk. He sympathised with me. 'Pity, lad. But this is nothing like when the last dauphin married. With the war, you know. No wine in the fountains, or street carnivals, or ship battles on the river. Poor, poor!' Maybe; but it was my own queen getting wed, and I ordered to stay in the office. I mumped about. Would anyone notice if I changed out of uniform, and slipped away? No, I couldn't disobey orders.

Suddenly a lad came running with an urgent message. Archer Hepburn had been shepherding his charge, a distant cousin of the queen's from Florence, across the Pont-Marie, when two stallions had started to fight. Hepburn was in hospital. The Medici, though slightly trampled, was determined not to miss the spectacle. But where was the place reserved for him?

I knew. I'd written out all the instruction lists. This Medici had a place right on the steps of Notre Dame Cathedral. I could send the lad back to tell him. But no frail foreigner was going to get through today's mob. Not without help. From somebody with authority. Like an Archer . . .

There was nobody else. This was an emergency. It was my duty to go. And I'd see the wedding, and from close up, in spite of my scars, ha-ha!

Some would-be-kindly souls had heaved my Medici up out of the crush right onto the balustrade of the bridge, in acute danger of being shoved off into the river. I squeezed him down, and then needed all my uniform's authority to force a way through the packed, revelling throng. We covered the three hundred yards to the cathedral in just over two hours, just as the band of the Swiss Halberdiers, in their crimson and gold, struck up. Drums and fifes, on top of the singing, shouting and cheering. God's wounds, what a din! My head was pounding. Was it worth it? Yes!

Blue velvet banners embroidered with white fleurs-de-lys covered the whole face of the huge church. For the wedding itself a stage with a twelve-foot high gilded arch over it had been built across the cathedral portal, above our heads, and a balustraded walkway had been constructed round the walls from the Bishop of Paris's Palace behind the cathedral, so that the royal party could reach the stage easily, and be seen by everyone. The members of the Parlement had seats inside the cathedral for the wedding Mass later. Some had gone up to the stage to look round, and didn't leave in time. When the trumpets sounded for the entry of the Court, they couldn't get back along the walkway; they had to clamber down the scaffolding like monkeys in their scarlet robes, to the mocking cheers of the crowd.

It took an hour for the Court to arrange itself on the stage. The Duc de Guise, who had organised it all, and two heralds were busy seeing to it that they didn't hide the wedding ceremony from the people. Or fall off.

Even after a year with the dauphin, I was amazed by the splendour.

The Bishop of Paris in purple and gold, his cross-bearer and fifty choirboys with lit candles in silver candlesticks, all scrubbed pink and on their best behaviour, crammed the centre of the platform.

Into one side packed a hundred rainbow gentlemen-in-waiting; half a dozen glittering Princes of the Blood Royal; eighteen purple bishops and archbishops; six crimson cardinals and the Papal Legate; the twenty-four Archers of the Bodyguard, a dazzling contrast in their white.

But for Lark, I might have been up there with the king's gentlemen . . .

Or dead, or crippled by the dauphin. That was possible, too.

The Dauphin Francois, in blue and silver, was escorted by his young brothers and his cousin Antoine de Bourbon, King of Navarre.

Queen Marie was led on by King Henri himself. She was nearly six feet tall now, as tall as her de Guise uncles, and towered over her puny little bridegroom. Her gown was an incredible pure white, stiff with shimmering crystals and pearls, with an immensely long train held by two ladies.

'White?' my Medici shouted. 'Is that not a colour of mourning?'

My head splitting from the deafening cheers and music, I yelled back, 'Madame de Poitiers helped her choose it, signior. There's nothing shows off red-gold hair better, except black.'

He grinned. 'You're wise, sir!' Who, me? 'Her jewels are very fine!'

'Her crown's new. There's one ruby worth half a million crowns on its own!' It had been part of the treasure I had been guarding at St Denis. He nodded, impressed.

Behind Marie, Queen Catherine, Madame Marguerite the king's sister, the young princesses, the noblest ladies of the Court, opulent and gorgeous as a bed of paeonies, filled up the rest of the stage.

The Cardinal de Bourbon conducted the wedding, and the king drew off a ring from his own finger for his son to set on Marie's hand.

At the end of the ceremony, as the new King and Queen of Scots led the Court away, I dragged my Medici against the wall of the cathedral. 'What is it?' he asked. I didn't need to answer; the heralds above us on the platform cried the traditional 'Largesse! Largesse!' and threw out handfuls of gold and silver. 'Diavolo!' my Medici cried in alarm and some disgust as the crowd hurled themselves howling on the coins. Some were hurt, and many had their clothes torn in the scuttle; and not all poor folk, either.

I looked at my Medici. He looked at me. What now? 'Signior,' I said, 'would it please you to honour my home with a visit, before the masques? It is simple, but cool and restful.'

He smiled, and set a beringed hand on my shoulder. 'Young man,' he said, 'I have seldom heard a more agreeable suggestion!'

With no hurry on us now, we enjoyed the gaiety of the crowds in spite of the din and smell. We bought two cold roast guineafowl from a stall on the way home. I was astonished how many people knew me, but of course it was the scars. There weren't many Archers with a face like mine. Well, there weren't many anybodies with a face like mine. Eventually I helped the Medici limp up the stair. Father was on duty, Pierre and Louis were out merrymaking, and Lark was at her final rehearsals, but shy Annette had stayed at home. She made us a refreshing elderflower tisane and produced a salad and a fresh, crusty loaf to go with the guineafowl, and while she mended a rip in the visitor's fine brocade cloak we sat in the parlour and discussed jewels, wine, Italian politics and terriers — rather to my surprise, Youpi liked the Medici. It was a pleasant afternoon.

In the twilight, we headed out for the grand masques at the Palais de Justice. I knew the secret password to get us in; but so did half Paris. Only my uniform, and a hefty bribe from the Medici, persuaded the guards to let us join the mob scrambling for spaces behind the tables. Many didn't get in at all, even some of the Parlement who were providing the banquet. We squeezed in near the centre of one long wall, where we had a good view.

The royal family took part in some of the magnificent and fantastical entertainments during the long meal. After a pageant of the seven planets, some of the young princes mounted gilded hobby-horses and drew light carriages round the room, filled with ladies singing. They were supposed to be pilgrims, but their gems would have paid for a new crusade. Who had talked about a poor show because there was a war on?

Later, six charming little golden ships on wheels were punted in by servants with silver poles. The six most important gentlemen in the room steered them, and each chose a passenger; the dauphin took on board his mother, Henri himself his new daughter-in-law, and so on. It was a magical sight, the silver sails billowing in an imaginary breeze as the delicate craft swirled round the room. Even Francois seemed to be enjoying himself, his pasty face smiling and happy.

As the ships were removed, a horde of tiny figures poured in, tumbling and leaping. All the dwarves in Paris must have been gathered there, over a hundred of them, in all shades of red, scarlet, plum, crimson, vermilion, puce, orange, cavorting down the long room to a tooth-grating discord of pipes and horns. Some were fire-eaters, spouting long gusts of flame to scorch the tapestries. Some were skeletons, some had animal masks. Many brandished tridents or whips. They screamed and threatened the spectators, while men wheeled in a fairy-tale castle, all silver and white trellis and turrets, with flowers of gold.

I didn't see Chicot at first, and was wondering whether he had a mask when he appeared by the castle gates. He and some other dwarves had a small cannon, which they fired with a deafening bang and a shower of blue sparks. Could he plan to burn down the castle? No, that was ridiculous. It must be too dangerous even for him to consider. Besides, there were men all around with wet cloths and buckets of water. But maybe Lark would be frightened by the fireworks; she still hated to touch the fire at home.

The first of the defenders, Faith, tall and striking in bronze armour and yellow satin, appeared on the six-foot high battlements. She sang in a rich contralto of the courage and greatness of the past, present, and future kings of the three lands. The audience were more impressed than the devils, who jeered, hooted and capered. The cannon fired again, with red sparkles. They set fire to a tablecloth, but the men had it out directly.

The Medici visitor tapped my shoulder. It startled me; I'd not been paying any attention to him. 'You are uneasy about the fires?' he asked. I nodded. Well, how could I explain?

Lark stepped forward to sing, small and delicate in her flimsy blue and silver veils. She ignored the fireworks and the grinning faces beneath her with a concentration which put a tense tremor in her hands, but none in her voice. She sang of the hopes that the countries had for their young king and queen, to join them all together in happiness and prosperity. Nothing could harm them then; all malice and envy must fade and die.

Indeed? I looked for Chicot; he was ignoring her, loading his cannon again, just as presumably he should be. The sparkles, green this time, fizzled out harmlessly. 'No trouble, no?' said my Medici. Not yet.

Lark must be mistaken; he couldn't be planning anything, or he'd have done it by now; all would be well. Surely . . . Somehow I couldn't relax.

Charity, a plumpish blonde in pink and gold, sang next. Something about love conquering all, of course. Francois smiled adoringly up at his bride, and enraptured by the day's wonders she smiled back down at him.

The devils knelt in surrender, joining the chorus of love and happiness. The verses were abominable, but who cared? The castle gates of silver trellis opened, and the drawbridge was lowered for the defenders to descend with wreaths for the happy couple. Lark stepped out with the others, head high, happy and triumphant, to walk down the steep little slope from the gate to the floor.

Each of them had a chorus to sing as they glided down. Faith welcomed the dwarves, and all those watching, to the glory of true loyalty to the young couple. Hope sang, 'All hopes are high on this wonderful day, joy inspires all at this splendid display —'

The handle of a trident slid between Lark's feet, and a strong hand jerked at her costume as she tripped. Thread snapped, silk tore, and her dress vanished under the drawbridge. As she staggered a harsh voice squawked a repeat of her song — 'Joy inspires all at this splendid display!' She landed flat on her back at the feet of the whole Court and half of Paris in silver slippers, a silver hair-ribbon and a storm of laughter that made the torch-flames quiver.

Jeering faces . . .

Queen Catherine was rolling in her seat. The dauphin was doubled up, squealing. The king, the nobles, the dwarves, the citizens of Paris — all of them were reeling and stamping, scarlet and purple, guffawing helplessly and heartlessly at the ruin of Lark's sweetness and charm.

Lark. That was my little sister out there, huddled too scared to move under their whistling and jeering.

I had to help her.

In front of them all . . . The king, and the Court. The other Archers. The other singers looking furious. The visitors from all over the world.

And the dauphin, who'd warned me that he never wanted to see me again.

To hell with the lot of them!

I started to push forward, reaching up to unclasp my white Archer's surcoat. But a hand on my arm made me pause. 'May I offer . . . ?' My Medici, smiling, was holding out his longer ice-blue cloak. Bowing thanks, I shoved through the crowd and strode down the hall with it, stopped beside Lark and draped the glossy brocade over her back as she sobbed beside my knee. I bowed stiffly to Their Majesties. Most were laughing too hard to reply, but young Queen Marie, though she was smiling, lifted a hand and nodded in approval. I reached down to help Lark to her feet, carefully wrapping the cloak round her. It hid her almost down to her knees. 'Come along, lass!' I whispered. 'Stand up! That's right! We'll show them! Up you come. Like a swan, mind, not a pelican!' I went on whispering, nonsense and encouragement mixed, as she gathered her strength to walk back down the long hall with me.

There was a change in the noise. Someone was clapping. Queen Marie. Then the king. More and more joined in. And then the whole hall, no longer jeering, was laughing kindly, applauding. Applauding Lark, and me.

Lark stopped beside me. I halted too, of course, my arm round her shoulders. She eased out from under it, turned to face the king and his family, and clutching the edges of the cloak together, her lips still trembling under the smile she fixed on them, the tears not dry on her cheeks, she curtseyed to them all. 'Bow, foolish!' she hissed at me. Amazed, I did so. The cheering redoubled. I found myself smiling.

As we bowed again to the roar of applause, Lark's disaster turned so unexpectedly to a minor triumph, I glimpsed Chicot's face staring among the swarm of dwarves. He was white with fury. That stopped my humour.

Queen Catherine's Service

Two days later Queen Catherine summoned both Lark and me to her levée.

'What can she want, John?' Lark kept asking as we walked through the streets, even so early in the morning echoing with the cries of sellers of water, fresh pigeons, polishing sand, eels all wriggling, sweet herbs. 'Look, my hands are shaking! D'you think the dauphin's told her —'

'How should I know?' I demanded. I was having trouble keeping my own hands steady. 'Don't admit to anything, or it could be a quiet cup of arsenic and a quick trip to the cemetery for us both, from what they say.'

'Oh, nonsense! I liked her, last year. And she liked me, I'm sure. And you.'

'What's that got to do with it? Henri's only king because his older brother died, and they say he was poisoned by his valet, who was Italian, like Catherine! If she's found out we hurt her beloved son, she'll want to crucify us, and who'll stop her? Not the king, even if I am an Archer. Nor Queen Marie. Just remember, whatever she asks, you don't know anything!'

As Lark and I walked through the high gates into the courtyard, we fell silent in apprehension. I remembered the first time, two years ago. I felt even worse today.

We were ushered to a crowded hall where, in the clear space behind a red silk rope barrier, a gilded, padded chair stood all alone on a carpet. The suitors weren't really very important, of course, for it was the king's mistress Diane who was the richer, more powerful lady.

Everyone knew me. If it wasn't the scars, it was that carry-on at the banquet. I exchanged bows with a dozen men I scarcely knew. A bell struck six, the door opened, and we all bared our heads and knelt as Catherine entered, in an under-dress of gold. The flat eyes swept round, and she nodded in response to our reverence. 'Monsignor.' As a bishop moved forward, her ladies offered gowns for her choice. 'Not that. The blue. And the sleeves with the sable. How can I help you, monsignor?' Her accent was stronger here, in her own rooms. She worked steadily through the assembly, beckoning this one and that, dictating letters, ordering gifts, arranging meetings, ignoring her ladies moving silently round her as they laced her bodice, skirt and sleeves, combed her hair and pinned it in under her pearl-trimmed cap. It was less formal, but somehow much more regal, than with the dauphin.

They brought three caskets on trolleys for her to choose jewellery. She had brought most of it with her from Italy in her enormous dowry, buying her royalty, the nobles had sneered. Diane had the royal jewels. With no glance at me, though I knew she'd seen me, she picked out the same rope of huge pearls that I had thought to be false that first day two years before. Earrings, rings, brooches, a final careful study of the result in a mirror. Though not ugly, she wasn't beautiful, but she was certainly impressive. Merchant's daughter or not, she had been a queen for ten years.

At last, after nearly an hour, she lifted a finger to Lark and me.

We advanced, quaking, as she gestured her ladies away out of earshot. Lark curtseyed. I bowed. 'You do not knock the table over this time, eh, Jean de Rouxelle, Sieur de Loyes?'

My throat was dry. 'I hope I have learned more grace, Your Majesty.'

'In my son's service?'

I bowed again in silence. I didn't feel like joking.

She glanced at Lark, and sniffed. 'That was unfortunate, at the banquet was it not?' Her lips twitched, and Lark blushed. 'H'm. I saw what happened. The dwarf concerned has been reprimanded.' Lark smiled slight thanks. Upsetting the dauphin's wedding celebrations would be frowned on. But he'd made them laugh, which was his job. They'd not have done much.

The queen turned abruptly back to me, her eyes hard. 'Tell me, de Rouxelle; why did my son dismiss you?'

Well, I'd expected it. 'I regret, Your Majesty, I may not say.'

She stiffened, frowned. 'Sir, you are an Archer of the Garde Royale of France. As Queen of France, I require you to answer, on your duty.'

Under the threat of the flat eyes in the flat face, my stomach quailed. Lord! I mustn't! 'It is by the king-dauphin's own orders, Your Majesty, that I remain silent. I deeply regret that even at risk of Your Majesty's displeasure I cannot say more.' Too true I couldn't — she'd have my guts for garters.

'So.' She turned to Lark. 'Do you know why your brother left, girl? I insist — I demand that you tell me!'

Determinedly, Lark shook her head. 'I am sorry, Your Majesty. Jean has never spoken of it.' Thank God she had enough sense, and courage, to stick to the story. She might escape.

99

'So.' She considered us. 'So.' She nodded slowly as we quaked again. 'You are discreet. Both of you.' It was the comment the captain had made. Horrible thought — was it the queen he'd discussed me with, not the king? 'As I thought the first time I saw you, de Rouxelle. You confirm my judgement. Let me tell you that I know what happened at Chambord.'

I gripped my cap rigidly, and my toes curled in dread. Lark blanched. Of course she'd know. How could we have been so foolish as to hope to avoid the spies she'd have in her son's household? Oh, God!

The queen smiled sourly. 'If you had spoken of it, you would not have returned to your home. Either of you.' A quick trip to the Bastille. Or the cemetery. 'But you can, it seems, remain silent even under some pressure.' She paused. 'I am not heartless. I can understand why you acted as you did, de Rouxelle. But I condemn it utterly. The person of a king, or a future king, must be inviolate, his wishes paramount. He must never be touched, whatever he does, however angry he becomes with a foolish maid, even if she is your sister.'

What had she said? Angry — what I had done . . . My breath caught. What about the slap? Was it possible her spies hadn't given her the whole story? The page had seen me holding back the dauphin, but not Lark hitting him. If he'd just thought that Lark had tried to scold the dauphin about the pups, and that Francois had been heading for her when I'd grabbed him . . . Could we get away with it yet?

Her face was severe. 'I myself would have punished you, but my son desired no action to be taken. I must follow his wishes. And I remember that you acted rapidly to save him when that foolish Scottish girl endangered his life on the river.' She knew about that too. Naturally. 'Of course he should not have been in any danger in the first place, but it was a typical boyish escapade. I was not displeased.' Thank — thank somebody. Her, or God, or the dauphin, I didn't care. We were going to survive!

She sniffed again, and lifted a finger. A secretary scurried forward from the side of the room. Oh, Lord, what was she going to do? 'A letter today to the Count of Montgomery, Captain of the Garde Ecossaise. Archer de Rouxelle is to be attached to my personal guard.'

My jaw dropped. What? A joke — surely it was a joke? 'I am overwhelmed, madame. Your Majesty does me too much honour.'

Her eyes glinted dully. 'Young man, you showed courage in aiding your sister in face of the dauphin, and of public laughter. My cousin Guido tells me how efficiently and considerately you attended him. My husband is impressed with your actions over an attempt on the Treasury, though I myself would expect no less from any Archer . . . However. You served my son well while you were with him. And you can keep silent. So. I need a new officer. I have selected you.'

What about Francois? I was bound to meet him. Her lips pursed, as if she heard my thought. 'The king-dauphin and the queen-dauphiness have their own household, of course, but it is likely that you will meet. His Royal Highness will ignore what has occurred, de Rouxelle. So will you.'

'I am grateful for Your Majesty's advice.' That was one problem solved — or at least postponed. My stomach was alternately leaping and sinking, with relief, dismay, pride; or was it a trap? Poison some time in the future . . . I felt ill. I couldn't show it, of course. God's wounds, how could I get out of this?

I had an idea. How to put it tactfully? 'Has Your Majesty considered . . . ?' I gestured to my scars. 'My appearance is scarcely handsome. It might bring adverse comment on the quality of Your Majesty's train.' From the Guises, for instance, who disparaged Catherine in

every possible way because she opposed their growing power.

'That is thoughtful of you,' she said graciously. 'But I
consider that wounds received in our service are badges
of honour, not a disfigurement. I believe you will serve
me well, as you did my son.' Well . . . it was unlikely
I'd be grabbing her to stop her yelling. Maybe it was
all right . . .

She moved her shallow eyes to Lark, and considered her carefully. 'Alice de Rouxelle — they call you
Alouette, the Lark, as I remember? You are personable.
You have a good voice. You are gently born, if not
noble. And you have been already in the household of
my daughter-in-law, Marie the queen-dauphiness.' She
wasn't going to send her back there, surely — to the
dauphin . . . 'I think you would prefer to remain outside
His Royal Highness's circle? Yes? Ye-es. So. You will join
my household also, as a maid-in-waiting, not merely an
entertainer.' It was a great honour, and not to be refused.
Lark curtseyed, smiling rather sickly.

About to wave us away, the queen paused, eyeing us
shrewdly. 'You are wary, de Rouxelle. I am glad to see
it. It shows intelligence. But you need have no fear. I
promise, as I hope for Heaven, I mean you no harm.'
Her smile was warmer than at first. A knot in my inside
relaxed. I believed her. 'I am sure you will serve me well.'
The knot tightened again.

As she left and we rose from our bows a man behind us
tapped my shoulder. He was all in black, with a scholar's
gown. I knew the face from somewhere. 'Monsieur de
Rouxelle? I am glad to meet you again.'

'Again, sir? I fear you have the advantage of me.'

He smiled, his black eyes piercing above his beard. 'In
a brief visit to Paris, I came here especially this morning
to renew our acquaintance, and make your sister's. For
she is of more importance than yourself.' What?

Lark, beside me, was as startled as I was. She frowned

up at him. 'Who are you, sir? And why am I so important?'

He stroked his beard. 'I am Michel de Notredame, called Nostradamus. The prophet, men call me. You have heard of me, mademoiselle?'

'Who has not, sir?' I said. I remembered him now, from my first interview with Her Majesty. Why did he want to meet us? 'Do we figure in your predictions?' I'd have thought Lark would be pleased and excited to meet the soothsayer, but she looked as if she'd been eating lemons.

His smile was wry. 'Your sister distrusts me. It is understandable. But like the queen, young lady, I mean you no harm.' Surely he'd been too far away to overhear . . . He nodded gravely. 'Young sir, you have a part to play in the fortunes of three kingdoms. But your sister has a greater one.'

Lark's chin was down on her chest and she was gazing mulishly up at him under her brows. He nodded again as if she had spoken. 'I understand what you think. But I know what I know.' The deep eyes switched to me. 'If I may offer a word of advice, monsieur; when your sister calls on you, answer her call. And do not despair. Seek out a way to help her, however impossible it may seem at first. God bless you both.' He smiled, turning away.

Mysteries, as if I hadn't enough on my mind!

Lark was furious. More so than was needed, I felt. 'Prophet, indeed! Mountebank! He prophesied that Prince Louis would have a long and prosperous career, and the poor baby died when he was only two. There's thirty thousand sorcerers in Paris, and every one a fake. And he's the greatest of them all!'

Maybe. But maybe not as she meant it. I couldn't get those dark eyes out of my mind.

I had a hard time persuading Walter Turnbull, the hard-bitten Archer who commanded Queen Catherine's guard, that I wasn't just a jumped-up pageboy; mainly because that was just what I was, of course. My scars helped. Eventually, we split the work; he saw to the military side, organising the guard, checking for intruders and thieves, and so on, while I took over the personal duties. He liked hunting, could bear boating and chatting to the queen's ladies; but it bored him to swearing to stand behind her chair for hours, silently attentive at church, banquets, christenings and funerals. It bored me too, but I didn't swear. Not so much, anyway.

My hair grew long enough to hide the fading scars on my head, and in spite of my face I kept finding myself surrounded by charming girls. Or maybe because of it; the Flying Squadron — Queen Catherine's dashing ladies-in-waiting — were fascinated, running their fingers over the ridged welts. Daft, I thought, but why should I complain? My first shyness melted swiftly, and the gardens saw not a few kisses and cuddles. I could fairly keep my end up in talk with my friends, till one day Lark asked, 'Which d'you fancy, then, big brother? Amélie or Perrine, or Célie?' She giggled. 'Have you not noticed, foolish, some of them are developing a serious, marriage-style gleam in their eye?' She laughed like a drain at my expression. 'Watch out! Pies and paramours are hot to handle!' She was getting away above herself. But the warning calmed me down a fair bit.

To my joy, my beard started to grow in. Thankfully, it was fair and so less noticeable, for shaving was impossible. It was fuzzy and scrubby round the scars at first, but five times a day Pierre rubbed in a special oil, and by the New Year he could comb and clip it to a respectable point. 'A vast improvement, John. It hides a lot of your face!' Lark approved.

The first time the dauphin saw me, he hesitated. For an instant I thought he was glad to see me, but then he brushed on by with his lips turning sulky. The next day he saw me before I saw him, spurred his horse and nearly rode me down. His mother saw it. She said nothing to me, but from then on he ignored me, except that he often turned his eyes, not his head, to watch me as he passed. I couldn't judge what he was thinking.

Wattie Turnbull taught me a great deal about the practical aspects of war: strategy and tactics; fortifications and the cannon and mines that could destroy them; control of food, water and civilians in a siege; the importance of always keeping open a way of retreat; how to choose your time and place for fighting, and get your soldiers there, healthy, trained, fed, well armed, paid, eager to fight. I learned how much more there was to winning wars than courage, honour and glory.

He helped me to recover my fitness, encouraging me to ride and run, swim and wrestle, exercise with the mace to strengthen and loosen my wrists and arms for fencing. As I toughened up, he started me jousting again, too, first with the barrel, and then the quintain. This was a wooden model of a Saracen with a shield and outstretched wooden sword. It was set on a post so that it could swivel easily when it was struck. If your aim was true, in the centre, you galloped safely past; if you hit it wrong, it flew round and walloped you. You didn't practise in armour; to save my head, I learned rapidly to aim well.

All in all, I enjoyed life with the queen's household.

So did Lark, at first. Although the finest painters, sculptors, poets, artists of all kinds flocked round Diane de Poitiers, the queen could call on musicians from Italy, and in this at least she was first. Even I could hear the growing maturity and control of Lark's voice, and her mastery of the lute to accompany herself. Our mistress often called on her to entertain guests.

The Court began to notice her. Now fifteen, she was thrilled to be a junior member of the Flying Squadron. I had to admit she was growing quite passable, with bright eyes a darker brown than her hair, clear skin, delicate hands and her impish smile. There was always a cloud of gentlemen round her like wasps round a honeypot. Considering how some of the Squadron acted with me in the gardens, I was a bit worried, but Lark just laughed, and boasted of her trophies. 'See what I've got today, John! A poem, flowers, a pearl ring! And a monkey!'

'Very suitable, Lark!' I commented rather sourly. The vicious wee beast bit my finger. Lark giggled. The monkey nearly drove poor Youpi daft, teasing and tweaking. He was getting old and stiff now, too old for such a carry-on. I was glad when Lark got rid of it quickly.

During her duty hours Lark stood or sat, walked or rode behind the queen with the other ladies, ready to run errands, sing, play chess or just talk to entertain the queen and her guests. Music and admirers filled her off-duty time. For a while, she was happy.

But behind the pleasant pastimes, the bright, silken hours, the exciting little flirtations, lay a nastier, darker side to the household. The queen's sorcerers hung around like blowflies, buzzing menacingly in corners. In long black and purple and green and vermilion robes with strange signs embroidered on them, they sneered and muttered to each other in what they said was Hebrew or Babylonian or Chaldean. It sounded like geese cackling. I wondered if they just made it up as they went along.

Soon after I arrived, I bumped into one on the stair. He smiled and nodded regally as I bowed a polite apology, but as I went on up he turned to a companion. I heard very clearly his comment; 'Oafish ignoramus!' That, about an Archer? From a dirty little charlatan? It was not to be borne; I whirled, and kicked him down the stairs. Montgomery would have cheered.

He glared up at me, climbing to his feet, rubbing his bottom, almost in tears; 'Curse you!' he screeched. 'Mael, Septentrion, Orolbagion, avenge this insult! Cower, fool, flee my wrath, for my obedient demons will bring you agony and death ere the new moon!'

They all talked like that. Just before I reached him he fled, his green skirts flapping.

Pierre scolded me. 'All very well, young master, had to clear yourself of insult, but now, slightest twinge in your belly this week, he'll claim it was his magic! Must hide it! And watch out for poison!'

True enough, and under all the eagerly intent eyes I was careful to eat and drink lightly, of shared dishes and wine. But two nights later, Pierre caught a lad climbing at my window with a bottle. 'No, sir, no thief,' he told me, grinning. 'Wizard's boy. Bringing it, not taking it!' I had a hard time stopping him beating the lad, for doing what he was told.

Next day I dared the boy's master, before all the other magicians, to drink from the bottle he had sent me, and when he refused I had the guards throw him out of the castle. Not as a murderer, but what was worse for him; as a fake. I had nothing but politeness from the rest after that.

The lad, Guy Laval, refused to go back to his old master however often Pierre kicked him out. He slept in the stables until at last his cheery grin wore me down. 'I'll not leave you, sir!' he said. 'I know I'm not clever, but I'm very, very determined.' True enough. I had to laugh, and took him on as a messenger-boy and page.

The wizards didn't bother me. I could walk by the doors of their foul rooms, eerie with glass retorts, sealed jars of swirly things in oil, black mirrors, bowls of ink and mercury, astrolabes, stuffed lizards and the like, and turn my head aside from the fumes; but Lark couldn't. One day in early October, in the queen's little château of Chaumont, I found her in tears, and could scarce calm her. 'I can't bear it! The poor doves and cats they kill, to poke about in their guts! And they come to the queen with the blood still black under their fingernails, and tell her that her children will have strength and good fortune! Oh, John! I'm choked with the stench of them!

D'you know what she has them doing? Spells to kill Mary Tudor of England! It's blasphemy!' Lark sobbed hysterically. 'The devil's work!'

Next morning she wasn't in her usual place. The queen called me over. 'De Rouxelle, I am told your sister is a touch over-tired. I have been working her too hard. And you, also. I forget you are both so young.'

'It's a mending fault, but Your Majesty is considerate,' I bowed.

She smiled. 'Let me add to my kindness. In November I return to Paris for the winter. Until then, I grant you both leave of absence, to rest and restore yourselves. You need a change. You might care to visit your estate.' She nodded to a secretary, who handed me a heavy little purse. 'To help with your expenses in setting Loyes to rights after the sad destruction of the war.' She was thoughtful and generous. When pleased.

Since dad was away in Rheims with the king and the dauphin, handing out medals like sweets to his commanders — it was cheaper than paying them — we took the queen's suggestion. Lark and I, with Pierre, Guy, Lark's maid, a cook, the three men of my lance and two grooms, and Youpi in a basket at Guy's saddle-bow, rode north high-hearted as children released from school. It was just as well, for when we reached Loyes after dark in the middle of a thunderstorm we found the house deserted and empty. No steward; no door, even, broken and removed for firewood like the furniture and shutters; the roof as waterproof as a winter tree. No stick of wood or wisp of hay in the barn, no scrap of food in the mouldy dairy or the cockroach-swarming pantry.

What was that the queen had said about needing a change?

Pierre and the men-at-arms splashed off cursing to the nearest farm to get us something to eat, while the grooms dried and brushed the horses, the maid whimpered, Youpi hunted rats and Lark, Guy and I hunted for a place to sleep. Lark cheered me gaily when I slipped and landed on my back in a puddle on the top floor. 'Do it again, Johnnie! I didn't see it properly that time!'

In a cupboard under the stair we found a bundle of tattered hangings. 'They're dry! Beds!' she cried gleefully, and had us sneezing in a cloud of dust, hauling them out to sleep on. When I stood on a more-than-usually rotten spot in the floorboards, and fell through waist-deep, she screamed with mirth. 'I've heard of having one foot in the grave, but this is ridiculous!' Guy helped me spluttering up through the powdery splinters, glad I'd not broken a leg; gladder to hear her laughter.

We pulled out rotten wood from the broken floor to burn. When Pierre and the others returned with cider, a very old hen, some onions, bacon, and hay for our horses, the kitchen fire was blazing high and the walls starting to steam. We slept well after the long journey, all huddled together for warmth among the curtains, with the horses in a corner to be safe from thieves. And then we started to be very, very busy.

The estate had been raided by the Spaniards and English, but the queen's gold produced a surprising amount of food hidden away by my tenant farmers. They'd had a lot of practice, of course, with tax-collectors.

As the new steward I engaged the unpopular younger son of one of my tenants. 'I'll get you your rent, my lord! I helped hide the grain and cider. I know how much they saved,' he offered eagerly.

'Don't press too hard, Jacques.' He looked rather disappointed. 'The rents are paid in produce? Corn, eggs and so on? But I don't want to live here. Can you change to a money rent? Good. In the meantime, here's five écus; buy some sheep and goats, a horse, a couple of cows, whatever they need to start the farms off again.' His jaw dropped. 'It's only sense, surely. Like sowing a seed.' He was still astonished. This wasn't how lords behaved! 'And we'll give you and your wife a hand to get the repairs started.' That shocked him again, and horrified Pierre, Guy and my men, who were also set to work.

Lark scrubbed stone shelves in the dairy, sewed hangings, sneezed happily as she stuffed feathers into mattresses. She sighed, one day. 'Maman would have enjoyed this, setting all to rights.' Yes, she would.

Youpi had a marvellous time, chasing rabbits as if he was young again. Then one morning, three weeks after we arrived, he simply didn't wake up. We buried him under an ancient oak tree. Lark shed tears for him, but not too many. 'He had a good life, Johnnie. I'll not grieve for him.' She was clearly much better and stronger.

Apart from the war damage, the whole place was run down. 'The last lord never came here, sir,' Jacques explained. 'The farmers haven't paid labour dues for years. But while your men-at-arms are here,' he smiled smugly, 'we can make them catch up. There are ditches to clear, brushwood to cut back, roofs and walls and fences to mend. And the house, my lord. That needs a lot of work.'

At the end of five weeks, when we set out again for Paris, we left a busy manor behind us, well set on the struggle to renew its prosperity. We were exhausted, but it was a productive, clean tiredness, of body, not of mind. Even Lark could face the return to Queen Catherine calmly. 'None of the wizards,' she declared firmly, 'could be worse than that dairy!'

In Paris the bells of Notre Dame were tolling. By the Porte St Denis, the Earl of Arran, captain of the first company of the Garde, was talking to a girl impressed by his uniform — it couldn't be by him. 'My lord!' I called to him. 'Who's dead?'

He jumped. 'Who — oh, Russell! Mistress Alice!' He bowed deeply to Lark. I had to repeat my question. 'Dead? Oh! Old Mary Tudor. We're in mourning, by

King Henri's decree. He's proclaimed Marie Queen of England.'

Lark was clutching my wrist. 'How did she die, my lord?' She started to shiver in spite of her fur-trimmed cloak.

He shrugged again, puzzled by her intensity. 'She just faded away. Lost heart, they say, after we took Calais. And all her burning of heretics didn't turn England back to Catholicism, either. She just — died.'

I could feel Lark's thoughts. Had Queen Catherine's spells worked?

The Challenge

We wore ostentatious mourning for weeks, but in vain.
The nobles and commons of England accepted Princess
Elizabeth as queen, though she had to threaten the bishops with imprisonment before she could get one of them
to crown her. After Mary's reign, they were all Catholic,
of course. Nobody paid any attention to King Henri's
claim on Marie's behalf. He probably hadn't expected
anything else for the moment, but there was always the
future . . . He had a set of silver-gilt plates engraved with
the combined coats-of-arms of England and Scotland,
and had Marie sign papers as Queen of England, Ireland
and Scotland. It drove the English ambassador wild.

Only a few days after Mary Tudor died, her husband's
father, the Emperor Charles, died too. King Philip lost his
remaining enthusiasm for the war. No-one in France had
any either, apart from the Guises, and in April of 1559 a
peace treaty was at last signed between France and Spain.
To confirm the peace, two marriages were arranged for
June. Elizabeth, King Henri's eldest daughter, now fourteen, was to wed the newly-widowed Philip, who had
offered for Elizabeth of England, they said, and been

refused. And the elderly Duke of Savoy would marry Henri's sister Marguerite; he'd been in love with her for years. The celebrations cost nearly two million crowns, mostly borrowed from Italian bankers. Much of it would go on the main feature of the double celebration; a great three-day tournament.

Lark started to look fretful again. One day I cornered her. 'What's wrong now? You're not as chirpy as usual these days. Throat sore? Or have the fortune-tellers been giving you more trouble?'

'Not me, John; the queen! Haven't you heard?'

'You mean the warning that the king'll die? You believe that rubbish?'

'Of course not, foolish, but Catherine does! She has nightmares about it. She's asked all her soothsayers, and for once they all agree. And it's one of Nostradamus's prophecies, that he made years ago.'

'You shouldn't be superstitious,' I said. 'It's unlucky!'

I'd thought she might smile, but she paid no heed, gazing past me at her own thoughts. 'If the old lion meets the young one on the field of battle, in his forty-first year, he'll be killed, his eye destroyed in its gilded cage. Something like that. The king's forty-one. The lion's the king of beasts. It's clear enough. The king's going to die.'

'Away! If Henri's the old lion, who's the young one? There's nobody among his opponents called Leo, or Leone, or even with a lion on his coat of arms. He's the finest jouster in the land, and his armour's the best. He's safer than anybody else out there.'

'She doesn't care. She's begged him to stop, but he won't listen.'

'Do you blame him?' I asked. 'She's bothered him about a hundred things before now, and not one of them has come true.'

'Well, this time she's worse than ever. I wish it was all over, John!'

The tiltyard was just in front of the Palace des Tournelles, a two-hundred yard stretch of the Rue St Antoine barricaded off for the occasion, with stands built on both sides for the spectators. At one end brilliant little tents were erected, blue and white and scarlet, to make the scene look like a picture in an old manuscript.

Three painted wooden barriers ran chest-high the length of the field. In a tournament, the horses galloped on the right of a barrier, so that they couldn't crash into each other. The knights aimed their light, often hollowed, lances to the left, across their horses' necks. It was a game, not a real battle. The aim was to show courage and style, break a lance honourably, and give a gallant show to the audience, not to kill.

A jouster nowadays didn't carry a shield, but he sat fully armoured behind a high pommel and in front of an equally high cantle to hold him in the saddle. He had a specially strong pauldron, a metal plate like a small shield, to guard his left shoulder, and often a gorget, an extra v-shaped plate bolted to his breastplate to protect his neck. In theory he was safe from anything but bruises. But in practice . . .

Early one morning the queen visited the tiltyards to watch the king and his knights practise. As she passed, workmen laying bright paint and gilding on balustrades and flagpoles, or hanging bunting, cheered her, for they knew she had helped bring the war to an end. For once she was popular, but even that didn't make her smile.

The king had his back to us as we approached, discussing with his friends a pretty suit of armour hanging on a stand outside one tent. 'I don't like so much fancywork, sire,' the Count of Montgomery was saying. 'He'd do better with more iron and less gold.' Henri was laughing.

The dauphin rode up behind them lance in hand, shoved up the visor of his plumed helmet and bowed stiffly, squeaking slightly. His armour was engraved, blued and gilded, even more decorated than the set the men were studying. Practising in armour? He must be trying to strengthen himself. A page who ran up to take his reins was nearly jerked off his feet by the powerful stallion. The lad was clearly as good a rider as ever.

Henri turned as the others bowed, his laughter dying. 'Madame,' he greeted Catherine warily, clearly wondering if she was going to embarrass him by begging him yet again to give up his joust. Rapidly he redirected her attention. 'Our son is doing excellently well. Francois, give Her Majesty the pleasure of seeing you ride at the quintain.'

Proudly, the lad snapped down his visor, gathered up his reins, and cantered off to where a superb Saracen gleamed. He attacked it enthusiastically, hit it perfectly, and pranced his horse back waving his lance in triumph to our clapping.

'Watch, Your Majesty!' he called shrilly. He took a finer, lighter lance, and rode to the far lane, where stood a row of six little gallows.

The quintain was stationary. To gain skill in precision, aiming at a moving target, you practised by trying to pick up on the tip of your ten-foot lance a two-inch ring swinging on a thread.

Most men would be pleased to collect one or two of the six rings. When the dauphin returned, his lance held high, and lowered its tip, four rings slid tinkling to his mother's delighted hands. It was a display of expert skill, and he was justifiably proud of himself.

He was bowing to us when his eye fell on me, clapping with the rest. His smile vanished, and then reappeared, malicious. God's wounds! 'De Rouxelle! You come and try. Show us how good an Archer is at tilting!' I knew it! And I couldn't refuse the challenge.

The dauphin was already beckoning to the grooms to bring up one of the spare horses. I bowed to the queen;

'With Your Majesty's leave?' She smiled permission. If I did well, it displayed the ability of her officers; if badly, her son's expertise would show up more clearly.

The eyes of the Count of Montgomery and the half-dozen Archers on duty were intent all round me. I had the honour of the Garde to uphold. I must do well, for their sake, as well as my own. I knew what they'd say later if I made a mess of it! Good thing I'd had a lot of practice with Turnbull. It was a cool, cloudy morning; why did I feel so hot?

In spite of my tension, I took a moment to halt the horse they'd given me and try its obedience; it was excellently trained, and moved at the slightest touch of my hand or knee. Good. My lack of spurs wouldn't matter.

Right. The quintain first. No problem here, though the lance was lighter than the ones I was used to, and a foot shorter. I got used to the balance as I cantered round to the lane where the Saracen was awaiting me. There was the bright red shield ahead of me. Lean forward; head down; lance balanced; urge on the horse. Straight into a canter, a gallop — faster — the shield close — there! In the last split second I tensed, gripped the lance rigid with fist and elbow, shoved my feet forward in the stirrups to wedge my back hard against the high cantle that supported me, felt the heavy jolt of a good hit, and swept on past in safety. The quintain squeaked angrily behind me, and I was reining round at the end of the course, with the applause of the little crowd and the watching Archers rattling between the high walls. God bless Walter Turnbull.

So far, so good. That was the easy bit.

Riding at the rings was much more difficult; and especially for me.

The quintain's colourful shield was an easy target. In hand-to-hand combat my opponent was just at

116

arm's length. I'd manage in a real charge of lances, even, aiming at the general body of men. But since the arquebus had exploded beside my face, my eyes weren't what they had been. I simply couldn't see the small glint of the ring soon enough to aim for it.

Oh, well. Do what I could.

While I changed my lance, the pages were jumping down from the barrier where they'd climbed to fasten the rings up again. I only had to ride down underneath them, looking as if I knew what I was doing. It was no great shame not to pick up a ring. And it would please the dauphin, blast him!

I turned along the barrier. Suddenly the sun came out. A brilliant light flared across the whole tiltyard for the first time that morning. As I cantered along, there in front of my lance was a tiny silvery gleam. I lifted my lancepoint, and over the gentle thudding of my hoofbeats I heard a faint tinkle. At least, if I'd not picked it up, I'd hit it. My personal best! I grinned to myself. Look, there was the next — give it a try — left a bit — steady — a little tug on my lance as the thread broke — I'd got one! The first ever!

It was the last, as well; and all due to luck, and the shorter lances. It was hard to hide my surprise and delight, and pretend it happened regularly. Lark was smiling broadly as she clapped behind the queen. My mistress was most graciously pleased with my performance. The dauphin sneered, and spurred his horse away to take out his sulks on the quintain.

For well over an hour we stood and watched, as the king's friends all took their turn. Two of them, in full armour, rode a couple of courses. Neither was hurt, although three lances were skilfully broken. It was a game, of course. The light lances here were meant to break easily.

117

One of them was Lieutenant Montgomery. When he dismounted, he grinned to me warmly, to my pleasure, as he turned to answer a call from King Henri. 'Well, lieutenant! Rumour has it that you are the finest jouster in the Garde.'

'Then rumour exaggerates, Your Majesty,' he bowed, 'though I may claim some skill. I'm not as good as my father.'

The count smiled deprecatingly. 'In my day, sire, in my day!'

'Aye, Montgomery, I remember when you'd have sent this lad flying!' the king laughed.

'He rode once against your own father, sire,' one of the other men said. 'Before he became First Captain.'

'You never told me that, Montgomery! Who won?' the king demanded.

'I have to admit it was I, Your Majesty.' Maybe beating a king wasn't the kind of thing you boasted about . . . Not to the next king, anyway . . .

I needn't have worried. 'Well done!' Henri had never been his father's favourite son, and was delighted to meet someone who had beaten the glorious Francois I in something. 'Would you care to try it with me?'

The queen stiffened.

'At my age? Pity my grey hairs, sire!' the count protested. 'Besides, as First Captain I'm your official champion! I can scarcely fight you!'

The king, not ten years younger, laughed heartily. 'My poor ancient! Well, then, I must break a lance with your son! Montgomery — ah, this is impossible! Two men with the same name! You have another estate, Montgomery? Lorges? Give it to your son — I'll give him a title to go with it! Well, Count de Lorges —' the lieutenant bowed deeply at the unexpected title so casually presented to him — 'you've got eleven days before the tournament to practise. I'll meet you, God willing, on the last day.'

Montgomery's eyes moved apprehensively to the queen. 'It is too great an honour, Your Majesty,' he tried to demur.

But the king had seen the glance, and his swarthy face reddened in anger. He glared at them both. 'I'll take no argument! From anyone!'

Montgomery bowed acceptance; what else?

The queen swung away, upset, but after a moment she smiled, trying to cover her loss of control. 'It is becoming unpleasantly warm. Let us return indoors.' The ladies began a general movement towards the palace. Some of the men moved towards the horses again. But a shrill voice that I knew very well called, 'A moment, Your Majesty! I have a challenge, too!'

'What, Francois?' the king's tone was suddenly rather cold, as if he knew, as I did, what the dauphin was going to say and disapproved. 'You have already two opponents in the lists, on the first day and the last.'

Queen Catherine had turned. 'Indeed, Francois. You must not overtire yourself.' I could have told her that was the worst thing to say to him.

He looked sullen. 'There are three days of tournament, aren't there? I want to fight de Rouxelle. On the middle day. Then I'll have one opponent every day. That won't tire me.' They weren't happy about it. He started to look mutinous, and his lip jutted. 'I wish it!' God's wounds, I thought he'd have grown out of his tantrums by now! But apparently not.

I could stop this, as they clearly wanted to do. 'Your Royal Highness,' I said respectfully, 'I regret that this meeting is impossible.'

His parents' faces brightened. His didn't. 'Why?'

'Unfortunately, sire, I have no armour. While I should be glad to please you by taking part in the tournament simply in my Archer's uniform, I fear the heralds would scarcely allow it.'

There were some half-smiles from the watchers. Lark

119

looked relieved, but the lieutenant was rolling his eyes in disgust. What had I missed?

The dauphin's face only fell for a second. 'No problem!' he squeaked. 'Many of the Archers borrow their armour from the king anyway.' God's wounds, it had slipped my mind, and I'd thought I was being so clever! 'Your Majesty will permit?' His father shrugged; no, he'd not refuse such a common request. The prince stared at me, grinning in nasty triumph. 'On the thirtieth, then, de Rouxelle. I'll look forward to it!'

Under all their glares, what could I do but bow and thank him for the honour?

Next day, Montgomery came with me to see my armour fitted. The Master of the Arsenal, de Girolles, greeted us cheerfully. 'Come in, Montgomery — Count de Lorges, I should say! Honoured to make your acquaintance, de Rouxelle! You've to be fitted with jousting harness, I hear! Well, well, I've had some looked out for you. This way. Mind your head. Oh, dear, de Lorges, you're too tall for these damned medieval doors!' Fat and jovial, he bustled us along past rooms piled with morions and bassinets, breastplates and cuisses, shields and gauntlets, halberds and hackbuts, stacked high as they had been returned at the end of the war. The hammering of smiths busy at repairs echoed up the stairwells.

In a room lined with complete suits, two men were working on a fine Italian armour. The tallest of the other three present was laughing exasperatedly, 'Will you stop that! Tickle me again and I'll stick this awl where it'll do most good! And stop jiggling about!' Not the way to talk to a gentleman . . .

The smallest figure, standing on a stool and hung like a dumpy maypole with gilded metal, bowed with a clinking flourish. 'Monsieur de Rouxelle! I came today especially to renew our acquaintance!'

Chicot.

My pleasure and excitement froze instantly to apprehension.

'Yes, yes, gentlemen,' de Girolles assured us. 'Chicot's going to run a joust too! We're fitting the dauphin's old armour on him.'

'The child had ambitions to be Sir Hercules and Sir Roland in one! At eleven!' Chicot's sarcastic tone mocked all dreams.

'Boy's fancy.' De Girolles snorted. 'Not for fighting, of course. Toy. Grown out of it, and not worn it ten times. Too slim for you, Chicot, eh? Never mind, new straps, patches, some gilding; we can fake it up. You'll look splendid, and that's the main thing, eh?'

Montgomery laughed. 'Don't try riding a real joust in it, though!'

The dwarf smiled again, posturing heroically on the stool to make them laugh, his teeth brilliant in his dark beard. 'Ah, my lord, when I fight, I choose my armour, and my place, and my weapons, with great care. My enmity brings the downfall of hope! I slap down even the friends of princes!'

My teeth were grating. The little horror was reminding me of Lark and the dauphin, threatening me again! Me, an Archer! But he'd not said a word I could publicly object to, though Montgomery was frowning. Chicot's pleasure at my frustration irked me even more. I turned brusquely away.

As I tugged on a thick padded shirt and the men started arming me, I was aware all the time of Chicot behind me. There was the quiet professional mutter of the armourers — 'Take in two holes . . . padding's worn . . . too high . . . bend your knee, sir . . . half an inch anyway, get a shorter pair . . . buckle's broken, what idiot passed this? . . . new sollerets . . . grease it up . . . try the other gauntlets, sir . . . thumb moves easily now? Good.'

Under it, though, ran a constant commentary that had the men chortling. It was apparently about Chicot's own armour, but I knew he was referring to me. 'Not a normal shape at all, are we? Talk about a tortoise! Fit like a glove? What a laugh! Ever fitted a breastplate on a cow's udder? Mind where you put that rivet! Don't want to be all scarred, eh?'

This was the magical moment I'd dreamed of; being fitted for armour. Me, Johnnie Russell, the sergeant's wee laddie! And now it was an irksome chore. Even when it was time to pick my helmet, I had no pleasure in it.

'Nothing fancy, Jean, just a plain closed helm.'

'Surely not, de Lorges! It's not stylish for a young gentleman —'

'No matter, sir. There's never been a helmet to beat it. No decoration to trap a lance-point, just the soft plumes. It's light, and you can breathe, and see well.' More or less . . . 'I wear it myself. It's ideal.'

Chicot's snigger rose behind me. 'Pity the old pig-snout style's out of fashion. It'd suit him perfectly, don't you think?'

It was too obvious, too coarse for even a jester to get away with. The Master of the Arsenal turned puce. I started to swing round, clanking, and stumbled on my newly heavy feet. Montgomery beat us both to it. 'Suit him? God's wounds, you'd dare mock an Archer?'

Chicot leapt down hastily, protesting, 'No, no, sir!' In a moment he was clattering and cursing out of the room.

We calmed down de Girolles, and after that things went better. My armour was taken away for the final adjustments while we had a glass of wine and discussed the recent news. 'Heard about the trouble in Scotland, de Lorges? Queen Marie's mother, Marie de Guise, she's facing a rebellion. The Earl of Argyle — do I

122

have the name right? With twenty thousand men, sent by Elizabeth of England.'

'Yes, sir. She's afraid Henri will send a French army to help beat Argyle and then invade through Scotland and take the English throne for young Marie, now the war here's over. Though where she thinks he'd find the money I don't know. A pity. It could have been a glorious enterprise.'

'Protestant, of course, Elizabeth. How that girl survived her sister Mary, God alone knows. And now President du Bourg of the Parlement is clapped in the Bastille.' De Girolles shook his bald head. 'Good man, du Bourg, even if he is a heretic. Respected. Bad, bad business. I blame the Poitiers woman. Guilt, maybe. Like Mary Tudor. Buying her way into heaven by burning heretics.'

'And the Guises.' Montgomery looked over to where I stood in my trunks and shirt. 'You know why, Jean? The old Duc de Guise accused Calvinists of poisoning him. Queen Catherine seems less harsh, though.'

De Girolles snorted. 'I don't credit anything that woman says, sir.'

'The Serpent Queen, some folk call her,' I said, forgetting to keep quiet among my elders. They looked at me for a long moment. I blushed.

But de Girolles clapped my shoulder to encourage me. 'Right, lad. Never shows what she's thinking. Foreign, of course. Can't trust her.'

'She can't help while Diane and the Guises have the king's ear.' Montgomery commented. 'There's no chance of reform, or even justice.'

I suddenly realised from his tone that he was in sympathy with the Religion himself. He must be newly converted, since maman died — maybe that had something to do with it. Awkward for him, serving a king who persecuted Calvinists . . . He seemed to remember that we weren't of his party, and coughed. 'Will your

123

men have finished the armour, sir?' And we returned to the business on hand.

Montgomery lent me his best horse for the jousting, 'For your mount isn't fully trained yet, Johnnie, and you mustn't disgrace the Garde!' I wore my armour for hours, to get used to the feel of it. When well greased it was easy to move in. Montgomery said it was because it fitted well, with the weight spread over me. Even so, if I overbalanced, getting up was an exercise in engineering. And weightlifting. I felt sorry for my horse.

One problem had been solved. I'd asked Montgomery one day, 'Sir, what do I do about the dauphin? I know the lances are light, but accidents happen. Do I deliberately miss, and disgrace the Garde, or do I my best to strike him, and risk killing him?'

He slapped my shoulder. 'You'll use a Garde lance, John.'

'Of course, sir,' I said. 'White, with a silver pennon.'

'Aye, but look here; be sure you pick one like this, with the pennon that bit down from the point. It's the Garde will be the esquires, and they'll know. But you check, too.' He eyed me hard. 'They've been very carefully selected, lad. Wood for lances should be straight-grained, for a knot snaps. But sometimes you want a lance that will break at a touch, almost. A tactful tactical weakness, you'll understand. No!' He raised a hand as I started to speak. 'No questions. A bit paint hides the answer to a lot of awkward problems. Remember — the pennon farther down the lance. And you never mention this to a soul.'

'No, sir.'

He clapped my shoulder. 'Good lad. You'll not be unfairly matched, either. The dauphin's lance will be the same, though he'll not know. Honour will be even on both sides.'

'Honour, sir? Is it not — well — cheating?'

124

'Honour can have facets, John, like a jewel. You've sworn solemnly to protect the king and his family. How can you risk hurt to the dauphin?' He eyed me quizzically. 'With his mother watching?'

That decided me. Tact was honourable, too.

The Tournament

On the afternoon of the twenty-seventh of April, 1559, the grand tournament began.

Henri rode a horse presented to him by his sister's bridegroom; a fine black called Le Malheureux, The Wretch, because a quirk of its mouth made it look permanently dismal. But it was well trained, and helped the king win all his bouts that day. He was delighted.

Queen Catherine sat tensely on the royal stand, built against the wall of the palace opposite the centre of the tiltyard. On her right sat her daughter Elisabeth, married by proxy and due to leave for Spain soon; to her left sat Queen Marie, and on Marie's left again was Diane de Poitiers, whose black and white the king wore as ever. Lords and ladies squeezed in on the padded benches. Pages fluttered with iced wine among the stiff, brilliant satins and glorious silks like butterflies in a flowerbed. The rest of the Court sat in the less favoured stands all round the tiltyard. Lark and I were in the room behind the queens, watching over the shoulders and fans of the courtiers at the window in front of us.

In the afternoon the dauphin ran a course, to the cheers of the crowd and the agitation of his mother. He won. The other lad's girth snapped. I wondered . . . a tactful weakness?

Lark pulled me back from the crowd by the window. 'John, this bout against the dauphin. What are you going to do? Oh, please be careful!'

'Don't fret, Lark!' The room was hot and airless. I took her fan, an expensive new one of painted chickenskin, and fanned her gently. Fans today, lances tomorrow; what next?

'Oh, I do apologise!' she snapped in frustration. 'I'm just a silly female, to be worrying about it.'

I couldn't tell her. Not even to calm her down. Give her something else to think about . . . 'Who gave you this pretty trinket?'

She snatched the fan back, blushing, and wouldn't tell me. That took her mind off, eh? This suitor must be more important to her than the rest, or she'd have boasted as usual. Hey! Was my wee sister growing up?

That night, Her Majesty's shallow eyes were intent on her husband, talking to Diane; and on her son; and on me; and back to her husband. Her face was a well-schooled, smiling calm, but her ring-armoured fingers tapped tensely. At last she beckoned me. 'De Rouxelle, I fully understand the situation in which you find yourself. I know that you have not sought this challenge. But harm to the prince cannot and will not be forgiven. You understand me?' Her dull black eyes were desperate and deadly.

'Madame, I would die myself rather than hurt your son.' Her hands and eyes relaxed a touch. She was a good mistress, within her limits. But touch her children, and . . . If I got the wrong lance . . . Or if Chicot ever told . . .

Next day I was in the stuffy dressing tent early. Pierre

came down to the tents to lace up my padded tunic. 'Good luck, sir,' he said gloomily.

'Cheer up, man! I'll be back for my uniform in an hour!' He didn't look convinced.

The armourers buckled me swiftly and expertly into my harness. 'Moving easy, sir? A touch of oil on this elbow? That it? Good luck!' Casual. They moved away through a welter of pages to the next man; the dauphin himself.

I clanked over to the door to get a breath of cool air and watch the spectators gathering like multi-coloured vultures. Dad came by, proud as a peacock of his son going to joust with the dauphin, and quite at ease. 'I'll give you the right lance, never fear! Good luck!' He winked cheerfully and marched off. Why was everybody wishing me luck?

The first two courses were both between beginners, like me. The first pair ran three times and missed each other completely. The crowd jeered. I mustn't do that, whatever happened! One man in the second joust was actually unhorsed, broke a leg as he fell, and was carried off on a stretcher. H'm. I'd rather not do that either. Maybe I needed the luck.

My turn. I sat down on the bench facing the dauphin. The armourers bolted on our helmets. I rose, my heart thudding, and clanked behind him out and up the steps of the mounting blocks. My groom led up my horse; 'Good luck, sir!' Another optimist. As I nodded thanks he tiptoed to whisper, 'Sort the wee hellion out for us, sir! Teach him to respect the Scots Guard!' At that, at last, my heart lifted in excitement, and in the silly laughter that so often bubbled up at just the wrong moment.

Two heralds arrived to lead us out into the open, to face the crowds. Their faces were pink and cheery above their embroidered tabards. Well, they weren't risking their necks. But nor was I; I must remember that.

128

Then we were on our way, the sun suddenly turning my armour into an oven, the crowd cheering my Garde white plumes and saddle-cloth, the dauphin's blue and silver. Montgomery was patting my knee, shouting up, 'Ride hard, look good, and let the lances break!' Through the padding in my helmet, his voice sounded muffled. I knew nothing was going to happen; why was I grinning, my heart pounding?

The dauphin's gilded armour glowed beside me in the sunlight. Mine was plain and workmanlike. Maybe some day I could afford a suit of my own ... Get my mind back on the job! We turned side by side towards the balcony, and bowed to the king and queens. Marie leaned over the balustrade and tossed down a blue scarf as her favour for her husband. A herald picked it up and came to tie it round his right arm.

Somebody was tugging at my arm, too. I looked down. It was my herald, with a scarf — no, a choice of scarves! When I raised my head, I saw a covey of girls leaning over, smiling and blowing kisses. The Flying Squadron! God's wounds! Which one ... ? Peering up, I just recognised Lark's new green dress, and thankfully chose the green scarf to avoid complications. I kissed it to her; if you've got to make a fool of yourself, do it thoroughly. As the herald fastened it round my arm, I turned my head. The dauphin was glaring from Lark to me, his podgy face pursed tight with spite.

I swallowed. I hoped he'd get the right kind of lance, too!

The King of Arms, the chief herald of France, reminded us of the rules. No lance must touch the other's horse, on pain of disqualification. We would run three times, unless either one of us was unhorsed or hurt so that he had to surrender, when his horse and armour would belong to the winner. What? The

129

armour was the king's anyway, but Montgomery might lose his best horse! I hadn't realised how great a favour he'd done me.

We turned away to our own ends of the course. My mouth was dry and my palms wet. What wouldn't I give for a cool glass of cider? Rough cider like maman used to make, kept cold in the well, with a dew of mist on the cup . . .

Here was the rack of slender lances. My horse was excited, and I was hard put to it to hold him in. This wasn't a practice, and he knew it. I eased my shoulders and reached for the lance dad handed up; the pennon was nearly two feet from the end. Right. Exchange a grin of encouragement with dad; snap down my visor; a deep breath; bend forward so that I could see up through the slots, three inches away from my eyes; find the King of Arms, and his flag a tiny white blur raised above him; a pause — why so long?

The trumpet sounded, and the flag fell.

My horse, more experienced than I was, surprised me by leaping forward before I spurred him. The squeak, clink and grate of the armour — the thunder of the cheering and the hooves. A gilded figure — aim right a bit — tight in the saddle — now! A cracking thud to my left shoulder, balanced by an equal jolt on my right arm. We'd both hit. The cantle nearly waist-high behind me held me in place. I'd felt far worse in practice. My light lance bent like a bow — snapped — the point with its tell-tale pennon bounced up past my shoulder as I rode on and fell behind me just as it was meant to!

At the far end of the course I dropped my broken lance and turned. At my end, the dauphin's blue-caparisoned horse was turning also. Its rider was still there, thank God.

The cheering was deafening. The dauphin had broken a lance honourably! Vive le dauphin! Vive le roi! Vive la France!

One down, two to go. I was laughing out loud, in sheer exhilaration.

The esquire here was offering me another lance. Check; the pennon was well down from the point. Pause; the trumpet; the flag fell. This time I was readier for it. The dauphin's horse, racing towards me on the far side of the barrier, was a very tall beast; aim a little higher — I must have nearly touched it last time. I was concentrating so hard on not hitting the horse that I nearly missed the small rider, my point glancing lightly off his pauldron, while his lance broke very showily against my visor. The clang was tremendous, and my head jerked fairly hard even though my helmet was bolted onto my breast and back plates. But the padding had saved my skull, and the bolts my neck. The visor couldn't lift, of course, at a blow from above. I was still in one piece.

Third run. There was some delay at the dauphin's end, but at last there he was, poised to charge. The herald's flag fell. I didn't hear the trumpet that time. The blue and gold plumes were spurring forward on that huge grey horse. The shouting rose again as I spurred on too, aiming for the pauldron.

Blue and gold? Not blue and silver?

In the second before impact I recognised the patched armour. Chicot! That damned jester! The brat! What to do? Dishonour to me and the Garde to touch him in a joust. Worse if I dodged. His armour was just for show, I might kill him, even with the fragile lance — too bad! I aimed straight for the centre of his breastplate.

Suddenly a shock slammed me back, twisted me, jerked me spinning right over the cantle as if I'd come to the end of a rope.

Even as I flew, I knew what had happened. I was using

131

the shorter tournament lance; Chicot, with his acrobat's training, was using a full-length heavy fighting spear. He hit me a foot before my lance could touch him. And his spear didn't break tactfully.

Then the ground threw itself noisily up at me.

When I woke I was in bed, mostly out of my armour, and Lark was wiping my face — my nose was bleeding. My back hurt, it was agony to move my neck, but I seemed to have no bones broken. There was a stiff, furious argument going on at the end of the hospital tent. King Henri himself, the King of Arms, two junior heralds, Montgomery, his father; the dauphin was surrounded, mumbling sullenly that he'd meant no insult to me, or the College of Heralds, or the Garde Ecossaise; it was a jest. Nobody believed him. I started feeling sorry for him, in a satisfied kind of way; everyone was blaming Chicot and meaning the dauphin, tearing him to shreds most politely. 'Not the action of an honourable person . . . disqualification . . . horse and armour of the dauphin forfeit to Monsieur de Rouxelle . . .' The little devil's malice had got him into real trouble at last. Good! The king's voice was gruff. 'An apology, Francois — only honourable course . . .' God's wounds, that'd please the lad!

He flung sulkily away from his father and the men, and glared down at me. Lark faded quietly away. He smirked. 'I'm told I must apologise to you, Monsieur de Rouxelle! For my dwarf's beating you!'

I shrugged, cautiously. I found I still couldn't help grinning. 'Don't let it fret you, sire. I must have got out of bed the wrong side this morning. It's just been one of those days!'

Suddenly his face broke. He dropped to one knee beside me. 'Jean! How can you joke about it? I could have got you killed!'

I saw his father and the men behind him exchanging glances. He'd refused to admit it a moment before. 'I told you, sire, Scots are tough.' He stood up, his face working. 'By the way . . .' It was difficult to think clearly. 'You'll need your armour — you have another course tomorrow.'

There was another general glance round. The King of Arms coughed gently. 'A ransom is usually paid for weapons and armour. Will you do me the honour of leaving it in my hands, Monsieur de Rouxelle?'

He'd salt the dauphin's tail for him . . . 'Most gratefully, my lord.' At least the little brat could ride again tomorrow. Maybe I shouldn't have done it, his mother would prefer him not to joust again. Oh well, too late. But what did he think about it himself?

He abruptly dipped his head to kiss my cheek. 'You'll come back to me. Today. Rejoin my household, Jean. I wish it!' He was panting with excitement. 'My mother will agree, you'll see! I'll go and tell her now!'

It's an odd sensation, your jaw dropping when you're lying down.

Francois leapt up and left so fast that his attendants nearly fell over themselves following him. His father nodded in approval, patted my shoulder and led most of the rest out while I tried not to yelp with pain.

Montgomery smiled. 'Well, Jean! I don't know quite how you did it, but you've made up with him again!'

Lark's mouth was open. 'What a — what a — well!'

Dad was scowling. 'That Chicot!' His words were pithy and powerful. I couldn't help chuckling, in spite of the aches. 'Don't be so cheerful! I think I'll just visit the wee man wi' a whip!'

'No, don't do that, Robert,' Montgomery advised. 'He did only what Francois ordered. Leave it. The prince feels guilty, but he's not been publicly blamed. He'll give your son anything just now.'

Dad considered. 'Aye. Good pals again, eh? Let's no

133

disturb the happy pair, then.' He grunted. 'But some dark night . . .'

Personally, I worried about Chicot. I didn't believe the idea had been all the dauphin's, though he might think so. That was the second time — no, the third — that the dwarf had tried to hurt me, and ended up by doing me a favour. He'd be raging. Dad might not be the only one out in the dark . . .

All that night Pierre put hot and cold compresses on my neck and back, and massaged me with warm oil till I could move again. With a stiff bandage to support my neck, I escorted the dauphin to the last day of the tournament.

The queen had again been begging Henri not to fight. He hurled himself into his seat on the balcony with a face like thunder.

The jousting was poor. The dauphin won again; his opponent's lance waved like a daisy in the breeze. The next pair were as bad. Henri finally lost the last of his patience and came charging down to the dressing tents where Francois was being unharnessed, shouting, 'God's belly, where's de Lorges? We'll show these wilting pansies some real jousting!'

He'd take no denial. Lieutenant Montgomery was summoned. The pair of them were harnessed side by side, almost arm in arm, the king constantly calling on the armourers to make haste. They rode out together. Henri would scarcely wait for the heralds; 'We know the rules! Get on with it!'

I suddenly saw the same green scarf Lark had given me, tucked into Montgomery's gauntlet. Well . . . !

The dauphin and I watched from the tent, his arm round my shoulders. 'Mother's in a state!' he commented with a smirk. 'Look at her fingers!' I couldn't make them out, but I did see Diane de Poitiers reach over to her in reassurance. Catherine stiffened and moved aside from the kindly hand.

In the first run, the king reeled in the saddle. The queen jumped up, but he recovered. Each man had broken his lance. Honours were even.

In the second run, they each broke a second lance.

They had to pause while Montgomery's girth was adjusted. The king was lounging in the tent drinking a cup of wine with Montgomery before the third run when a page entered, and nervously knelt. 'Sire, Her Majesty begs that you will not joust again. Your Majesty has done enough for honour.'

For a moment I thought the king would throw the cup at him. 'God's belly! Am I the king or is she? Women! Besides, we're even. We must settle the match. Tell her — tell Her Majesty I'll break one more lance. In her honour!' He snorted, pleased with the idea. That should keep her from bothering him; honour for her, instead of Diane!

Montgomery shrugged. 'Maybe, to respect Her Majesty's fears . . .'

'Don't be a fool!' The king was scornful. 'Come along, man!' He leapt up to the saddle again with the ease and energy of an athlete twenty years younger, not bothering to use the mounting block, and seized a lance, laughing. 'Come on, de Lorges! Let's not keep the ladies waiting!' He cantered off, waving to the cheering crowd, turned at the far end of the field and shut his vizor ready for the charge.

Montgomery grinned at the rest of us. 'Keep my wine for me!' He hesitated as a lance was offered him. Should he pick a weak one? No, it would be an insult to his king. He winked at me as he rode off.

We watched the great horses thunder towards each other. There was a crash, and both lances were broken again. Everyone cheered — and stopped.

The king wasn't riding on. He dropped his reins, so that the well-trained Malheureux slowed and halted. His hands were at his face. The queen was standing, screaming, a tearing scream that ripped through the sudden silence. Francois gripped my arm in horror, whispering, 'No! No!'

Henri fell, slowly, to crash to the ground.

Montgomery's lance had not snapped cleanly as it should have done. As a weak one would have done. Its tip had shattered against the moulded and carved decorations of the king's visor, and splayed out, driving long, twisted splinters with dreadful force through the slits into his face.

Montgomery was a Scot. The Royal Arms of Scotland were a lion rampant.

The young lion had killed the old one, in single combat in his forty-first year; his eye smashed in its golden cage.

I half-carried the dauphin, white and trembling, behind the stretcher bearing his father into the palace, but I couldn't go with him into the king's room. As I stopped, I found Lark, shaking violently, grasping my arm. 'Come on, love!' I whispered. 'Steady!' I put my arm round her waist to support her. 'It's maybe not all that bad.'

'What'll they do to him?' She murmured so low I could barely hear her.

'He's not dead. The physicians —'

'Not the king! Gabriel!'

'Gabriel?' I pushed to find her a seat, for she was near collapse.

'Gabriel Montgomery!'

It was worrying me, too. 'He didn't mean to do it. It was the king's own command. They can't blame him.' I hoped. But since when did my wee sister call him by his first name? I didn't, and I was his friend.

Diane de Poitiers, white as her own stiff silks, hurried past us. She was a good nurse, who had once saved the life of Catherine herself from childbed fever, but she had stood on the balcony, calling anxiously to be told how the king was, while the queen had thrust through the crowd like a madwoman to her husband's side. As Diane reached his room, the queen's voice sounded inside and the door was shut in her face.

She stopped dead.

The crowd round us froze, patted at its tears to hide its expressions and give itself time to think, and started doing frantic calculations about who was, or would be, in, or out, of power if the king died, or lived.

La Belle Diane drew a deep breath to recover from the rebuff. Her huge violet eyes glanced round the hall. Few met her gaze. What now? She was a duchess in her own right, and a great lady who would not demean herself by behaving with less than dignity. Turning away, she said quite clearly to the duke beside her, 'We must not disturb the physicians at their work. Pray you, d'Aumale, send for my carriage. If I am needed, I shall return immediately, of course. But now we must go and pray for the king's health.'

Which naturally produced a scatter of courtiers, none wishing to be thought unwilling to pray for the king, all desperate to spread and discuss the news. Her retreat was easily covered in their departure.

Lark and I sat waiting for word, staring at the medieval murals. The wall in front of us showed the Death of Hercules. Pages and physicians scurried with hot water, bags, notes, bundles of gilded armour.

Lark fidgeted, sniffed, rose. 'I must see how he is. Gabriel. I —'

'Sit down!' I hissed. 'You're the queen's attendant. You can't go wandering off, any more than I can. Wait, and maybe soon you can run to him with good news.' She nodded reluctantly, her hands twisting together.

The inner door opened again. We all half-rose in anticipation. Count de Montgomery came out, grey and grim, his white satin stained with blood, and gazed round rather blindly. I moved forward, for I thought for a second that he was going to faint, but when his eyes lit on my Archer's uniform, his mind seemed to clear. He swallowed, but spoke loudly for all to hear. 'The King's Majesty is conscious, and calls for my son. Fetch him at once.'

Lark gasped with relief. It couldn't be so bad, surely!

As I turned to go, Montgomery himself marched in. He'd taken off his armour and was in uniform again, the silk scarcely whiter than his face. Lark leaned forward, but he had no eye for her. 'Sir? How is the King?'

His father stood aside. 'Come in. He wants speech with you.'

I glanced back at Lark. She nodded urgently, and motioned me forward. I took my chance and followed them in, leaving her sitting there alone.

The bedroom was crowded. Nobody could send the queen away, or the dauphin, or Queen Marie, or the Cardinal of Lorraine, or the Dukes of Guise or Bourbon. Catherine was sitting holding the king's hand, while the rest stood round his bedposts like church statues. The window was closed, and the heat stifling. Four physicians were muttering together in the far corner. Two of the bodyguards were carefully not catching Montgomery's eye.

The king's face was mostly hidden by red-stained bandages. As we entered he called, 'Is that him? Montgomery! Have you brought your son?' His voice was surprisingly strong.

'Yes, your Majesty. He is here.'

The hurt man's free hand crawled across the coverlet, feeling out towards us. 'De Lorges? Are you there?'

The lieutenant stepped forward, taking the reaching hand in his. 'Here, sire. I beg your Majesty's pardon. I had no intention —'

'No, no. I know that.' Unwisely, the king moved his head on the pillows and cried out. The queen drew in her breath hissing beside him, and the dauphin bit his lip, cowering in to Queen Marie's side like a beaten puppy. When the pain had died down, the king turned his hand in his wife's grasp. 'Catherine — you are there? Catherine, he is not to be harmed. You hear me? It was an accident. Accident. I order — Agh!' He had moved again. 'Diane! I want Diane! Where is she?'

There was a pause. I was the only one there who actually knew what had happened. I stepped forward and bowed. The queen's eyes glinted sharply. 'Sire, she has gone to pray for your recovery.' Catherine nodded approval.

Henri moaned, 'Diane! Call Diane! Diane, I need you! Diane!'

The queen rose, wiped the tears from her cheeks and looked down at him. 'Soon, my dear. Rest, now.' She laid his hand gently on the cover. 'Come, let us allow the physicians peace to tend His Majesty.' She swept us out into the hall again, leaving her husband groaning on his bed.

Outside, she gazed, as Diane had done, round the attentive faces. 'It would be a pity to disturb the prayers of Madame de Poitiers, of which the king stands in such need,' she said flatly. 'I shall send for her myself when the time is right.' Her olive skin was pale, but her expression was hard as any rock. Her beloved husband was all hers now. Whatever he wanted he should have; except his love, since that was not herself.

She stepped slowly up to Montgomery, looking into his face, and spoke without moving her head. 'Count de Montgomery, you will hold the Count de Lorges strictly confined until the king's further pleasure be known.'

We gasped. Lark, on the far side of the room, clasped her hands over her mouth. The count protested, 'But your Majesty, his Majesty said —'

Unmoving as a statue, never shifting her flat eyes from his son's face, she interrupted. 'His Majesty is at present unfit to make decisions. Until his recovery, his assailant must be kept safe, in case any charge may be laid against him.' Her fingers were twined in her rope of pearls, and as she spoke it snapped. The great jewels rolled like tears down her crimson satin and pattered over the floor. She spared them not a single glance.

The count bowed stiffly to her, and to his son. They turned together in a single motion, and marched out side by side. Lark was biting her fingers. Oh God, what would happen to him? What would the queen do to him?

Queen Catherine turned to the rest of us. 'Your Graces — in the morning, if the king is still unwell, I feel the Council should meet.' She had no right to call it; but then she wasn't, exactly. The Dukes of Guise and Bourbon bowed. 'Your Eminence, I beg your prayers for my husband's recovery.' The cardinal bowed too. Her eye moved on. 'Your Majesties —' my heart jolted, but of course they were King and Queen of Scots — 'perhaps you will go and rest? There is nothing you can do for the present. I shall send word if there is any change in his Majesty's condition.'

The dauphin beckoned me to follow him. Lark was weeping, but I had to obey orders. As I went out, Queen Catherine was handing the remains of her necklace to a page. 'Here. Recover the rest. One hundred and eleven pearls, and ninety-two crystals.' And she turned back to the door of the room where her husband lay crying for Diane.

Love, I thought. Henri, torn between Catherine and Diane. Montgomery and Lark. My sister was — she was sixteen, now that I thought of it. More than ten years younger than Montgomery, but dad aye said I was a cold-blooded Scot, like him; Lark was more French, like maman, soon a woman. I was glad of it; I could do without love.

The Warrant

The king grew worse, better, worse again. The doctors bled him, dosed and poulticed him, probed agonisingly for fragments of splinters that they thought must remain in the wound, beheaded four condemned criminals and thrust lance splinters into their eyes to study the effects. All in vain.

Queen Catherine spent her time either devotedly nursing her husband, or on her knees praying for him. Francois visited his father daily, tired, frightened and overwhelmed by the sudden tragedy. Queen Marie came often. The Council and Court, foreign ambassadors, half of France, it seemed to me, trooped in silent reverence through the small, stuffy chamber.

The one person who was never admitted to the king's room was Diane.

Instead, the day after the tournament, she received a letter demanding that she return to the treasury all of the royal jewels Henri had given her, which if he died would become the property of Marie, the new Queen of France. No-one was sure who had sent it — Catherine or Marie.

To my relief — and, I have to admit, chagrin — Francois no longer needed me so much. His wife comforted him through his nightmares, he had new friends and attendants, and the Guises took up much of his time. I had more freedom than I'd expected to see Lark, who was also unneeded, and together we often visited the Conciergerie beside Notre Dame Cathedral. Montgomery was lodged there instead of in the Bastille because it was the nearest prison to his father's house. He was on the first floor, in a pleasant enough room, with his own servants and his meals sent in from his father's kitchens. He always welcomed us eagerly — he wasn't a reader, and the time hung on his hands, for only his fellow-Archers, fiercely defensive, visited a man who might be charged with killing a king.

Dad came up with us once, when he was free. I could see him keeping a thoughtful eye on Lark. After we had escorted her back to the palace, 'It's a bind, lad,' he said ruefully. 'There's no a soul I'd have liked better to see her take up with. He's a grand match, a good man, old enough to bear with her flightiness, well born an' well set up but no too rich nor too noble; just perfect. An' here we have to keep them apart.'

'You noticed, then?'

'Notice? A blind man runnin' from a bull would be hard put to it no to notice,' he grunted. 'Sittin' as close as she can get, she'd be in his lap if she could, an' quiverin' like a jelly whenever he speaks to her? An' she can't keep her eyes off his face, an' can't meet his glance. Aye that wee smile, an' pick-pickin' at the braidin' on her sleeve. Dod, I mind it fine when I was courtin'. She's the image o' your mother, God rest her soul.'

'What about Montgomery, though?' I asked. 'He doesn't show much.'

'Well, he's older, an' more in control o' himsel'; but did you no see him makin' excuses to touch her hand, come close enough for his foot to brush her skirt? I know the signs, son. I've been through it. An' you'll come to it yet! Aye, he's smitten. An' he's an honest man. If he was free, he'd be in to see me, to ask for her hand honourably. But what can he say, in prison, with the rage o' a queen threatenin' him? He can't ask her to join him at risk. No, all he can do is wait until he can speak freely.'

'When will that be?' I muttered, and he shook his head doubtfully.

We parted; he walked on to the barracks, while I went home. As Guy hung up my cloak and sword, Pierre came smiling down the stair. 'Friend of yours come to visit, sir!' he said cheerfully.

I ran up to the hall. By the window stood a small, shy figure in a bright green dress with flowers all over it. 'Nicola!' I cried, my heart somehow lifting at the sight of her. 'Nicola la Jardinière! How are you? You're looking well, my dear! God's wounds, Nicola, you're like that song they used to sing about Mary Tudor! What is it? *Mary Mary quite contrary, how does your garden grow? With silver bells and cockle shells, and pretty flowers all in a row!*'

Her sweet little voice joined mine halfway through, and we ended up laughing together. 'I'll have to remember that one, sir!' she chuckled. 'I can easily get shells, and I've silver bells already for the moresco dance. That would make a good piece for me! For a happier time, maybe.' We both fell silent for a moment. 'He's worse again,' she sighed. No need to say who 'he' was. 'Not more than another day, the physicians say.'

'And then the dauphin'll be king. King Francois.'

'And you his friend again,' she nodded. 'It's that I've come to see you about. When your sister — well, when she . . .'

'Slapped him. Aye.'

'Yes. When she did that, she put your neck under the axe.'

I snorted. 'You've no need to tell me that, Nicola! I've just been waiting for Chicot or somebody to tell the queen. And then God help me!'

She took my hand comfortingly. 'Never fear, sir. The dauphin has Chicot gagged. He's warned him he'll have him hanged if the tale gets out, for he's terrified that Marie'll hear of the blow, and then ask why a young girl should dare do such a thing, and find out about him. You did exactly the right thing, sir, threatening to tell her. Chicot'll hold his tongue, and make sure all the rest of us do too, for fear of his master. You know the lad's never done anything like that since? The fright you gave him seems to have scared him out of his nasty ways.'

'Oh?' Pierre, serving wine, looked relieved, but I was doubtful. 'Did he not put a page's eye out with an arrow in Fontainebleau last winter?'

'A sheer accident, sir. It was terrible weather, and they were playing at archery along a corridor. Guillaume de — de — I forget. Oh, it doesn't matter, he was an idiot, he simply walked out just as the dauphin loosed. The prince even shouted to warn him! That's something, now, for last year he'd have cheered. The change in him! He's still sulky, and if he's angered he'll strike out, but who doesn't? But not the sickly, deliberate evil! There's not one of us who knew him before, or has heard about him, that doesn't bless your name. If you ever need help, just ask; all the palace servants will do anything we can for you.'

I was flattered, but didn't believe her. 'Even Chicot?'

'Well, no,' she had to admit with a smiling shrug. 'Not him. He's tried to hurt you, and failed, and he'll never forgive you. That's what I came to say.' Her pretty face became deadly serious. 'It's the dauphin. He's still not well. They say — you know they're making bets on how long he'll live? Well, if he dies — when he dies — beware! Run for your life. For there'll be nothing then to hold back Chicot from telling the queen. You've bested him three times now; he'll take his revenge. Never doubt it!'

I didn't.

At first she perched shyly on the edge of a chair, but gradually relaxed as we spoke like friends. She was well informed about the Court, and thought it a pity that the king hadn't pardoned the Protestant du Bourg, as a gesture of mercy. 'But then, he never did think for himself. It was Diane, always, and now it's the Cardinal of Lorraine makes up his mind for him. The Guises will rule the dauphin too, through Marie. Her mother's a Guise, and she always does what her uncles advise.'

'Yes.' I hesitated. 'I've wondered should I ask her for help for Montgomery, do you think? Though he's a Calvinist.'

'Better not, sir.' Nicola was quite definite. 'She'd maybe suspect a fanatic's plot, like her uncles. You'd probably make things worse.'

Next day the king died quietly, just after dawn.

It had been expected, of course. Messengers were away with the news within minutes, and a meeting of the Council was set for that afternoon. But first, Queen Catherine had something to do. She prayed, her son and his wife beside her; and they wept together. And as her son left the room, holding Marie's hand, Catherine walked into her office and came out with a sheet of paper, signed and sealed in red wax. She beckoned Walter Turnbull, who now attended her again in my place. Her voice was dull and flat. 'Tourneboule! The Governor of the Conciergerie is expecting this warrant. As he loved his king, the execution is to take place immediately.' She turned back to kneel by the bed again. Turnbull saluted, and marched out.

Lark left her place, slipping away like a black velvet shadow behind the other attendants while the queen's back was turned, to patter away after Turnbull. I should have gone with the dauphin, but I followed her. 'Stop,

Walter! For God's sake, stop!' she begged him, seizing his sleeve to halt him. 'You know what that is! It's Gabriel's death-warrant!'

He looked down at her regretfully. 'I'm sorry, lassie,' he said. 'There's nothing I can do. I like him too, but I must obey my orders!'

She turned to me. 'Oh, Johnnie! Help me! Help me!' Her eyes were huge and desperate. But what could I do?

For my wee sister? I had to try.

I looked over at Turnbull. He looked at me. He was a good soldier. If I did anything open, he'd defend himself; and it wouldn't help, anyway. But if I could delay him . . . At least it would give me time to think.

'Be quiet, Lark!' I snapped. 'He's got to do his duty!' She cried out in horror at my refusal. 'Stay here, and keep quiet!' I opened a door half-hidden in the panelling. 'Wattie, come down along here. It'll let you out right at the side of the stables, and avoid the crowd in the anterooms.'

It was a stupid story, but just barely possible. I'd been here more than he had; I might know the servants' passages better. But as we rounded the first corner, he glanced sideways. 'It'll do no good, son,' he told me. 'The message'll get through sooner or later. And then you'll be for it!'

He knew what I was at, and wanted to help, but saw no hope for it. I saw little enough myself. I nodded. 'Maybe, Wattie. But later's better than sooner. And I'll take my chances.' I opened a door. 'This way.'

He walked in immediately, stopped, turned round in the middle of the little store-room and shook his head. 'I wish you luck, son,' he said. 'You're goin' to need it!' He stood and watched while I shut and locked the door. As I hurried back to Lark, I could hear him knocking, as was his duty, on the door, and calling 'Let me out! Let me out!' But quietly.

Lark was standing where I'd left her, dazed and unbelieving. 'Wake up, wee sister, and tell me what we can do now!' I whispered, tugging her into a window embrasure. 'That's the message stopped, but just for a while.'

One of the chamberlains passed, and I thought of what Nicola had told me. I caught the old man's arm. 'Duvallier, will you aid me? I need help.'

He stopped at once. 'De Rouxelle? What's wrong? What can I do?'

'The passage in there, down the back stair to the kitchen corridor. Can you stop anybody going along it for an hour? It's important. Vital.'

He frowned, but didn't waste time asking questions. 'Stop anybody? Anybody at all? I'll see what I can do. H'm. Noircy!' A passing servant stopped. 'Noircy, stand here and don't let anyone go through this door. They've all to go round by the blue room. Say the stair's cracked and dangerous, if anybody asks you. I'll go and block the other end.' He raised an eyebrow at me, and as I smiled and nodded, and the servant took up his position importantly, he hurried away. With a touch of luck, and Walter doing his bit by not shouting too loudly, we might have that hour.

To do what?

'There's only one person can stop that warrant,' I said grimly to Lark. 'And now's the time to find out just exactly how he feels about me.'

'The dauphin?' she whispered as I led her off along the corridor.

'No. The king!'

The lad was standing looking out of the window at the gardens when I entered, Lark behind me, and knelt. He beckoned me with a faint smile, waving away his equerries and pages. I gestured to Lark to wait by the door. 'It's you, Jean! Thank God! I thought it was the Duc de Guise back again. He and the cardinal haven't left me alone for days. They tell me I should be praying, but I've prayed till my knees ache. And surely my father's in heaven already, so what good will my prayers do him?'

What could I say? 'Well, sire, the cardinal probably knows a sight more about it than I do. At least he says he does!'

He looked startled, and then almost laughed before pulling his face straight again. 'Don't make jokes, Jean! Not with my father lying dead.'

'It's a blessed relief for the man, sire,' I said quietly. 'I'm sure he's happy about it. It's a pity you can't feel that too.'

He nodded. 'I do, Jean. But they all say I should be mourning.'

'And you will, sire. When your time comes to do it. When my mother — when maman died, I was very ill; I didn't weep for her for weeks. Then suddenly I realised my loss, sire, and the tears came. They'll come for you, too, in God's good time.'

He took a step towards me, put his arms round me, and hugged me close. 'Thank God you're here, Jean!' he whispered. 'All the rest are — they're so — they say what they think they ought to say. I need you, Jean. Stay with me! You're the only one that's honest. You always have been.'

This was my chance. 'I'll be glad to stay, sirc. But may I ask you a favour, in return?'

He drew back, his face changing to a sneer. 'A favour? You, too, Jean? Well. What is it?'

'Sire, it's not for myself. But the Archer. Your father's opponent in the joust. Gabriel Montgomery, Count de Lorges. You'll remember that your father himself said it was an accident, and he shouldn't be harmed?'

The sneer had vanished. 'Yes, Jean, I remember. What about it?'

This was the difficult bit. 'Your lady mother, sire. Her

Majesty Queen Catherine. She has sent a warrant for his execution.'

He thought about it. 'Well — he did kill my father.'

'He didn't mean to, sire. He didn't even want to fight — I was there, and so were you. You heard him try to refuse. Even on the day itself, it was your father who insisted on that last joust. It was pure mischance.' The thought came to me. 'Like when you hit the page with your arrow.'

He bit his lip. 'You heard about that? It was an accident, Jean.'

'I know that, sire. And so was your father's death.'

He turned away, back to gaze out of the window. 'Maybe. But . . . I can't go against the Queen of France!'

I drew a deep breath. 'No, sire. It is your wife who is the Queen of France. As Your Majesty is now the King of France. Your mother is the Queen Dowager.'

He'd known, of course, but it seemed he'd not appreciated it. His jaw dropped. 'Yes — that's true! I'm king now! She wanted to be regent, but the Guises said I'm fifteen, I'm of age to rule alone. And it's true! So she has to do what I say!' He seemed delighted.

'Then if Your Majesty will grant a pardon to Lieutenant Montgomery . . .'

But thinking was one thing; actually doing was another. He hummed and hawed; and time was passing. Had Turnbull been freed? Was he halfway across Paris already? I pressed Francois as hard as I dared, but he'd not call a secretary to write the pardon. He was growing sulky. I was near despair.

Suddenly the door was opened, and Queen Marie was announced.

She swept across the carpet, to bend and kiss her husband's cheek before she turned to me. 'De Rouxelle, I am glad you are here with us again at this dreadful time. His Majesty my husband values your friendship.' She noticed my tension. 'But what is amiss?'

Would she help or hinder? Nothing to lose now. Except my position . . . That didn't matter, compared to Montgomery's life. Before Francois could stop me, I repeated to her my plea for Montgomery. As I spoke, I heard Lark, unsummoned, walking up to kneel beside me. She joined her voice to mine. 'Your Majesties, this is the first day — the first hour of your reign. I beg you, let it commence with an act of both justice and mercy.'

Queen Marie sat down on a chair by the window. It immediately became a throne. She turned regally to the puny little figure standing by her like a pageboy, or like a child by its mother, and said, 'Well, Francois? Your Majesty? What shall we do?'

He fidgeted. 'I don't know, Marie. Jean says the Archer didn't mean to do it, but — he did kill the king — and the queen — Queen Catherine — she's very angry . . . What do you think?'

She looked thoughtful. 'Well, it is a good argument that we should be merciful. And I'm quite sure it was unintentional. I do feel sympathetic, especially as the plea is from a Scot for a Scot. But it's you who must decide. I have no right to make the decision for you, or sign a pardon. Just as your mother had really no right to sign a warrant of execution.'

Not that anyone would argue with her. Except Lark and me.

That hadn't struck the dauphin — the king — either. 'No, no she hadn't, had she? Not really. No. Well . . . If you think I should . . .'

'I applaud your good judgement,' she said, taking the hesitant agreement by the scruff of its neck and firmly turning it into definite approval. Lark beside me nearly sobbed with relief as the young queen decisively beckoned a secretary and dictated to him the five lines of the pardon. It was written out at once, for she could see how urgent the matter was, and the desk was held out to the new king, the pen dipped for

151

him, the paper all ready, the wax for the seal heating over the candle.

He hesitated, chewing his lip. Marie smiled brilliantly, encouraging him. Suddenly, like leaping into water, he snatched the pen and scribbled 'Francois R', his hand and chin both trembling. He stood back after this, perhaps the first time he'd ever defied his mother, watching the seal being attached; and his wife, having persuaded him with charm and understanding into doing what she wanted, praised him for his courage and clemency.

Glowing at the praise, panting with the excitement, he took the parchment and held it out to me. 'There you are, Jean. Take it, and go and save your friend. And tell him from me he has a good friend in you!'

'As you have too, Francois,' Queen Marie told him, as I bowed away.

Lark slipped back with me to the door. 'Oh, thank you, Johnnie, thank you! Come on, now!' she urged me. 'If we give the pardon to Walter Turnbull we can save him a journey! And he'll not make any complaint about being shut up, either!'

We raced off through the rooms and corridors to where Turnbull was locked up. The servant was still keeping guard at the little door, and tried to stop us. 'It's all right,' I assured him. 'We know about the staircase! We'll be fine!'

Joyfully, we ran down the passage, round the bend.

The door was open. Walter Turnbull was gone.

Gone to the Conciergerie.

And the warrant for Montgomery's immediate execution with him.

I didn't even stop to tell Lark to go back to the queen. I was off like a coney down its burrow along the passages, through the crowds, across the yard to the stables, grabbing the reins of a fine mare from a startled, groom. 'In the king's name! Clear the way!' I yelled, and kicked the equally startled beast for the gates.

Everybody looked round and leapt for their lives. Just as well; I wouldn't have stopped for a dozen of them.

The Rue Saint Antoine was packed with mourners; I'd have to go by the back streets. There wasn't far to go; less than two miles. How far behind Turnbull was I? Could I catch him? Would he be hurrying, to prove himself dutiful? Or dawdling, in hope that I'd succeed in thinking of something? God's wounds, I had to save Montgomery! Thank God he wasn't in the Bastille just round the corner!

My horse was excited, entering into the spirit of the race, its hooves clattering, sparking and slipping on the cobbles. I was taking the narrow, crowded streets dangerously fast, shouting to clear the road. Between two carts, the donkeys braying in fright. A man with a tall pile of baskets on his head jumping for safety, the baskets toppling but I was past. Ragged children playing leapfrog, scattering with a cheer.

A small market, packed with elderly gossips, slow to move. Stalls of fish and leeks overturned, the owners cursing. Screams — my mount, rearing and neighing, had trampled a beggar. 'Make way, in the king's name!' God's wounds, I couldn't get on! I'd be too late!

Some Archers at the far end of the street saw my urgency and started to shout, clearing a path for me. I waved, drove forward towards them, cut into the path they had opened, one was dad, no time to stop, charge past.

Three monks nearly martyred for the dignity of their order. Two nuns with more sense, leaping nimbly, black habits flying, outraged pink faces upturned under huge white coifs, red mouths shouting, the noise lost in the din of the hooves echoing off the walls.

More din than there should be?

Another horse behind me. Two. Lark, black skirts hitched up, riding astride, screaming white-faced. And dad, cursing a kidnapped carthorse as first cousin to a snail, riding bareback, whipping it along with the long reins. I was clearing the way for the three of us, so that they could keep up, and their extra noise made folk jump quicker. And to have them behind me was somehow a comfort.

'Is it a pardon?' dad bellowed behind me.

I'd no time nor voice to reply. Lark screeched, 'Yes! From the king!'

'Thank God! On you go, son, we're right with you! Clear the way!'

Past the Hotel de Ville. The Place de Grève — any sign of an execution? No, thank God, but barges unloading. Carts, piles of grain and wood everywhere. Two men carrying a huge beam — too close to avoid. I kicked my horse on, and he flew over it as if we were out hunting. Hang on like a monkey. The beam fell behind me, and Lark and dad jumped it as it bounced and rolled. Porters cursed, dodged, dropped sacks like dandruff.

Thundering over the bridge. The Conciergerie ahead. Thank the Lord, the gates were open. Yelling, 'In the king's name!' again, I rode straight for them. The Swiss Guards hadn't time to lower their halberds — not that they'd have dared against an Archer, anyway — before I was past them, clattering through the gatehouse tunnel into the prison yard. Nobody there but the duty officer waddling out of the guardroom.

'Turnbull! An Archer! Is he here? Wake up, man! Has an Archer just come with a letter for the Governor?' My voice broke, hoarse with shouting.

The officer was a slow thinker, but his sergeant was quicker. 'Yes, sir, ten minutes ago. Went right up to Governor de Villeville's office.'

I was already running, and to the devil with dignity, across to the main entrance, along the hall, up the stairs three at a time, Lark and dad left far behind. Down the corridor to the office, fling the door open —

The clerk at the wide table looked up in fright,

big head wobbling on his long neck. 'Goodness, sir, what a start —'

No time to waste on politenesses. 'The governor! Where is he?'

'Oh — er — he's — er — he's not here!'

'I can see that!' I pulled myself together just before I started to shake the silly fool. 'I've a message for him. Where is he? Hurry up, man!'

'Oh — er — he'll be back shortly, sir! He's just gone to — er — to see to an execution. Your — er — lieutenant — er —'

'God! I've got to stop him! I've got a pardon! How can I stop him?'

It took him a long moment to understand. 'What was that? A pardon? For Lieutenant Montgomery? Oh dear, how — er — how unfortunate!'

'Why?'

'Well, it's — it's too late, sir! Look, there they are!' He pointed to the glass window and babbled on. 'The governor had his instructions days ago. The priest was called yesterday, and all ready when the message came.'

Down below was a small green square, not the main yard at the entrance but a private lawn with bushes and gravel walks. And at the far side a black block of wood, with a little cup cut out of one side, I knew, for the chin to fit. And a man all in red, leaning on a long-handled axe — Monsieur of Paris. A line of crimson and gold soldiers, Swiss Guards, at attention. Two drummers starting a roll while a priest was praying, and the governor and an Archer, Walter Turnbull, and a tall young man with fair hair who was handing his white doublet to Turnbull, laughing, giving the executioner something — a purse, to encourage him to strike cleanly — and my hoarse voice wouldn't reach them, nor my knocking on the glass, over the drumming, Dear God why didn't the man have shutters like everybody else, and I couldn't get the window open, and the tall gangling clerk behind me was worrying, 'No, it's jammed, hasn't been opened this past year, you'll not shift it, I'm afraid, oh dear oh dear,' with his bad breath stinking round me, and Montgomery was untying his shirt collar and kneeling before the block, and the priest moving forward, and the executioner hefting his axe, and as I drew my sword to smash the window two more guards staggering backwards into view from a gate at the side, a Scots Guard forcing them in with drawn sword, and a girl in a black gown raced past them, across the green grass, and flung herself on top of Montgomery.

King Francois II

'Aye, son,' dad said an hour later, brushing his moustache smugly. 'You were a bittie quick off the mark there, eh? Just shows you, the old dog can still show the young one a trick or two! When you're wantin' somethin', you're aye best to ask a sergeant. I just said, 'Where's Montgomery, quick?' an' the sergeant pointed us the way while the ensign was still drawin' breath. So we just went straight for the lad, never mind the governor. Mind you,' he added, starting to huff slightly, 'they two Switzers had no business stoppin' a Scots Guard like that.'

'Trying to, you mean, dad,' I suggested, and he chuckled and relaxed.

Lark was sitting by us in the window seat of the Count of Montgomery's house, gazing silent for once out at the garden. Montgomery was standing near her, but not touching. Messengers had been sent to find and reassure the count, and bring him home. My sister and Montgomery had scarcely said a word since she'd saved him. They didn't look at each other. The governor of the Conciergerie had been, I think, quite disappointed

157

by how poorly Montgomery had thanked her. But even I could sense a tension, a magnetism between them. And dad was nodding in satisfaction.

A bustle outside in the hall; the count had arrived. He bowed to us, politely, but his eyes were seeking his son and he nearly collapsed into Montgomery's arms, struggling to restrain his tears of relief and joy. I was shocked at how old he looked, so suddenly.

It took us a long time to stop him thanking us.

However, at last he turned to practical matters. 'Gabriel, the queen dowager is confounded for now, but —'

'She never forgets.' Montgomery's voice was dry. 'I've small desire to stay in her vicinity, I assure you, sir. I'll be away from Paris by night.'

Lark gasped once, beside me. I took her hand.

The count glanced over at her inquiringly. 'Mademoiselle de Rouxelle?'

Montgomery returned to the window and knelt down at her other side, his fair hair and white surcoat dazzling in the sunlight against her mourning black, all his attention on her, ignoring us all. 'Alice, I have to go. You must see it. It would be madness for me to stay within Catherine's reach.' He lifted Lark's hand from mine gently, and she clung to his long fingers. 'I will send for you. As soon as I can. I swear it.'

Dad cleared his throat, but the count was before him, his tone formal and chilly. 'Send for mademoiselle? I am sure that Mademoiselle de Rouxelle is of good birth. I know she is lovely, and talented. But I was not aware that you had formed an understanding with any young lady.'

My temper prickled, but Montgomery was already on his feet between us, facing his father. 'No, sir, there's no 'understanding' between us. Yet I believe we understand each other well enough. I owe her — you owe her more than I can say. That I'm alive now is due to her heroism, for she flung herself between the axe and my neck.'

Well . . . A slight exaggeration, the executioner hadn't actually lifted the axe higher than his knees, but why spoil a good story? It was having its effect on the count, too.

'When I'm with her I see no other, and when I'm apart from her my heart longs for her. No, my lord, I have never spoken for her, but I do so now.' Lark was pale. He knelt by her again in front of us all. 'Alice, I should ask you this in private, I know, but time is short. If your father will give his consent, will you do me the honour of becoming my wife?'

She wasn't yet sixteen. But Princess Elisabeth was wed, at fourteen. I took thought and hauled my jaw off the floor. We all waited, the count's face frozen, dad smiling again, till at last she lifted her head shyly. Her brown eyes glanced up for an instant, and she nodded. Her voice was so soft I could scarcely make it out. 'Yes. Oh, yes, Gabriel. If you please.'

God's wounds! This was my cheeky wee sister?

Montgomery kissed her hands, and turned still holding them. 'Sir —'

'Aye, aye, man, I heard you,' dad grinned. 'Nothin' like an axe for concentratin' the mind, eh?' He chuckled, and the atmosphere in the room lightened. 'You'd be just the ideal man for her. I'll no say other.' The count's eyebrows rose, but before he could say anything dad was reaching to separate their hands. Lark gasped again, shocked, as he held her firmly. 'But that was then. This is now. You're a man o' good birth —' that was a dig at the count, dad wasn't blind or daft — 'an' estate. You've also the enmity o' a queen, that means you must flee your family an' regiment, an' seek a new position.' He tugged his moustache thoughtfully. 'I'd be failin' in my duty to my daughter if I let her wed any man in your present situation. She's young; she doesn't know

159

the difficulties, but you've seen it yourself, I'll swear, soldiers' wives at the tail o' an army, startin' out with hope an' pride an' slippin' down an' down into wretched misery. My lass'll no leave me save to a settled house. You see my point?'

'Father!' Lark was outraged. 'What does it matter that he has to leave? I'll follow him anywhere! Gabriel —'

'No, Alice!' Montgomery interrupted her. 'Your father's right. We can't wed now. Not till I make a home for you. You don't know what he and I have both seen. No, my dear,' he insisted against her protests, 'no! You'll stay here in Paris, under the protection of your father and brother, while I go and find a general who needs an officer. And then, when I have a commission and a house, I'll return for you. Queen or no queen!'

'Have I nothing to say in this, then?' The count's tone was stiff.

Montgomery bowed formally to him. 'My lord, I would have told you before, but while I thought I was to be executed, there was no point. I'm twenty-seven years old, sir; old enough to know my own mind. This is the lady above all others whom I wish to marry, dowry or none.' Lark was blushing all over again.

I spoke before dad could. 'On that matter, my lord, you need have no fear. My sister is well provided.' If I had to sell the house and estate, go in debt up to my ears, I'd see my sister well dowered and properly respected. Dad grumphed in his moustache, and nodded approvingly.

The older man's pursed lips suddenly relaxed. 'Gabriel, you're quite right, and I beg your pardon. It's only the surprise that has made me so ungracious. I welcome your choice, I truly do. The young lady is indeed lovely, and I owe it to her bravery that I still have you.' He came over and stooped to take Lark's hand from dad. 'My dear, I wish you all joy!'

She rose and curtseyed. 'I thank you, my lord.' Her

voice was stifled again, and I knew she was near crying as he kissed her cheek.

I bent to kiss her too. 'Good fortune, and many years together, Lark!'

In the meantime we gave them half an hour, murmuring in the windowseat while the count made plans. 'My estate in Normandy first, I think, while I gather some money for him. Then — who knows? Scotland, maybe. Or England.'

'England would be better.' I shrugged as they looked at me. 'For a Protestant, my lord. Queen Elizabeth seems to favour that religion. Queen Marie's mother, the Regent of Scotland, still follows the Catholic Church.'

The count nodded, after a sharp look, but dad tugged doubtfully at his moustaches. 'A Calvinist? I didn't know. H'm.'

'Does it matter, dad?' I asked. 'Lark may change her mind. Or he may. Anyway, I don't believe she'd care.' Evil, hating faces, she'd said once.

Dad made a face, but accepted it. 'Well. Aye.' He rose. 'Come, now, Lark. You mustn't keep your man back. She'll wait for you, Montgomery —'

'For ever, Gabriel!' she assured him passionately.

'— But for now, I'll take her home. Never mind nightfall, you'd be best outside the walls of Paris in an hour. Send us word, mind!'

It was good sense; but Lark still wept all the way home.

I was worried about her. She'd deserted her post, to aid the man the queen hated. What would Catherine do?

We found out immediately we arrived at our door. Annette was fussing over two chests, three sacks and a letter. Lark, trembling slightly, broke the seal. The Dowager Queen understood that Mademoiselle de Rouxelle no longer served her. Under the circumstances, her immediate withdrawal from the royal household was not merely

161

permitted, but required. Lark's clothes, hats, shoes, fans, all her belongings, had been bundled up and returned. It was cold, abrupt, thankless; but at least Lark was away safely.

'Oh, well,' she sniffed, trying to put a brave face on it. 'I can have a while to myself at last! Oh, dad, I'm so glad to be home!' She burst into tears all over again. 'Dad, I know why you said I had to stay. I do know. But — but — I wish — I wish —'

'We can never have all we wish for, lass,' he said gruffly. 'An' if we could, it wouldn't be good for us.' Then he surprised me. He sat in his big chair, pulled her, velvet, whalebone and all, gently down onto his lap as if she was still a little girl, and held her lovingly while she wept.

I left them sitting there together, closer than they'd been for a long time. I had to return to my own duty, with the king.

Most of my friends seemed to be holding their breath for the next few days, to see if the queen would have me arrested or just poisoned. I didn't blame them — well, not much; I'd probably have felt the same. But it showed me which were really friends. Walter Turnbull turned out to be one of them. He didn't report my attempt to stop him. The king's message excused my stealing the mare, Lark's romantic gallantry made her the toast of the city, never mind the Garde, for weeks, and the carter was happy with a denier as hire for his horse, so we got away with it. But I was constantly aware of an itch between my shoulderblades, as if malevolent eyes were fixed on me all the time. Eyes a bit less than three feet off the ground.

Francois enjoyed being king for a while, but soon he was sick of Council meetings and his Guise uncles and running the country. He'd burst out, complaining, 'God's belly, I'm stiff! Papers, always papers to sign, and taxes and treaties and appointments — why should

I care who's Bishop of Beaune? Are the horses ready, Jean? Let's get out before I die of boredom!'

The funeral of his father in August was a huge procession, led by the Garde de Paris; over three hundred churchmen in red and purple; the funeral bier itself, surrounded by the Parlement in their scarlet robes, with an effigy of Henri in gilded armour above the cloth-of-gold canopy. After it rode the king, princes and nobles. To the rage of the Bourbons, the king's cousins, the upstart half-foreign Guises had the place of honour beside him. Behind them was led Henri's warhorse, royally harnessed in violet velvet with gold fleur-de-lys. And last of all, the Garde Ecossaise. The badge on our surcoats had been changed from an H with linked D's to one with linked C's. Only a few stitches, but significant.

At one window, a figure in black watched us pass. La Belle Diane was denied any place in the funeral of the man who had so greatly loved her.

In September Francois was crowned by the Cardinal de Lorraine, in the cathedral of Rheims. From respect for the dead king — and also because there was no money to pay for new clothes for the Court officials — everyone was dressed in the same black mourning he'd worn for the funeral. Only Queen Marie again wore white, and shone in the glow from the huge red and green rose window like a good deed in a wicked world. Which of course she intended. The little figure of the king seemed bowed and bent under the weight of the crown, though the ceremony was cut short for his sake.

I was in the cathedral too. For I had been promoted to be one of the twenty-four Archers of the Royal Bodyguard. Our uniform was all white, with the little king's new badge; a flaming sword between two circles, to represent the earth and the sky. His motto was 'Unus non sufficit orbis' — 'One world is not enough'. Big-headed, I thought, but nobody asked me. Three of us stood on each side of the king on all official occasions with ceremonial silver halberds, very fine but as much practical use as a candle in a snowstorm. And far too tall for me, of course. I felt a proper fool.

Dad nearly burst with pride, and Pierre's self-esteem expanded enormously. He engaged more servants for me; I now had twelve. I'd have had to have many more to keep up my position, but I didn't need a house of my own; I was given rooms near Francois wherever the Court travelled, for I had to be on hand whenever he wanted me, day or night. I attended him, as I had done Queen Catherine, to church and state occasions, and also I went hunting with him whenever he could dodge his Guise uncles-in-law.

I was beside him when he signed the warrant for the execution of the Protestant du Bourg, without a second thought, among a heap of papers he didn't bother to read, hurrying to get out to the chase. So du Bourg was burned. And the Guises stoked up persecution of the Religion again.

I found that Nicola, with her sweet temper and earthy humour, relaxed me. Since the tournament, Chicot had been very subdued. Nicola dared even let it be seen that she liked me, and found that now he fawned round her as much as round me. Disliking it and him, we avoided him as much as possible.

One fine afternoon in October we were in the gardens at Fontainebleau, enjoying the sun and sharing a basket of cherries. I was leaning on the marble balustrade of one of the pools which gave the palace its name. Nicola was perched up beside me, bouncing cherry stones off my head to plop into the water. We laughed as the big carp which lived there swam gravely up, engulfed them with a slurping noise in their huge mouths, considered for a moment, and then spat them out again reproachfully.

The Cardinal de Bourbon strolled past. I bowed. With a casual nod he passed on along the wide gravelled walk, between the clipped and manicured trees, friends and clients fawning round him, a couple of the Flying Squadron on his arm. Two others, painted and elegant, perfumed, jewelled and exquisite, stopped to talk to me, ignoring Nicola. 'Monsieur de Rouxelle, all alone here? May we bring solace to your loneliness?'

Now that I was back in favour, they were all after me worse than ever. Bitches! 'You do me too much honour, ladies. But I am not alone. I already have most charming company.' As they frowned in dainty perplexity, I gestured to Nicola beside my shoulder. She smiled and bowed lavishly.

Their beautifully painted eyebrows and lips arched in artificial surprise. 'Charming company? Nicola? Dear sir, when will you be serious?' Their tinkling silver laughter rang through the splashing of the fountain.

That really annoyed me. And, I could see, Nicola. Before I could speak, she held a hand to her mouth and gasped in horror. We tensed. She gasped again, straightened with a look of wild alarm, opened her mouth and with a huge burp spat out a dozen cherry stones, which bounced off their embroidered skirts. 'I begs yer pardon, me dears, I'm sure!' she apologised effusively, her voice suddenly rough and hoarse. She leapt to her feet like a multi-coloured monkey, grimacing and twitching crazily. 'But ye're too late, dearies, it's meself that's his true love — ain't I, Jean honey?' She danced along the balustrade to clutch my neck in her short beflowered arms and give me a smacking kiss. Then, as I thanked God for my beard to hide my flush, she turned her face up beside mine to leer at the girls. 'But he's a big strong lad, so he is, and I only need half of him.'

'That's true, ladies!' I smiled invitingly. 'Nicola's got the top half, but the bottom half's still free!'

Nicola winked broadly. 'Aye, plenty for all. Help yerselves, I ain't greedy, me dears!' She waved a short arm generously to beckon them closer. Naturally, they drew back and glided off huffily.

I disengaged myself, and eyed Nicola severely. 'Nicola, that was disgraceful! And you're making me as bad as yourself!'

'I'm making you bad? Little you ever needed, sir! But what did you expect? I'm a jester. It's my part, to shock, tease, amuse; dispel boredom. I seem to have dispelled yours, at least!' We rocked with mirth together.

'My lord?' My page, Guy, puffed stiff and splendiferous in his new uniform — green, for sentimental reasons — was offering me a letter.

'From a lady-love, sir?' Nicola inquired archly.

'God's wounds, I hope not!' I cried. 'No, I'm wrong. It is from a lady I love!' She looked intrigued. 'My sister.' She threw a cherry at me in disgust. 'Thank you, Guy. Let's see. Her writing's worse than mine, and that's like a hen scratching. Um. Dad's well, apart from a bull on his neck. A bull? Oh, a boil! Gabriel — that's Montgomery — he's in London, with a recommendation from the English ambassador. Good. She's happy, and going on with her lessons in singing, privately. That's all right, then.'

Nicola glanced over. 'It seems to me she might change her faith, sir.'

'Yes. It worries me. But . . .' I'd respected and loved maman; I loved, and yes, I supposed I respected Lark too. I shrugged. 'If it's what she thinks is right . . .'

Nicola nodded approval. 'It's her choice, sir. Her soul. And she'll be safe enough from harm, as your sister, as long as she's discreet.'

Discreet . . . I shivered suddenly. 'Are you Calvinist, Nicola?' I asked.

'Me?' she laughed. 'Can you see me arguing with bishops? Me, I think God cares little for men's words; it's their hearts He'll judge. And their actions. I'll stay with my mother's faith. But when two men of religion scream at each other, 'You're wrong and I'm right!' well, they can't both be right. But they could both be wrong. I always feel, what arrogance, to try to force anyone else to believe as you do! What if you're mistaken?'

She was saying what I'd thought for a good while. But — 'The Cardinal of Lorraine wouldn't agree with you!' She used a rude word that I'd only heard before in the stables about the Cardinal of Lorraine, and startled me into laughter again. 'Nicola! I'll tell him!' I threatened her.

'Spare me, merciful lord!' She pretended fear, climbing a stone triton to grin down at me from a safe perch over my head. 'My, what a change in you, Jean, since we first met! Did you ever think you'd be chatting to cardinals, and gossiping with Guises, and bowing to Bourbons? Easy and natural, as if you'd been born to it!'

'No, Nicola, not that yet!' I said, musing. 'I can't believe it's real, somehow. That this grand personage in the fine white satin, and the rings, and the perfume is really me, Johnnie Russell, the sergeant's lad.'

'Keep it that way, sir,' she advised, climbing down, her smile fading. 'For when you start to think it's natural, you'll have become the same as the others, foolish and frippery. Just you keep on wondering how you got here, with your fancy uniform, and your estates — how many is it now?'

'Four, now!' I boasted. 'Another last week in Provence somewhere. And with being the king's friend the bribes — well, presents, eh? — I get for a word to him are fantastic. It's usually a word to his secretaries, though.' I grinned. 'I'll be as rich as the Guises if it lasts!'

She laughed with me at the incredible idea, and then suddenly was serious again. 'Jean, you know there's many folk jealous of you?'

'Apart from Chicot, you mean? Yes, I know it. I've

come up so far, and so fast. They can't hurt me. Unless I fall out of favour.'

'Not unless, sir. Until. Be wary, sir! You know what he's like!'

'True enough, Nicola. True enough. I've had that feeling for a good while. I'd better start preparing my retreat. Or escape!'

She nodded approval, but wasn't finished. 'In case anything happens to him, either, sir. You know they're betting he'll never see twenty? And they say — Jean, have you heard the rumours? About the king having leprosy?'

'Is that what it is? I heard somebody shouting at us yesterday while we were out hunting, but I couldn't make it out. Leprosy? Filthy nonsense!'

'I'm glad to hear it,' she said. 'But that's not all of it.'

'Oh? Well, go on, don't stop there. I'll hear sooner or later.'

She bit her lip, and checked that no-one was close enough to hear. 'The peasants say Francois has leprosy, but his mother has found a cure for him.' She hesitated again. It must be something very bad, I thought; and it was. 'They say she kills children, and bathes her son in their blood.'

'What?' I couldn't believe it. 'Surely nobody could be that stupid!' She'd not go that far — surely not — God's wounds, I was as bad as the country folk!

'Little you know, sir! They've seen how he's grown, this past year, and he's not ill quite as much. And with her sorcerors and all . . . That's what they say. They're sending away all their children, wherever the king goes. You'd best warn him, sir. For if he comes suddenly into a village —'

'They'll shout, like yesterday. And when he finds out what they're saying he'll burn the place round their ears!' I sighed. 'God's wounds, warning him'll do no good — he'd do it all the quicker. I'll tell the Archers to try to keep folk away from him, but . . . How did this tale start?'

She drew me close to whisper, even out by the fountain, away from anyone else. 'The Guises. Trying to turn him from his mother. I think, anyway. He'll hear about it some time, he's bound to, and if he thinks she's to blame for his unpopularity —'

'He'll turn even more to the Guises. God, they must fear her!'

'Don't you, then, sir?' The quiet question stopped me. Yes, I did.

But I'd keep my tongue tight in my teeth. I'd be discreet, and so would Lark.

Amboise

In early February, 1560, we moved to Amboise. It was never one of my favourite palaces, perched high on a cliff above the Loire, sneering over the peaceful woods and meadows all around it. Inside two corner towers wide tunnels spiralled down among the dungeons, steep and dark as mole runs, leading to the town below.

That spring certainly justified me in my dislike of it.

Queen Catherine's household was six miles away at the Château of Chenonceaux. One day she came visiting, and found the young king almost hysterical. The Duc de Guise had just sent warning of a Calvinist conspiracy. Chewing his fingernails, Francois didn't even wait for his mother's curtsey of ceremony before shrilly accusing her. 'You've heard? This de la Renaudie leads a revolt against me! And it's your fault! You let these heretics discuss their foul ideas with you, and see what happens!'

Marie agreed. 'Your Majesty's countenance encourages them. They must be taught that their duty and salvation lie in obedience to the commands of their king and their church!'

'Your Majesties, you express well the opinions of the

de Guise family; will you not now hear mine? Or am I so stupid that my thoughts are worth nothing?' Catherine's tone was biting, her hands clenched. She was very upset, to lose her usual control. Taken aback, the king nodded. 'Thank you, sire. You know that my sole care is for your good, and that of France. So. You say these heretics must be taught obedience. So.' She paused, and glared at them. 'Exactly how?'

She didn't wait for a reply. She spoke more slowly but no less urgently, her high heels clacking on the parquet as she paced in agitation. 'For years the Calvinists have been cruelly persecuted. Has it defeated them? No. It makes them martyrs. It strengthens them. Mary Tudor burned hundreds of heretics to make England Catholic. Did she succeed? No. So tell me, what more can you do? Kill them all? So. But consider. They are not all mere peasants. Conde, Coligny, Navarre — these are princes. Unless you can kill every single one, wipe them out all together, without warning, they will fight. And then you have a civil war.'

She held out her hands to them, her voice strained as I'd never heard it. 'Listen to me, Francois, Marie, for God's sake! For the sake of France! There is nothing worse than a civil war. Nothing.' She drew a deep, hard breath. 'When I was eleven my city of Florence rebelled against the rule of my family, the Medici. So. My uncles besieged the city. I was trapped inside. God, what I saw! I will not sicken you with the dreadful details. Dreadful! But the suffering, the horror of that civil war, I can never forget. I will do anything, anything, to avoid that. Nothing can be worse!'

Her son was shocked. 'But they're Calvinists! Blasphemers! Their souls are damned to eternal flames —'

'That is not the king's business! It is their responsibility, not yours!'

'But that is not right, madame!' Queen Marie interrupted. 'The king is chosen by God to lead, to rule his people — and that must mean their souls as well as their bodies. For their own good.'

Catherine sighed. 'Madame, I think not so. The king is responsible for the safety of the state as a whole. He must ensure that all men have peace to live and work as they please and as will best profit themselves and their neighbours, and so benefit the state and its ruler. But each man is responsible for his own soul, as for the colour of his own coat. It is his affair and the Church's, not the king's.'

'This is — it is no less than tolerance of evil! Wicked, weak, contemptible tolerance!' The young queen was outraged.

'No! It is good government! And if I, the niece of a Pope, say so, you can believe I mean it. Madame, it is for the Church to deal with matters religious. It is for the king to govern the state. He cannot see men's souls. God will not hold him responsible for what he does not know! While men do not act against the state, it is worse than wrong, it is foolishness to act against them.'

'But that is just what they are doing, madame!' Marie argued.

'They're in revolt!' Francois wailed. 'They want to kill me!'

'I hear not so. I am told they oppose only those who urge you to persecute them — the de Guises, my son. And can you blame them?' Marie looked surprised, and then thoughtful. Francois started to protest, but Catherine talked right over him. 'Yet however justified they feel themselves to be, it is an act against the king's authority, and so it must be stopped now, before it can spread. Men call me the Serpent Queen, and say I cannot be trusted — oh yes, I know! But trust me in this; civil war destroys everything, good as well as bad! I have seen it!'

Francois was gaping, overwhelmed by the urgency

of his mother's plea. Marie was frowning. There was a long silence.

At last a chair scraped as Queen Marie rose. 'Your Majesty,' she said quietly, 'your views are far apart from those of my uncles of Guise, but I promise you that my husband and I will think well on them. However, I understand that we shall act together against this rebellion?'

'Of course, Your Majesty.' Catherine's voice was again under control. 'For the king's sake — for my son's sake — I will spare no effort to find a way in which all men, even heretics, can live at peace together. I will not stand by and watch a civil war come about, if I can by any means avoid it, whatever men say of me. But whoever acts against the king must be shown no mercy. For the good of France, whatever must be done will be done.'

Throughout February reports of de la Renaudie's plot continued to come in from the duke's spies. He gathered in all the Archers and half the Scots, French and Swiss Guards. Even dad came, called away from his parade ground to organise the billeting of so many men in Amboise town and in tents by the river below the castle walls. The Cardinal de Lorraine arrived unwillingly, and he and Francois panicked together. Pistols, long cloaks and even wide boots which might hide a weapon were all banned. Francois once ordered all the gates to be locked permanently, till I pointed out that meant we'd all starve.

Early in March the king made the de Guises announce an amnesty to all rebels, on condition that they lived in future as good Catholics. No-one accepted. He couldn't decide whether it was because there weren't any rebels, or because they were incorrigible. But at least he'd offered, he felt; whatever happened to them now wasn't his fault.

To be on the safe side, Francois and Marie slipped away in secret to join Queen Catherine at Chenonceaux, leaving the Court in Amboise to draw any attack. I went with the king. The Earl of Arran was officially in command of the Amboise garrison. Chicot made up a song about him: 'Flustered by the hustle and the bustle'. It was very popular among the Garde, in spite of all dad could do.

On the twelfth of March some men were arrested in the forest. Under torture in the dungeons of Amboise, they said de la Renaudie had called on all true Frenchmen to gather at Amboise on the sixteenth, to arrest the Guises. But it seemed to me that the men weren't villains; just simple men trying to save the king from the Guises who they felt were ruining the country. And maybe not far wrong.

On the fifteenth, one of the greatest of the Protestant nobles, the Prince de Conde, arrived unexpectedly at Amboise. In a mask. Quite natural, of course — many travellers wore them to protect their faces from dust and wind. But . . . he declared that he had heard of a plot, and had come to defend the king. Acidly, Nicola suggested that perhaps he'd come a day too soon.

Next day, we had no word by noon, and in a fidget the king sent me to Amboise to find out what was happening. A mile from the castle, cantering quietly along the straightest path, one of the hunting rides cut in the forest, with Guy and two men-at-arms of my lance, I found myself catching up with about twenty men in worn uniforms, poorly armed and badly disciplined, straggling casually; when I reached the head of the troop I'd have a word with their sergeant. Then one of them started a song about hanging a duke and a cardinal side by side, and they all roared the chorus, laughing and cheering.

God's wounds! This was the revolt! These half-armed, half-organised, half-witted ex-soldiers, arguing even now, on their way to the castle, about exactly what they were going to do. This was the revolt that had the cardinal and the king holding hands for courage!

I hastily drew aside into cover. 'Guy, Alan, ride back, tell Turnbull the rebels are here. Charlie and I'll try to warn Amboise.'

The men ahead started shouting. They'd met a larger group, of about two hundred, and they all stopped while one man, presumably de la Renaudie, made a speech. They were cheering, shouting oaths of loyalty to the king and death to the Guises, blocking the road completely.

I had to get past. Blast this eye-catching white uniform!

I took thought. Montgomery would charge them, and die gloriously. Not my idea of sense. What would Turnbull do? Disguise! At my order, Charlie rapidly unhooked his uniform. His white shirt and blue trunks were common enough — not all that clean, under the doublet, but even better so; I'd not blame him this time. But what about me? Then one man turned his horse among the bushes, and dismounted. I caught Charlie's eye. We waited a considerate minute before riding in beside him. As he looked up I smiled, 'Finished, friend? Good!' and Charlie stunned him with his dagger-hilt.

He was much bigger than me. I dragged on his long leather jacket to hide my doublet and trunks, and his long boots hid my white hose. Our horses, thank God, were unremarkable brown. We rode openly out to join the crowd. I found I wanted to laugh with the excitement. It fitted the part, so I did. Charlie looked sideways at me as if I'd gone crazy. Unobtrusively we circled round them, shouting and waving whenever they did. Then we rode quietly off into the bushes again.

Unfortunately, somebody else had gone aside too. A squawk rose behind us; 'Wait for the rest of us! Stop! Who's that? Hey! Stop those men!

The alarm was raised. We spurred hard. Still laughing

— how daft can you get? — I dropped my heavy borrowed jacket. The boots, naturally, had to stay where they were.

Several people were trudging towards the castle. Not armed men; just ordinary men and women, come at de la Renaudie's call. Some even raised a cheer as we galloped past, God knows why. God help them!

We headed straight for the upper gate above the town, waving to catch the sentry's attention. 'Rebels behind me! Shut the gates!' I shouted as we galloped over the drawbridge, through the gates into the courtyard, and looked round for the garrison.

The court was full of ladies and gentlemen. Silks and satins, fluttering fans, laughter and chatter and calls for a glass of wine for madame ... 'What in God's name ... ?' I spluttered. 'The rebels are on you!'

The cardinal, in scarlet satin and linen-white face, screeched, 'We were told they'd fled!' He raced for the nearest door.

Men and women were tugging at my reins and boots, demanding news, screeching till I couldn't make myself heard. I drew my pistol from my saddle holster and fired into the air. In the sudden hush I shouted, 'The rebels are here! Close the gates! Charlie, get everyone inside, and bar the doors! Man the walls! Get those damned gates shut!'

As they scattered in shrieking confusion I rode back to the gateway. A couple of the Garde joined me, heaving at the gates; but too late. We dived for the door of the guardroom as the first of the rebels galloped onto the bridge over the ditch, and twelve score behind him.

Maybe the honourable thing for one of the Royal Bodyguard to do would have been to stand in the centre of the archway to face them, and forbid them entry in the king's name; but maman never raised me to be a fool.

'Where's Arran?' I shouted as the door slammed at my back. 'The duty officer? Your sergeant?'

'Out lickmadowpin' the lords an' ladies as usual!' a Scots voice called in the crush. Twenty Guards, mostly blue Scots, a few yellow Swiss and crimson Guises, were rattling arquebuses and halberds, jostling to get near me and find out what to do. Not an officer in sight.

God's wounds! If I stopped to think, I'd laugh again. 'Silence! Who's that needs his tongue clipped? How many firearms have you?'

'Mason, sir, corporal o' the guard, sorry, sir! Most o' the men's out on patrol, sir. We've ten arquebuses, but no ready to fire, sir! By order, for fear o' accidents, sir!'

'May your duty officer sit on the hot hob of hell for a hundred years! Right, sergeant! Wind up and prime your pieces! Bring them up to the roof! Where's the lever for the portcullis?'

'Up the stair there, sir, thanks, sir! Come on, ye Calvinists, into line! Attention! Set your piece! Wait for it, Hay! Dismount your key!'

In the rebel's heavy boots I stumbled up the narrow spiral to blink in the sunshine beside the excited sentry. 'I fired, sir, I did! I got one, I swear! Well, I think! Maybe!' He nearly set me off giggling again. Behind me the ex-corporal was racing through the drill, winding up the springs of the arquebuses; they'd be ready in a minute.

The courtyards were cleared. The cardinal would see that the doors were barred. The only people to be seen were rebels, riding round in excited frustration. Heads began to appear at the windows, and shots were exchanged with the riders as the soldiers of the garrison woke up and started to do what they were paid for. A window smashed; a rebel was hit. They didn't know what to do. They were lost.

Clattering on the steps behind me. 'Ready, sir! An' that's the lever for the portcullis by your hand, sir!' The sergeant grinned expectantly.

One jerk, and the heavy barrier would roar down its stone channel to trap the rebels like rats in a ring for the dogs. I couldn't do it. Those fools down there were honest, in their way. Give them their chance. 'Leave it, Mason,' I told him, still grinning. 'Get your men up along the parapet. Aim at the leader. Ready to fire on my command.'

I stood up, my uniform announcing me as one of the Bodyguard. 'De la Renaudie! I'm commanding here!' And hell mend the Earl of Arran. 'The king's not here! You've failed! Surrender!' He was due his chance too.

'Never!' he yelled back, and fired his pistol up at me. It was a good shot, or a lucky one; the ball hit the parapet just along from me, and chips of stone flew up to cut my cheek, ear and neck. That stopped my grin.

'Fire!' I shouted. Ten wheel-locks beside me belched smoke and flame; not one ball hit him. He waved a cheeky hand, but must have seen that there was nothing left for him to do. He rode round the yard again, gathering his men, and then they just trotted away, back through the gate, across the bridge, off into the forest.

I blew out a sigh of relief. I'd done my duty. I'd saved the castle, and the honour of the Garde. I sat down, beckoning the sentry to pull off those ton-weight boots, as cheering rose from all the roofs and windows round the courtyard. It was hard to stop myself taking a bow. My grin came back, wider than ever.

Something was bothering me, though. The noise of the wheel-locks . . . and the amount of flame . . . and not a stir in the gravel behind de la Renaudie . . . 'Sergeant!' He looked nervous. I knew there was something. They'd not been primed or wound up, but I wondered . . . with Arran in charge . . . 'Sergeant, were there any balls in your weapons?'

Surprised. 'Of course, sir!' Too surprised. And his eyes were shifty.

'Oh, aye?' Dad's very tone of disbelief.

At that he gave up. 'Sir — I, er . . . No, sir. It slipped

my mind, sir. In the rush. I just forgot. An so did the lads, sir. I'm sorry, sir.'

God's wounds! Oh, well. I'd have liked to have been the one to get the glory of killing the rebel leader, but ... I should have checked, too, not trusted a man I didn't know to keep his head. I started to laugh, free at last to let it out, and after a moment he grinned rather nervously. 'Don't worry, corporal.' His face fell, but it was the least he could expect. 'Just make sure it doesn't get out, or the Switzers'd jeer at us till the Last Trump. But I'd not be laughing then. Nor you. You'll keep it quiet, won't you?' He nodded vigorously. So did the sentry. 'Right. Close the gates. Reload your pieces — fully. Find me a pair of shoes. And send someone to tell the duty officer, and your sergeant, to report here. Now.' His face brightened again as he saluted and marched off down the steps.

I heard his voice rising up the stairwell; 'Willie, just step over to the castle an' inform Archer Gordon that John Russell, o' the Bodyguard, requests the pleasure o' a wee word with him. Immediate. An' old Sergeant Gobbleguts as well. Though I'd no care to wager that either o' the pair o' them'll find much pleasure in the meetin'. There's no flies on that lad.' Which pleased me considerably.

The Earl of Arran, when at last we found him, had been in one of the far rooms with a young lady the whole time. He'd thought the shooting was fireworks; he said. He went home to Scotland quite soon.

For me, the whole day was a comedy. The cardinal was extremely impressed by the blood which had gushed all over my doublet — ears bleed incredibly, and it showed up well on the white. I was given an estate near Rheims and made commendator of two abbeys; their incomes would come to me. He'd take no thanks. 'No, no, my son! It is for me, and your king, and all France, to be grateful for your dedication and courage, which drove off the traitors and averted a catastrophe.' His death, he meant. 'An old head on young shoulders!' He gave me a huge ruby ring, and gifts and kisses showered on me from the ladies and lords I had saved — even Conde, smiling rigidly.

The king was impressed, too, and Queen Marie. Queen Catherine was less so, perhaps because she didn't see me in all my gory glory. But from the king I got yet another estate — I was losing count of them — and the promise of a title of nobility at Christmas. And Queen Marie promised me an heiress for a bride. That stopped my giggles. I protested, but in vain. A rich, beautiful bride for my nineteenth birthday, in February.

Nicola laughed like a drain at my dismay, till I had to grin with her.

It was the last time she, or I, laughed for a good while.

The royal household returned to Amboise. The Garde were busy rounding up all the poor, silly people who had come to support de la Renaudie, tying them in dozens, and driving them in to the dungeons of Amboise. Queen Catherine drove over from Chenonceaux, and she and her son spent all day, day after day, down in the torture chambers.

Francois was still fascinated by cruelty, as he had been years before. He was, I think, ashamed of it. But now he had a perfect justification; he must discover all the traitors. His mother walked down the dark steps controlled, cold, determined; he slunk down with greedy anticipation. His young brothers went too, sometimes. I went once, was sick, and begged to be excused from further attendance. I will not describe what I saw. Francois was furious, and angrily dismissed me to attend on his wife, since I was too lily-livered for the necessary work of government.

Queen Marie rode out to hunt or visit friends, or

played the virginals, her head gallantly high; or worked quietly on her embroidery, her eyes downcast, with no word of criticism for her husband or her mother-in-law even when the husband of one of her ladies was arrested. She winced sometimes at the sounds that escaped from the tiny gratings. I wondered if she remembered Queen Catherine's words about the dreadfulness of civil war.

De la Renaudie was captured. It would have been better for him if my men had shot him.

Hundreds of the prisoners were tied into sacks, after their torture, and thrown into the river to drown. The banks of the Loire were covered with stranded bodies and ravaging dogs. The stink could be smelled ten miles away downwind. Many others were sentenced to the galleys for life, after Catherine herself appealed for mercy for the ordinary folk. But there were plenty left, and more brought in daily, gathered for a special day when de la Renaudie and the main conspirators were to be tortured to death as an entertainment for the whole Court, and a warning for anyone who might think of treason. Conde, for instance.

I would have to attend that. As one of the Bodyguard, and known to be a friend of the king, I couldn't get out of it. When I heard, I spent the evening in dad's room in the town. He'd not tell anyone how sick I was.

The day before the mass execution, Walter Turnbull and I rode out with Queen Marie. We took out the king's cheetahs to hunt hare, but when we were a mile from the castle the young queen looked round at the fresh green of the spring forest, and the birds singing. She sighed deeply, stretched frankly as a child, and sent the rest of the hunt away. 'I'll cause no death this day, John. Let me have one day of peace, at least!'

It was a pleasant, quiet day. We rode gently, or walked, or sat and talked and sang among the groves and streams of the beautiful countryside. We seemed to be alone; yet if we wanted cool wine, a cushion, a picnic, a lute, my page Guy or one of the queen's servants would appear, and vanish again, as if by magic. We recalled the old, simple jokes of two years before when Queen Marie was not yet wed, and I was still whipping-boy to a little prince; and what was different for me, I wondered? Or for her?

Wattie Turnbull spoke Scots to us, recalling to us words and phrases that had drifted into the dusty corners of our memories long ago. My mother had been French, and I had spoken mostly French at home; the queen had been in France, her tutors and all her attendants French except for her friends the Maries, since she was four years old. Yet we both began to find the tongue again. We sang old Scottish songs. The Marie with us that day, Seton, had a soft, sweet voice that reminded me of my sister's, I told her.

'The Lark! Yes, John, I remember her well,' Queen Marie said.

'She's in Paris, keeping house for my father.'

'Will I find a dowry — what's that, Wattie? — a tocher? A tocher, and a braw laddie for her, as well as a bride for you?' the queen teased me.

'No need, Your Grace,' I assured her. 'She's got one.'

'Oh? Who's that, then?'

Well, I had to tell her. 'Gabriel Montgomery, Your Grace.'

She was silent for a moment. Then, to my relief, she nodded. 'How fitting! She saved his life. Do you know what he's doing now?'

'I'm not sure, Your Grace. I've not heard from Lark this past month.'

Her large brown eyes were steady. 'He is in England. Don't look so surprised. A queen must know where her foes are.'

'He's no enemy of yours, Your Grace,' I protested.

'No? He seeks to serve Queen Elizabeth, who sends

gold to the Calvinists who oppose my mother in Scotland. He who serves my enemy is my enemy. And your sister, out of love for him? And maybe you, out of love for her?'

I gasped at the unexpected attack. Suddenly temper flared. I drew my sword, knelt, and with a flourish presented the hilt to her. 'I am Your Grace's loyal servant. If you doubt it, strike to the heart!'

Her eyes opened wide, and her mouth, and as my foolishness deserved, she collapsed onto a grassy bank, helpless with laughter. 'My God!' she wailed. 'Oh, thank you, Jean, for the melodrama! I've not had such a laugh in weeks!' I blushed and made some play about sheathing my sword, avoiding Wattie's sardonic eye.

It was some minutes before she sobered and sat up. 'Oh, dear, see how low the sun is! It's time we went back to dress for dinner. Fleming will be scolding me.' Her smile faded, and she sighed.

It was dusk when we turned in to one of the dark tunnels up from the town. Our horses' hooves echoed on the cobbles as they paced steadily upwards. Halfway up, a Scots Guard stepped forward from under one of the torches at the side and saluted. 'Sir! I've a message for you.'

The queen waved permission. 'Yes, take it, Jean.' She rode on with her attendants.

'Well? What is it?'

The Guard shrugged rather doubtfully. 'It's a girl we brought in this morning, sir, she gave me a teston to tell you that hope was high to make folks' hearts rejoice at the splendid display. Something like that. She said you'd understand.'

My head was spinning. 'A girl, in the cells here? In Amboise? One of the Calvinists?' Oh, God have mercy . . .

'Aye, sir. High hope, eh?' He cocked his head sideways. 'Know her, sir? Does she think you'll help?'

183

Somehow I grinned. 'Some lass I used to know, I suppose. Not that I'd help a rebel. She must be mad. But I'd rather not have it known — you understand? Here — another teston for you. Keep it quiet, eh?'

He saluted, and went off whistling. Automatically I turned my horse on up the passage, the lines spinning in my head, that neither she nor I would ever forget; that no-one else would remember. Hope's words, in the masque; 'All hopes are high on this wonderful day, All hearts rejoice at this splendid display.'

It was Lark. It must be. Arrested, and dragged here among all the Calvinists. In the dungeons, facing torture and execution next day.

What I do not know . . .

Half an hour later, we were all gathered in dad's room; dad, me, Pierre, Guy, dad's valet Louis, and, at Pierre's suggestion, Nicola. 'Could be very useful, sir. Jesters can go anywhere, do anything, without question.'

Dad and I suggested everything we could think of, and Nicola poured scorn on everything. Frontal assault? 'Don't be silly!' Sneaking in among the workmen setting up the torture implements for the next day? 'They all know each other.' Bribe the guard? 'More likely to take the bribe and betray you. Besides, bribes are dishonest.' Ease her out of the herd when the prisoners were driven out of their cells and into the courtyard, in the crowd and the dazzle of sunlight? 'And then? She'll be stinking, filthy — how could you get her away?'

'What, then?' Dad was on the point of explosion with worry and tension.

After her first cry of consternation and concern, Nicola had sat quietly, perched like a child on one of my brocade stools with her green shoes swinging inches from the floor. Now she sighed and shook her head. 'Men!' she said in vexation. She cocked her head

185

to one side to look up at us standing round her like goats round a kitten. 'Sir, what are you thinking of? You've been at Court two years, and your father longer, and you still don't understand it? Scots are so slow! I'm surprised at you, Pierre, though!' Pierre actually blushed at her scolding. 'Don't you know that short of open murder, maybe, one of the Bodyguard can do almost anything! Who'd dare question him? Now, Jean, sir, after dinner Chicot's doing his ventriloquist act. You know the one? His big servant pretends to work him, while he works a dummy, and you know how the king loves it; you can slip out quietly and not a soul will notice, or stir. And you'll go straight down to the duty officer — no, you'll go to the dungeon and send for the duty officer . . .'

Her plan was so simple, we laughed in relief. 'It's foolproof!'

She grinned. 'Be sure you get it right, then!'

'Oh, Nicola! You're a wonder! You've a mind like a corkscrew!'

'Isn't that just what you need, sir, with your sister stuck like a cork in a bottle? Besides, I'm a jester! It goes with the job!'

While the messenger was away seeking the officer, I perched one hip casually on a corner of the sergeant's table and caustically tore him to shreds, in front of his men, for stains and a loose braid on his uniform. Well, it kept him off balance, and hid the tension tightening in my chest, and helped me ignore the moans and weeping and prayers echoing dully under the low ceiling that hung black above the few torches.

At last the duty Archer appeared, slightly out of breath; a good sign. I sighed, to let him know he'd kept me waiting and fluster him like the sergeant, and I didn't rise to meet him. I gave him my haughtiest stare and chilliest tone, copied faithfully from the Duc de Bourbon. They had him jumping to obey the king's friend. 'I don't know you, Archer?'

'Henderson, sir! I joined the Garde two weeks ago.'

A rookie! Good! 'An agent of the Duc de Guise has been brought in with the heretics whom she was watching. Yes, Henderson; she. A woman. Small, brown-haired, young, scarce more than a girl, I'm told, who sent the very first word of this rebellion.'

'A brave woman, my lord!' the Archer said admiringly. Eager to please, the sergeant nodded with vigour.

'Indeed,' I conceded superciliously. Time to relax, be friendly, all in the same regiment after all ... 'A dirty business, spying, but necessary, I suppose. I am to remove her from here. A pity if one of the king's best servants should end up on the rack tomorrow with his enemies, eh?' We all laughed.

The women, a score or so, were all together. They were singing a hymn. Lark's voice, even though hoarse and tired, rose above the rest. I glared at her to keep her quiet while I beckoned her out. 'Mademoiselle, I am to escort you to the Duc de Guise.' I was afraid for a moment that she'd not play up to me, but then a spark of life came back to her eyes and she bowed silently. 'My page has fresh clothes for you there by the door.' I ushered her rather coldly, as a gentleman would treat a contemptible spy, however clever, to the shadows behind a buttress where she could strip and pull on Guy's spare hose, trunks and shirt.

Meanwhile I returned to the guards. 'This woman's very existence is to be forgotten. She has never been here, you understand?' They nodded, rather doubtfully. 'Archer Henderson, I shall mention your name to His Majesty for loyal obedience. Here — a token of his appreciation of your discretion.' A purse of a dozen gold écus. His eyes lit up at its jingle. 'And something for the sergeant and men-at-arms to drink his health.' A score of testons, enough to make them thoroughly happy. 'Discreetly, you understand! I must again stress that this is a secret of state.' They all hid their grins, and looked impressed and solemn.

I turned to Lark, emerging from the alcove. A cloak hid her boy's clothes; even the soldiers wouldn't be able to describe her. 'Mademoiselle? You are ready? Then let us go up to the duke's presence.' I waited for the soldiers' salutes, nodded in response, and we walked quietly out.

It was that easy. No ifs or maybes. They'd keep quiet till Judgement Day. And if they did speak up — who, me? One of the king's own Bodyguard, aiding a criminal to escape? How ridiculous! They'd made a mistake, or they were trying a crude bit of extortion. Some suspicion, maybe, but no proof. We were safe; as long as we got Lark away without being recognised!

She was weak, white and shaky, but she managed to follow me up the stairs beside Guy, as another pageboy would. Not a soul lifted an eyebrow at her. A nostril, maybe, at the dungeon stink, but we were past by then. Within two minutes, Lark was wrapped in dad's arms. Nicola, Pierre, Guy and I were grinning in triumph, and near tears.

'God's wounds!' I said, to cover my emotion. 'I thought we'd never get out, she took so long getting dressed!'

Lark was stiff and white, her eyes huge and circled with black rings of strain. Pierre had everything prepared, and Nicola chased the rest of us out while she got Lark washed and fed, and the whip weals on her back and the rope marks on her wrists salved and bandaged. When she let us return, Lark was wrapped in the blankets on Guy's pallet at the foot of my bed.

'You'll not be angry with her?' Nicola advised. 'She's worn out.'

'Don't be stupid, woman!' dad barked in a whisper. 'Of course I'm angry with her! But I'll not beat her. Not here and now, anyway!'

He bent over Lark. 'Better now, lass? Well, then. What are you doing here?'

She bit her lip. 'I came to warn some people in Tours that their plan was known.' She looked up pleadingly. 'My friends! I had to, dad! I told Annette I was going to stay with friends. And I wasn't entirely daft. I found an old suit of Johnnie's, to travel safer.'

'Bird-brained!' I said. Pierre nodded, smiling as he remembered.

'Oh, dad! I was too late! So many of my friends were arrested! And then we were caught the day before I planned to start back. But I managed to save a teston, to bribe a guard to take John a message.' She was so proud of her ability to cope! 'I knew you'd remember that horrid song, Johnnie. I knew you'd save me!'

She was clutching my hand as I knelt by the pallet. I smiled down at her, trying not to show how grieved I was by the state she was in. 'Well, Lark, I had to come.' She frowned slightly, puzzled. 'D'you not remember the wizard? Nostradamus? I was aye to come when you called me, he said.'

She started to laugh weakly, and fell asleep, still holding my hand.

We looked at each other. Dad sighed. 'Should I be angered, or proud of her?' he whispered.

'Proud, sir!' Nicola murmured firmly. 'For she risked her life to save her friends. Just as your son did, to save her.'

'And as you've done too, my dear,' I said quietly. My throat was tight, and my voice somehow not quite under my control. 'We had little choice, for we're her family. But you did it from sheer bravery and goodness of heart.' I leaned over where I knelt, and kissed her cheek.

She flushed vividly, scrubbing at her face with the back of her hand. 'Away with you, sir! There's no call for that nonsense!'

Dad looked from one to the other of us. 'Well, son, duty calls.' His voice was a touch loud, and Nicola shushed him. He eyed me. 'John, you'll not disgrace the Garde tomorrow, will you?'

'I'll manage, dad.' I hoped. 'I'd best return to the hall now. The king might call for me, and I'd better be there. Pierre, will you — ?'

'Yes, sir, I'll see to the lady,' Pierre nodded.

'I'll stay too,' Nicola said. 'For a while, in case she wakes.'

'Aye. Come along, then, Guy,' I said. 'You know not to say —'

'Not a word!' he assured me. 'And I'll sleep on the floor, sir!'

'Don't be a fool, boy!' Pierre's tone was dry. 'Get you a mattress. Enough martyrs suffering tomorrow!'

He was right. From the hour I dulled my brain with brandy for breakfast and walked grimly out to join the king's party, the whole day was filled with sounds and sights I wish I could forget. I stood behind the king's chair all through that morning and afternoon, trying to shut my eyes and ears, while Francois leaned eagerly over the balcony to cheer on the executioners and point out the best horrible sights.

Queen Catherine, the Serpent Queen, watched with no visible emotion as the enemies of her son were punished and destroyed. The young Duchesse de Guise broke down and wept hysterically, to her husband's annoyance. Three of the ladies-in-waiting, including the Marie on duty, were sick. Queen Marie herself sat rigid, white and stiff in a red gown to show her happiness, and stared out above the agonies in the courtyard like a statue. She was seventeen. Francois complained several times that she didn't seem to share his enjoyment of his triumph, but she scarcely answered him. She seemed almost to be in a trance.

I wished I was. The brandy flask emptied far too soon.

But I managed not to disgrace the Garde by any show of a weak stomach.

The window of my room, fortunately, did not give onto the courtyard. I'd told Lark to stay inside, and keep the panels closed. For once she did as she was told. When I returned to prepare for dinner, she was rested and keen to be away. She kissed me, and thanked me again for saving her, but she didn't ask what I had seen. I had no intention of ever telling her.

'We'll get you out this evening before the gates are locked,' I told her. 'When Queen Catherine's leaving, I'll send Guy for you. He'll take you down the back stairs and you'll both just walk out with the crowd. Dad will meet you at the Garde office. He's sending a letter off to Paris, and you'll ride with the messenger. Don't let him know you're a girl. Can you do that?'

She nodded. 'I'll manage. Don't worry, Johnnie! After all you've done for me, how can anything go wrong now?' I touched wood. She gave me a wavering smile. 'You once said it was unlucky to be superstitious!'

She stood up to show me how she looked, her hair cut short, smart and boyish in Guy's old uniform. 'I'm most grateful, Guy!' She smiled at him. He bowed to kiss her hand, her slave for life. 'My name is — er —'

'Georges Laval,' I told her. 'If anybody asks, you're Guy's cousin. You came to visit, to see if you could get a post with me, but I didn't like you. You were too cheeky!' She stuck her tongue out at me. It was hard to be cheerful . . . For her, too. But we had to try. 'You'll be sore, I'm warning you — the Garde ride hard.'

'I'll be all right,' she assured me. 'Pierre's given me an ointment that he says will ease my aches. If I can get some privacy to rub it in!' I tried to smile. She glanced at me sideways. 'Was it so bad, Johnnie? No, don't tell me!' Her own smile had gone; but she forced it back. 'I'll part from your soldier at the Orleans gate, and go straight home. And I promise you, I'll stay there!'

I took her hand. 'Lark — be careful. And — look, lass, I don't want to alarm you, but —' I was unsure how to go on. Eventually I spoke to Pierre instead of to Lark. 'Pierre, I want you to prepare for the worst.' His eyes sharpened above his red whiskers, more like a fox than ever. 'Anything could happen. At any time. The king — he's not well. Did you see his colour tonight? And he's malicious, as you know. I want you to be ready to — to —'

'Run for it?' He wasn't surprised. Why should he be, after all? He knew the Court better than I did.

I nodded. 'At two minutes' notice.'

He didn't argue. 'Where to, sir?'

'England.' It was Lark who said it. She wasn't surprised either. 'We'll go to join Gabriel. And dad too. Then we'll all be safe, thank God!'

'Well.' I was rather taken aback at how easily she'd accepted it. 'We can think about it again later. I must go down now. Good luck!'

Chicot kept us all entertained during dinner with repeats of the funniest moments of the day's events. Francois laughed like a jackass, and when he noticed my frozen face he laughed even harder, till he nearly choked. I forced myself not to wish that he would.

At last Queen Catherine rose to leave. I nodded to Guy, who slipped away quietly. The halls were full of people saying farewell to their friends who had come over for the day to see the executions. There was a kind of hectic gaiety; I think most people were more shocked by the tortures than they could admit to, in case they were thought sympathetic to the Religion. Amid the crowds of guests and their servants Lark would never be noticed, I was sure.

The dowager queen's train clattered out, and we all stood aside while the king and queen led the royal household back indoors. Francois was over-excited, talking loudly and fast, patchily flushed. 'Come on, Marie!

They've hung traitors all along the balcony, and stuck heads on the spikes of the railings! Come and see!'

The young queen looked down at him and sighed wearily. 'Very well, sire. But allow me a moment to rest quietly. It has been a long day.'

'A great day!' he argued pettishly. He started to wipe his nose on his sleeve, saw me, flapped the hand away sulkily, finished what he'd started with a defiant glare at me, and snapped, 'I'll await Your Majesty's convenience in the Great Hall! Don't be long!'

Chicot, clearly in great favour again, was beside him. The pair of them danced off across the hall to the stairs, gold-embroidered violet and black-striped orange close entwined together, giggling and singing a horrible song about the devil in hell getting the Calvinists' heads mixed up. Behind them, chatting and yawning in a twinkling haze of gems, filtered the rest of the Court.

I was about to follow when I saw the duty Marie, Fleming, with an arm round her mistress's waist, looking round anxiously. The queen's face was paper-white and blank. She mustn't show weakness, not on the day when her husband's enemies were executed! Hurriedly I stepped forward. 'Your Majesty? Take my arm.' Good, there was Guy in his green uniform. I gestured to him to open the nearest door, to give the poor lady some privacy.

As we passed, I nodded thanks.

It wasn't Guy. It was Lark.

How? What had happened?

My God! She'd been in Queen Marie's household for months! She'd be recognised!

The queen sank down on a chair in the side room, Fleming fanning her. I had to get Lark out of the way. 'Guy,' I said, 'go and fetch a bowl of hot water and a towel.' She'd have the sense to go straight back to my room and send Guy down, I thought.

Marie, sitting gasping and blinking on the chair, had

opened her eyes wide, trying to recover her senses. Suddenly her whole figure tensed. 'Guy?' she shrilled, not in her normal quiet, firm voice. 'That's not Guy! Stand, there, boy! Fleming, I'm right, am I not? That's not de Rouxelle's page Guy, surely? Or — no, I'm sure I'm right!'

'His cousin, Your Majesty,' I assured her. 'Georges. The name got tangled in my teeth. Go on, boy! Hot and cold water! And some wine!'

Lark bowed and turned to escape, but the queen called again, 'Stop!'

We froze. The queen tried to push herself to her feet, but failed. She sank back, holding the Marie's arm, and shook her head to clear it. Then she beckoned.

Lark stood still.

'Come here at once, boy!' Fleming snapped, appalled at the insolence.

Lark slowly stepped forward and knelt. Dad was at the Garde office. There would be horses saddled. If we could reach it, I could commandeer two — one for dad — three of them.

The queen was peering up at Lark with disbelief in her face. She let go and sank back. 'Lark! Isn't it? Lark Russell. In boy's clothes.' She drew a deep breath. 'Here, today of all days. And you love Montgomery, who is a Calvinist . . .'

'I'll call the guard, madame!' Fleming said, and turned to the door.

But the queen snatched at her wrist. 'No! No, Fleming, be still!'

There was a long, cold pause. The young queen studied me, and Lark, and me again, gathering strength in the quiet. At last she sat up.

'Madame, I can explain —' I couldn't, but I had to say something.

'No!' she interrupted urgently again. 'No, you'll explain nothing! Not a word! You told me once —

194

Dear God, only yesterday — that you and your sister were not my enemies. I will believe you. I will! Don't speak! If your sister chooses to wear boy's gear, well, I've done so myself for a masquerade. Her reason is without doubt sufficient.' Fleming was frowning.

The queen smiled slightly. 'It was said to me some days ago that God would not blame anyone for what he — or she — did not know. So. I choose not to know about this.' She nodded, and repeated it to herself. 'What I don't know about I can't be blamed for. I refuse to add to today's — triumph. Never again . . . Never, never again . . . Not that I have any reason to believe that you have anything to hide. No. My conscience is perfectly clear.'

She leaned only a little on Fleming's hand as she rose to her full tall height, towering eight inches above Lark and me. 'I have to go and — and look at heads. Go in peace, Jean de Rouxelle. And you, Lark. When we meet again, I hope it will be in happier circumstances.' I knelt in gratitude, and Lark, after a foolish bob of a curtsey which made the queen's lips twitch nearly into a smile, copied me. Then Marie walked smoothly, once more in control, from the room.

As the door shut after Fleming, Lark collapsed to sit on the floor. 'Dear Lord God Almighty Jehovah! She knew! She knew, but she didn't betray us! We're safe! Oh, thank God!'

'Thank the Serpent Queen,' I said absently. Then I came to myself, and grabbed her shoulders. 'What happened? Why aren't you half way to Paris?'

'I couldn't, Johnnie!' she protested. 'The crowd in the courtyard — we got separated.' She hesitated, and bit her lip. 'I couldn't think. I was scared, Johnnie!' Silly panicky female! Oh, well. I'd been nervous myself. 'I was going back to your room to wait for you, but then I saw you, and headed for you, and you called me, and . . . That's how it happened.'

'God's wounds!' I puffed in exasperation, and stood

195

up. 'Dad must be hairless with worry! Come on. I'll take you down to the office myself. Just remember you're my page. Walk behind me!'

The summer came, and passed. The king still had his bouts of illness. His mother and wife nursed him together, for though they disliked each other, they were both devoted to the sickly boy. He turned from me to his other friends, especially Chicot, while Queen Marie drew me more into her circle. We never mentioned how she had saved — or spared — Lark and me.

In June Marie's mother, her regent in Scotland, died. Marie's first terrible grief made her really ill. She was upset again when in August the Scottish Parliament declared the Reformed Faith the official religion. I was proud that while she held her head high in front of the Court, she trusted me enough to weep again when only her Maries and I were present.

In July Queen Catherine arranged the Treaty of Edinburgh, by which Marie and Francois would recognise Elizabeth as the Queen of England. In return, Elizabeth withdrew her invading armies from Scotland, and promised to stop supporting the Scots Protestants.

But Mary and Francois never actually got round to signing the treaty; there was always pressure of affairs, or some such excuse. True enough, Francois was busy, but not with work. He spent more and more time hunting. If we could persuade him to sit still for two hours in a week to sign papers, we were doing well.

As time went by, Nicola started avoiding me again. I was dismayed; I liked her, owed her so much, needed the relief of her earthy, caustic comments on Court life. But what could I do? Order her to be friendly? Charge through the back corridors after a dwarf, demanding why she didn't speak to me any more? I'd make myself, and the Garde with me, ridiculous.

Her reason, of course, was that Chicot was riding high in the little king's favour, and as the weeks passed it became clear that he was working against me again. Francois and his cronies started to giggle whenever I approached them. My saving their castle of Amboise was forgotten. Tricks Chicot played on me — loosening my girth when I came to mount, 'accidentally' spilling jellies and wine over me, tripping me to fall with a clatter of my daft ceremonial halberd in church — they all brought him laughter and applause, not punishment for his clumsiness or insolence.

It came to a head in mid-November.

The Jest

We were at Blois, dancing after dinner in the Great Hall. I had by now learned how to move with some grace and style, and confidently led out one of the Flying Squadron. People behind me started smiling, snickering. My partner stiffened. I moved her out of the lines of dancers, and asked her to check. As I'd suspected, in the crush someone had pinned a notice to the back of my white silk doublet. 'Wife wanted. Must be good laundress. Apply at front.'

My partner smoothly removed herself from the vicinity of the butt of so many jokes. It might be catching. I looked round. The queens, Marie and Catherine, were dancing, but the king was in his high seat at the end of the hall, Chicot by his side, both watching me, sniggering.

I was too angry for sense. I walked up to face them, and bowed. 'With Your Majesty's permission, I should be glad of a word with your jester.'

The two faces grinned up at me together. 'What's wrong, de Rouxelle?' the king squeaked. His voice hadn't broken yet. 'Can't you take a jest?'

'He'd like to choke the joker! He's so manly when

198

he's angry! Perhaps he lacks the wit to see the wit, Your Majesty!' Chicot smirked.

He maybe hoped I'd strike him. Right, I wouldn't. 'Wit? If I saw any, I'd know it well enough. All I see is impertinence. Small dogs yap loud.'

'Hoity-toity, sir mastiff! And you so tall!' he jeered. 'We'd best find a wife for him, sire. He looks as if he needs somebody to whip!'

The king chortled with glee. Behind me the dance was over. I'd get nowhere while the little man clung to his royal protector. But later . . . I was stepping aside when the king cried, 'Don't go away, de Rouxelle! I'm sure Chicot can find a suitable lady for you!' Spluttering with mirth he gestured to Chicot, who waved to the musicians. They started a solemn bridal hymn, the same one that had been played at the king's own wedding.

This had been all planned. I could guess what was going to happen.

The queens were conducted past me and up to their seats, smiling at me in a rather puzzled way. 'De Rouxelle? What is going on?' Marie asked.

'A jest, Marie! Sit, sit! You need no longer concern yourself about a bride for Jean. See — here she comes!'

From the far end of the hall, between the pillars, advanced a bridal procession; of dwarves. Two women parading in the red and yellow of the Swiss Garde; two bearded men prettily gowned in pink and white, throwing sweets and dried flower petals round the audience; and then a little figure in a copy of Queen Marie's own white wedding gown, heavily veiled. Whispers and chuckling rose to the gilt fleurs-de-lys on the high vaulted roof.

As they reached us, the 'Swiss Garde' and the 'flower girls' parted to let the 'bride' come up to my side. Chicot pranced forward, bowing deeply. 'Monsieur de Rouxelle, allow me to introduce you to your bride! Mademoiselle! Honour us! Allow us to admire your beauty!'

She didn't move. Making a face of mock sympathy, and gushing, 'Dear sir, I fear the bride is shy!' he reached out and lifted the lace veil.

It was, of course, Nicola; painted in a white clown's face of black eyes and huge scarlet lips and cheeks, staring at me in mute apology.

However, I'd had just enough warning. The king's gleeful malice had made me aware of the joke just too soon, in time to think. If I reacted angrily, complained of being insulted, Francois could lose his unsteady temper — and Queen Catherine was sitting only five feet away. In childish anger Francois might let Chicot speak. I'd smile, join in the joke. And turn it on them if I could.

I knelt, smiling and winking where only Nicola — and Chicot, to my satisfaction — could see it. 'Mademoiselle la Jardinière,' I said clearly, 'save only the queens here present, I have never met a lady of your honesty and courage, wit and kindliness. Mademoiselle, these make you more truly noble than many of taller stature, or greater standing. I am honoured!'

That should loose a fox in his fowl-house! It was true, too, I realised with some surprise. Nicola flushed deeply, and her eyes filled with tears. I drew my lace kerchief from my sleeve and wiped them away, taking the opportunity to remove much of the face paint as I did so.

When I looked up, there was a priest standing beside me. No, not a priest; the dwarves' servant, the hugely fat man who acted the ogre, the puppeteer. He was dressed in soutane and stole, and held a Bible.

'Everything's ready, de Rouxelle!' the king cried cheerfully. 'I'll be witness at your marriage! And Marie, too!'

Queen Marie half rose, her lips pressed tight in irritation, but Catherine beside her patted her hand. 'Only a jest, my dear!' she reassured her, and the young queen sat back.

I looked at Nicola. She raised her eyebrows slightly

in resignation. 'If it keeps them happy!' she whispered so that only I could hear.

Well. I'd decided to play along; silly to break out now. It would ruin me with the king, anyway, to wreck his stupid prank in public. So I stood still while the 'priest' read a service over us, answered 'Yes, I do,' when I was asked if I would take Nicola, called la Jardinière, to be my wedded wife; smiled as Nicola stated that yes, she would take me as her husband, and kissed the 'bride'. She clung to my hand, unhappy and ashamed, and my anger rose. It was bad enough that the king should play silly japes on me, but Nicola was only involved because she was small, she was a servant, she was my friend, she had no wealth or position. It wasn't her fault . . .

The young queen seemed to agree with me. She rose finally, when the jest seemed to be over, and gestured to the musicians. 'Music! The Pavane of the Queen of Scots!' As the slow, stately melody began she gripped her husband's hand like a vice. 'Francois! We will dance!' she declared in a tone that would have quelled a rebellion on its own. 'De Rouxelle! You and Nicola, pray lead the dance.' What an honour!

The queen's taut face clearly showed her anger, and her action showed approval of mine. Francois — odd, that! He should have been glowering, sulky at having his jest spoiled. But he was still smirking.

The hair on my neck rose. Something was wrong. Very, very wrong.

Chicot skipped forward to present a long, prettily-wrapped parcel to Nicola. 'From my humble self and your late colleagues, Madame de Rouxelle, to remind you of us! We are sure they will be of use to you!'

Queen Marie frowned again. 'Chicot, this becomes boring,' she said firmly. 'Let the jest die, now.'

He mimed astonishment. 'Jest, Your Majesty? What jest?'

'This false wedding!' she snapped.

The king could no longer hold in his mirth. 'It's not false, Marie! That's the heart of it! It's a real wedding! That man — he's really a priest! They're really married!' He leaned on Chicot's shoulder to hold himself up, hicupping and helpless with laughter. 'He's a hedge-priest Chicot picked up years ago — thrown out of his church for drunkenness! But he's still a priest! And he's read the banns for them! They're truly wed!' He peered up at me. 'How do you like your bride, Jean?'

I saw how I'd been trapped. I'd done what I thought would annoy Chicot, spoiling his fun, and the clever little man had foreseen my every action. Murmurs of mirth were rising, growing into a roar of derision. Queen Catherine, always a coarse woman, was reeling with laughter. I was burning, scarlet with humiliation.

Nicola was white as paper. 'Oh, God!' she whispered. 'I'd no idea — I'm sorry, sir! I'm sorry!' Her lips were trembling in mortification.

My hot rage froze. Favour with Francois was past; I didn't care. If his breeks had been burning I'd have blown on the blaze. Right; what would annoy them most, without getting me arrested?' 'Dear Nicola,' I said, 'we are holding up our wedding dance.' I smiled, and took her hand.

The sight of the king's jaw dropping was the only pleasure I had that day, and it only lasted a second. I got another shock.

Nicola tugged her hand out of mine. 'No, sir!'

'My dear sir! Not even a dwarf wants to be wed to you!' Chicot jeered.

I ignored him. 'Nicola, it's the only thing to do. Come along.'

'No, sir,' she repeated sturdily. 'Don't be foolish!'

The jester crowed with glee. 'Scolding your husband already, madame?'

'Sounds just like a wife, doesn't she, Chicot?' the king snickered.

'Indeed?' his wife said icily above his head. She was quite unaffected by the laughter, or the hushing so that folk could hear better. The music had stopped. 'Nicola, I should imagine that that parcel is another stupid jest. Pray throw it away.' Nicola took her at her word, and hurled the bundle right at Chicot. Unfortunately, it hit his shoulder, not his face. The brocade wrapping came undone as it clattered to the floor, and a pair of stilt shoes about two feet high fell out. Marie gazed at them in disgust. 'As I thought,' she said scornfully. 'Vulgar.' The king's face was a picture of embarrassed annoyance.

The young queen wasn't finished. 'I promised you a well-dowered bride, Jean,' she told me. 'I shall make good my words. Here is a small token of my good-will.' She beckoned a Marie to unfasten her necklace of emeralds. There was an indrawing of breath all round the hall as she presented it to me. It was worth an estate all by itself; a magnificent gift. Nothing could have shown more clearly that she disapproved of her husband's action. She glanced briefly at Francois and his mother. 'They are my own, not part of the jewels of France.' Catherine and her son both looked furious.

I knelt to kiss Marie's hand. Right. Annoy them some more. I drew Nicola forward. 'They match your gown, my dear.' Still kneeling, I fastened the jewels round her neck and kissed her. The beginnings of a sound that wasn't a jeer murmured among the enthralled audience.

'Thank you, Jean,' Nicola whispered, her eyes flooding again. 'I shall always remember that.' She drew a hugely deep breath and turned resolutely to Queen Marie. 'Your Majesty,' she said, 'I beg you to accept me into your service. Immediately.'

'What? Nicola, you're my wife, and —'

She tutted at me. 'Oh, sir, that's foolishness! You know it's not possible! Your Majesty, I pray you ask His Eminence of Lorraine for an annulment for us as soon as may be, and let me stay with you till then.'

'Nicola!' I might as well have held my tongue.

Marie held up a hand to silence me. 'Certainly, Nicola. You may come tonight to my maids' room, and remain with me as long as you wish.' She turned back to me. 'Monsieur de Rouxelle, though I enjoy your company, yet I feel you might do well to visit your estates for a while.'

Thoughts floundered through my mind. It wasn't a bad idea — with Nicola safe in the queen's care. If Marie got me an annulment quickly, and with a cardinal for an uncle she could, the marriage would be only a minor annoyance. Again Chicot had missed his full mark. But though I had many acquaintances, I also had many jealous enemies, and no powerful friends apart from Marie. Now that Francois was against me again, the jester had heavy bombards against my single arquebus. A period of exile would help the joke, and the king's temper, and people's envy, to die down. Yes, sensibly, I should go. I didn't want to. It would look like running away. But . . .

The king's mouth had tightened unattractively. He didn't hide his bad side from her as carefully these days. Another reason I should leave. Suddenly he smiled. God's wounds, what now? 'Very well, he can go. But after tomorrow. We'll arrange a farewell hunt for him!' He grinned at Chicot. 'Something special!'

Marie turned and looked at him fully. No flies on her, either; she had heard the threat as clearly as I had. 'What a good idea, Your Majesty,' she said calmly. 'De Rouxelle can escort me, give me the pleasure of his company again before he leaves. Jean, tomorrow you'll not leave my side.'

Francois pouted sulkily. 'Well — all right.' He made an effort. 'To give you pleasure, Marie!'

She smiled more fully. 'Thank you, Francois.' But

she'd not forgive him so easily. She smiled at me. 'Jean! Nicola! Take your place in the dance!' She raised a hand to the musicians, and the music started again.

As we moved into the pavane, I glared at Nicola. 'Why?' I hissed. 'Don't you want to be married to me?' I held my hand low for her comfort.

She sighed, stepping long not to hold back the royal couple. 'It's not that, sir. It's just — you must see it's impossible! You, an Archer, with your way to make. And me — look at me! Everybody would laugh at you. They do at me, but I'm used to it. I make my living from it. It would ruin you.'

It was true, but I didn't want to give in. All through the steps and turns and stately balancings, which she managed with more ease than I'd expected, I argued, but in vain. 'You're kind, sir, but you're cutting off your nose to spite Chicot's face. No, it's not possible!'

When I threatened, 'I'm your husband! I'll drag you off!' she snorted.

'No, you'll not, sir! I'd scream for Chicot to rescue me!'

I wouldn't have, of course, anyway.

She drew down my head at the end of the dance, kissed me, wished me well, and scurried off to the queen's apartments.

I felt lost, somehow. My face was wet where our cheeks had touched.

Pierre, hanging up my suit that evening, sighed. 'Two minutes, sir!'

I had to laugh. 'You're that prepared, Pierre? You're wonderful!'

'Just what you said, sir. Horses kept saddled in an outside stable. Debts paid, as you do insist. Sensible, I suppose. Nobody'll be chasing us except whoever's chasing us, if you see what I mean. Creditors stick tighter than nits. House and most of your goods sold off, quietly, and hired back. Didn't know, did you, sir?

Nor nobody else does. Money in bank with branches in England. Jewellery and papers in a saddlebag at all times, ready to lift. Clothes — pity, that!'

'I'd rather save my skin than my shirts, Pierre!'

'Suppose so, sir. Leave them for servants. Estates paying rents to banks, not here; you'll get the money, if he doesn't whip them off you.' No need to say who 'he' was. 'Two minutes, sir. If we have to.'

'I hope we don't. I'm getting out now, before I'm shovelled out.'

'Good.' His approval was emphatic. 'Pity about the little lady.'

Yes, it was. Whatever he meant.

It was indeed a special hunt next day. We were late in starting, for the king had a sore ear, but at noon he insisted he was well enough, and we put up a fine stag not far from the town. Queen Marie rode astride, as Queen Catherine had taught her, with breeches under her flying yellow skirt. I galloped close by her side as she had commanded, thinking myself safe from whatever malice Chicot and His evil little Majesty had dreamed up. When the attack came, it took me by surprise.

Just ahead of us, Francois was shouting in excitement as he drove his horse along one of the open rides specially cut in the royal forests for the hunt. The stag suddenly dodged aside among the trees, the hounds after it, and Francois whipped round fast enough to unseat a worse rider, flicking through a gap in the bushes like a bat in a belfry. I drew rein for a second to let the queen in ahead of me, and a pistol fired.

It had its effect, though not on me. I often practised shooting on horseback, and my mount was used to sudden bangs. But the queen's wasn't. It shied violently, tripped in the undergrowth and fell.

There were a dozen riders behind me. I reined mercilessly round to block them, yelling to them to stay clear. Thank God she wasn't strapped into a sidesaddle — she'd certainly have been injured. Before my horse had stopped I was off him and down astride the queen, swearing, though I didn't know it, and pushing at her horse struggling to its feet beside her. The frightened beast smashed one hoof down on her cap, an inch away from her head, actually trampling on her hair. I hit out at it as it reared, and managed to drive it aside. Then someone grabbed its reins and hauled it away, and I could drop to my knees to see if she was hurt.

Amazingly, she was laughing. She lay and giggled breathlessly up at us. 'Jean!' she gasped. 'What language — before your queen! Appalling! I've never heard anything like it!' She paused for breath. 'No, no, man, I'm all right! Just winded! Oh, and a root right where I'll be sorest when I sit! Oh, dear me! Oh, stop looking so worried, all of you! I tell you I'm well! Look — arms, legs, all working! Just give me a hand up, Jean, will you?'

I helped her rise, gently, watching for the sudden wince of any unknown hurt. She came to her feet grunting slightly, but standing straight. I sighed with relief — we all did.

Then she asked, 'What's wrong with your doublet, Jean?' Surprised, I glanced down. It was hanging open like a gutted chicken.

The shot hadn't missed completely. If I'd not reined back, it would have hit me. The ball had slashed like a knife diagonally up across the front of my uniform, without touching the skin beneath.

Marie had heard the bang, but not known what it was. Within seconds, furious, she had the hunt turned to hunting the assassin. She mounted my horse, since hers was lame, and I took one of the spares led by the hunt servants. At my suggestion the bloodhounds were set to the bushes where the stag had unexpectedly leapt aside. 'Look for a very small person,' I said; everyone nodded in angry comprehension. They found a trail, and we trotted off eagerly, but it simply led to a place by the river where a boat had been moored. We'd lost him, whoever he was.

In spite of her courage, the queen was drooping now. She'd had a bad fall and a shock. In the cold wind she was at last shivering with reaction, so I gave her my cloak, on top of her own. The cold gave me an excuse for the trembling of my hands. I'd had a fair shock, too.

There was a cry among the trees. 'Where have you all been? I lost the stag, because there was nobody with me! Couldn't you keep up, you idiots?' The king came cantering up, very annoyed till he saw his wife on a new horse. 'What's wrong? Did your horse go lame, Marie? Is it all right?'

'Yes, Francois,' she said grimly. 'And so am I, and de Rouxelle here. No thanks to whoever shot at us.'

'Shot at you?' He seemed genuinely amazed. 'Tell me! My God! He could have hit you! And then — you say it was Jean kept the others from riding you down, and saved you from your own horse!' There was mud on her cap, and he inspected it in growing agitation. 'You in danger, Marie! No — I never — I mean — I never dreamed —' He finally fell silent. I wondered just what he'd never dreamed; that Chicot would put the queen at risk, to get fully even with me? He rode quietly beside us all the way back to the town.

As we clattered under the arches into the courtyard, his hand went up to the ear he'd complained about before we set out. 'Ow!' he cried. 'Oh, it's sore! Oh!' The pages led his horse to the mounting-block and helped him down. His knees buckled. 'Oh, God! Marie!' he cried, and started to scream in pain.

Queen Marie forgot her own state in her worry. 'His Majesty rode hard till he was heated, and then returned beside me slowly, in a cold wind,' she told the physicians. 'I blame myself! I should have known better, and sent him on ahead.' They reassured her, and started the well-practised round of fomentations, hot and cold pads, warm mustard oil . . .

It seemed to work. Next day he was better. Had we found the assassin? When he heard there was no trace, he sighed, maybe with relief. But there was no trace of Chicot, either. Francois bit his lips nervously.

I planned to leave next day, but that night at Vespers the king fainted, and could not be revived for hours. He called for his mother, who came as fast as a horse would carry her; and for Marie, who nursed him, as usual, devotedly; and for me.

I entered his room, I admit, with a sinking heart. Queen Catherine, sitting at one side of the bed, gazed at me levelly, showing no emotion, though her eyes were swollen and red. What had he said to her? What had he, and she, in mind? Queen Marie, resting by the window, smiled wearily. The physicians in the corner muttered as physicians do. The heat from three braziers would have baked bread. That must be why I was sweating.

I nodded to the Archers on duty by the bedhead, and knelt by the little figure lost among the embroidered brocade curtains and coverlets. His eyes were closed. Maybe he was asleep? I glanced over at his mother, who gestured for me to speak. 'Your Majesty called for me?' I said quietly.

His dark eyes were deep-sunk, with blue shadow below them, and his face looked grey and less puffy than normal. The fur cap he wore was bulged out at one side by the cloths over his ear. 'Jean,' he whispered. 'Oh, Jean, it hurts.'

'That's just because it's sore, Your Majesty,' I tried a joke. Catherine's eyes flashed menacingly at the impertinence.

'No, truly . . . I'm dying.'

Poor, horrible little lad . . . 'God's wounds, sire, I wish I'd an écu for every time I've heard you say that!' I grinned cheerfully. It was true; but he might

209

be right this time. There was a pinched look about his mouth.

He tried to smile, in spite of the pain. 'Jean, I've been a bad king.'

'Well, that's what I came here for, sire. To be your whipping-boy.'

He nodded very slightly. 'Yes. But — no. Not any more. To cheer me. To speak honestly to me. Honest. Not like the rest. Not like —' He stopped.

'Like Chicot?' I ventured.

He nodded, and sniffed dolefully. Then he gripped my hand, his nails digging in. 'Don't tell her! Please! Never!' he breathed.

'I won't tell, sire,' I assured him, and he relaxed. He whimpered in pain, and Queen Marie was at once up beside the bed with a damp cloth.

The dowager queen was frowning. Any hint of a secret, and she was alert. But there was a bustle at the door; the Cardinal de Lorraine had just arrived. I slipped quietly away as he blessed the little king.

As far as I know, Francois never mentioned Chicot again.

Rumours flew. A Huguenot barber had poured poison in the king's ear; a Huguenot cook had poisoned his dinner; a Huguenot servant had poisoned his wine. Few believed them; we thought it was the Guises who started them.

I was called for twice more. Once, the king was moaning in pain, his ear leaking black pus. 'Jean!' he whispered. 'Jean, have I done right? He bothered me so . . . He told me . . .'

Wondering what he was talking about, who 'he' was, I reassured the poor lad that of course he'd done right. What else could I say?

'He taught me a prayer, Jean,' said the wavering little whisper. '"Lord, pardon my sins, and do not blame me for those which my ministers have committed in my name and by my authority."' Queen Marie, holding his hand, murmured approval. 'Do you think God will listen?'

'To a king? Of course He will!' I assured him. 'If He doesn't, just give me a whistle and I'll see to Him for you!'

'Whistle . . . I haven't got a whistle. Not any more . . .' His eyes closed.

As I left, I heard that the Cardinal de Lorraine had brought in the warrant for the execution of the Prince de Conde, the Protestant leader, who had been arrested some weeks earlier, for the lad to sign before he died. I understood the prayer then.

The next time, Francois was almost lively. I'd made a new willow whistle for him, and he blew it, and thanked me, laughing faintly.

But after that he fell into darkness and unconsciousness. On the fifth day of December, he died.

His wife Marie was no longer Queen of France. He was succeeded by his younger brother Charles; King Charles IX, aged ten.

His mother Queen Catherine was made Regent.

And if Chicot dared to reappear, there was now no reason why he shouldn't tell her about Lark . . .

Two Minutes

If Chicot had been still at Court, I'd not have given
way, but there was no trace of him. So when Nicola
begged me, 'Sir, Queen Marie's ill with grief and weariness. She asks you to stand by her. And so do I,' I
didn't refuse.

I wasn't happy, though. 'What if Chicot comes back?
Have you seen the way the old queen eyes me? Like a
snake at a frog.'

'With her face she can't help it!' I had to laugh, but
under the flippancy Nicola was deeply earnest. 'Sir, you
and the Maries are the only true friends Queen Marie
has now. All the rest, even her uncles, are crawling
round Queen Catherine and young King Charles. You
can't leave her alone in her misery! Not after what she's
done for you and your sister!'

True, we both owed her our lives, and Montgomery's.
Though I didn't like it, I had to agree. But I made sure
Pierre remembered; two minutes . . .

Queen Catherine certainly grieved for her son, but his
death wasn't unexpected; he'd been a disappointment,
and Charles was younger, healthier, and would obey her,

not the Guises. She had real power at last. She quietly freed Condé.

Five days after the little king's death, I attended her levée, packed now with the greatest in the land. I was almost the last to be called. 'De Rouxelle? How is your lady wife, eh? My God, that was a jest!' She chuckled silently, not to shock the crowd. 'Well? What do you want?'

I expressed my sympathy for her loss, which I shared; and then asked straight out, 'Your Majesty, may I have your permission to resign from the Royal Bodyguard? The Dowager Queen Marie —' I knew that would please her, and it did — 'has honoured me by asking me to join her household.'

'You feel grief, de Rouxelle, and wish to avoid people who might arouse memories of my son?' Well, yes . . . She sighed, rather theatrically. 'I cannot indulge my own feelings so much.' Her eyes slid past me to study the throng, and returned to fix on my face. 'I was angered by your rescue of Montgomery. Unwillingly I had to bow to my son's liking for you.' My heart sank, till she smiled. 'But seeing your devotion to poor Francois in his last days, I decided to forgive you.' Thank God! 'So. Yes, you may leave the Bodyguard, de Rouxelle, but be assured I shall not forget you.' God's wounds, that was the whole idea!

I cut my servants down to four. I really only needed one groom, but I kept two, one young, my own size, and one burly like dad. Then Guy, and Pierre, of course. I'd half expected him to leave and find a position with a more important man when my state diminished so much, but to my pleasure and relief he stayed. 'No, sir! Too used to arguing. Friendly house, no stiff pride, spoiled me for French service! Be whipped out within a week!'

I sank gratefully back to a more normal life, escorting Queen Marie as I'd done Queen Catherine two years before. Now that Chicot had vanished, Nicola was a good friend again. There was no sign yet of the annulment.

Back among the Archers, there was some ill-feeling, but I soon dealt with it. I admitted ruefully that high life wasn't for me. Fashion drove me daft — silver bells on my shoelaces! My back was nearly broken with all the bowing. And the company! Well, I asked, how would they like to be constantly fleeing from the Flying Squadron? They laughed and made the expected bawdy comments, and their envy faded. I polished up my fencing, jousting and pistol shooting. I was useless with a long gun now, I couldn't see the targets, but with a pistol at short range I developed some skill.

Queen Marie was exhausted and ill. Over-emotion always upset her. However, after a while she recovered her usual courage and spirit, and turned her mind to the question that had been asked all over the Court even before Francois had died; who would she marry next?

She and her cousin Elizabeth of England were the two most desirable unmarried ladies in Europe. Few men, however, were eligible to marry a queen in her own right. One day, as I came in from duty at the Hotel de Guise, where Marie was staying, I found dad and Lark discussing it.

'Queen Catherine could get young Charles a papal dispensation to wed his brother's widow, no bother,' dad was saying as I gave Guy my swordbelt to hang up. 'But I don't like the idea. Nor does Catherine — she's aye disliked Queen Marie, an' wants her away. Nor I don't fancy her English cousin, Henry Stewart o' Darnley.'

'A tall, pretty, smarmy lad about my age?' Lark shook her head. 'He came to visit her last year. None of the Flying Squadron could stand him. He sneered at us as if we were dirt, but he kept trying to get us in corners and paw at us. Calm down, dad, he's gone! Oh, hello, Johnnie! We've just refused Darnley and Charles for Queen Marie.'

'Fair enough,' I said. 'They're betting on Don Carlos, the son of Philip of Spain by his first wife. Catherine's against it, with her own daughter queen there now; Marie would soon outshine her again. I'd not mind Spain. If I stay in Marie's service. I'd do better for myself than here.'

Why was Dad's face a picture? Oh. All my life I'd never wanted anything but to join the Garde. And now here I was, almost casually considering leaving it. I'd changed. Funny that I'd not noticed it!

'Mulled cider, Johnnie?' Lark asked. I took the hot cup gratefully She shook her head. 'I'm not for Don Carlos. His mother was mad. He's — what — twelve? And even less healthy than poor Francois. He may be Catholic, and make her Queen of Spain if he lives, but it's too much like what she's had before. I think, anyway. What does Marie say, Johnnie?'

I did my best to imitate that clear, decisive tone. 'There's but one place in the world now where I can be all that I may be.'

Lark was enthralled. 'Where did she mean?'

'Scotland! She's decided she's going back to Scotland!'

'Scotland? What do her uncles o' Guise say to that?' Dad was shocked.

'They're against it, but now she's not Queen of France any longer they don't care as much for her, so she's not caring for them. She says she's Queen of Scots in her own right. She'll go home if she likes. Unwed.'

Lark frowned. 'But how can she hope to rule alone? She's Catholic, the Scots are Protestants now! And they're always rebelling against the crown!'

'She says she's noticed a bit of trouble here too! She knows she can't force them into obedience, but she thinks she can charm them into it. And once she's on her throne, she'll pick herself a husband that suits her.'

Dad puffed out his cheeks in doubt. 'A French kitten

rule Scotch terriers? It's no easy, as her mother found out. Ach, well, she'll learn!'

Queen Marie's half-brother, Lord James Stewart, visited her that spring. She liked and respected him, and he seemed surprised to find her intelligent and reasonable. Marie promised not to try to enforce her faith on her country as long as she, in turn, was allowed to continue to worship as she pleased. He agreed that was fair, and invited her cordially to return to Scotland.

In June, then, we returned to Paris to make the final preparations for leaving. As a formality, Marie sent to Queen Elizabeth of England for a safe-conduct to sail across the North Sea without hindrance, and settled to a last round of farewell visits and banquets with her friends and family.

Early in July Lark called to me excitedly as I got home from duty. She was singing and dancing round the hall as I'd not seen her do for months.

'Don't tell me!' I said. Dad was grinning behind her. 'It's a letter from Montgomery. We'll get rid of you at last, thank God!'

'Oh, clever-clogs!' She threw a cushion at me. 'He's bought a small estate, in a village called Fulham, near London. He's building a house, and he says it'll be ready for me in a month. He'll come for me himself, to Calais, on a ship called the *Martha*. The captain's called William Hackins, or Hockins. Isn't it wonderful!' She whirled me round and kissed me, and dad, Annette, and Pierre, and would have kissed Guy as well but he dodged.

We were all pleased for her, even dad. 'But I'll lose you, my own wee lassie,' he sighed in regret, sitting down in his big chair. 'Daughters an' dead fish, you'll no keep them long.'

'Who's dead fish?' she snorted. 'You'll not lose me! You'll come and give me away at my wedding! You'll stay with me, and fight the London men when they

216

don't believe your boasting, and we'll have to bail you out twice a week from the sheriff!'

She was laughing, but he shook his head. 'No, lassie. Johnnie's going back to Scotland with the queen, an' I'll just go back with him.' He smiled rather sadly. 'I'd have stayed here for Martine's sake, but ... It's aye in my mind's eye these last months, the broad slopes o' Strathmore ... Aye. I've enough put by for a good house, an' Johnnie'll be the great soldier, Captain o' the Queen's Guard, eh? An' come to visit me, an' I'll show him off to my brother, an' have that satisfaction in my old age.'

After a silent moment, Lark pecked a kiss on the top of his head, and patted it. 'Aye, granda, you're getting old an' done! Near bald already!'

Roused by her mockery from his sudden dejection, he slapped her bottom to make her squeak. 'That's no baldness, you hussy, that's my brains growin' through my hair. Maidens should be mild an' meek, quick to hear an' slow to speak! Granda, eh? I'll give you a year! No longer!' She giggled.

Guy was grinning shyly in the corner. 'Well, Guy?' I asked. 'Will you come with me?'

'Of course, sir! I'm your man! You'll not get rid of me that easily.'

'Pierre? Would you come to Scotland with us? Or England, with Lark?'

The foxy little man snorted. 'Me, sir? Leave France? Don't speak English, or Scots. Money put aside, bought a couple of houses to rent.' He hesitated. 'This one, sir.'

'What?' We were all astonished. 'It was you bought this house?'

He turned as red as his hair. 'Fair price, sir! Fair rent too, assure you!' he protested.

'Oh, I don't doubt you, Pierre!' I laughed. 'It's just a surprise, that's all. Will you find a wife, then?'

He nodded, grinning. 'Annette. Good enough girl. Not much brain, but a good cook.' Annette blushed. 'See to your affairs here. Fair commission, sir! But Scotland? Never, sir! Too cold! Too wet! Worse than England!'

Dad, of course, didn't care about England, but couldn't let an insult to his own land pass. While they wrangled amicably — Pierre was quite right, he'd never have got away with it in any purely French household — Lark and I drew off towards the window. 'Happy, my dear?' I asked.

'Oh, Johnnie! I'd started to think he'd forgotten me, or found somebody else. I should have known better. Trusted him.' She was all soft again. Love seemed to turn your brains to mush.

We packed and sold and gave away, ready to go with Marie to Calais whenever the English queen changed her mind; she was refusing the safe-conduct because Marie had still not signed the Treaty of Edinburgh. Dad bought out his contract and I resigned from the Garde, though I was still in attendance on Queen Marie. They held a huge farewell party for us. I don't remember a lot about it, except that dad's worst rival kissed him and dad punched his nose.

The very next morning I was reaching for my sword-belt to leave for the Hotel de Guise, where the queen was staying, when there was a banging at the door. 'It's a Guard, sir, in a great hurry!' Annette called in alarm.

Dad and I dived out to the landing, and the messenger started speaking halfway up the stair. 'Message from Archer Turnbull, sir. There's a wee bird singin' about a wee bird, at Chambord an' Amboise.' God's wounds! Lark — and Chicot telling about her. How had he found out about Lark at Amboise? 'Mother's no amused by the jest, an' she's sendin' a letter for a lock.' That would be a lettre de cachet from Queen Catherine, to imprison us. 'Fast as I could gallop, he told me. He said you'd understand.'

218

'Aye. I do indeed.' Lark and dad were watching open-mouthed. Pierre was flinging open chests in my bedroom. 'Thanks, man! Tell Wattie Turnbull thanks, too, he's a true friend, an' then forget all about the message, eh?'

He caught the teston I tossed him, and grinned. 'What message, sir?'

As Annette shut the door behind him, I looked round. 'Two minutes!'

In the passing of the months they had relaxed, and started to flap about in a kind of panic. 'Quiet!' I yelled. 'God's wounds, we've had this planned for ages! Alan! Vincent!' The grooms appeared at the kitchen door. 'Saddle my charger, and the two next best horses! Guy's to carry an urgent message, and you've both to go with him! Move!' They ran for the stable. 'Annette, cut Lark's hair, short as Guy's, and get her into her lad's gear, fast!' I was already stripped to my shirt. 'Dad, never mind about your pistols yet. Get the saddlebags down the stair!'

We dressed fast, Annette sniffing but for once moving briskly. 'Right, Guy. Where d'you take the letter? How d'you go? And what d'you say when you're caught?'

He'd been well drilled. 'To your agent at your estate near Nantes, sir. The horses are at the livery stable in the next street. We'll ride as fast as we can, but keep away from roads, as if we were trying to avoid pursuit. When they catch up with us, I say you sent me off with these instructions, and I just did what you said.'

I was hooking up a plain brown suit. 'Right, good lad! They can't prove anything against you. You know nothing about any warning. You know nothing, full stop!' I took time to clasp his shoulder. 'It's risky —'

'Never fear for me, sir!' he interrupted. 'I'll lead them away as long as I can, and then — well, I know I'm not clever, but I can keep quiet!'

'That's smarter than most, lad.' Dad was checking the

219

priming of his pistols. 'You'll give us hours, maybe days, to get away.'

I gave Guy silver, and five gold ecus. 'Hide them in your boots, even from the grooms. There's many will kill for less. When you're free, make your way to Scotland. I'll welcome you. Go on now, and God go with you! Here, don't forget your cloak!' God's wounds!

'Lark, are you ready? Now, mind, we're going to ride as obviously as we can out towards Loyes. Chicot will think nobody could be so stupid as to make such a fuss; so we must be a decoy to draw attention away from the real Russells; and he'll find traces of Guy and the grooms, who look fairly like us, going secretly, and follow them. I hope. Pierre —

'Know nothing, like the pageboy,' the thin little man assured us.

'You're a good friend, man. Tell Nicola we'll join the queen later.'

There were tears in his eyes as he nodded, clasping my hand. 'Trust me, sir! Do my best for you. Go on, sir! You're losing time!' Annette kissed Lark, weeping, and we ran down the stair.

In the stable, my best horses were waiting. Leather saddlebags with my bank papers, gold and jewellery, were strapped to my saddle. Dad and I each had our pistols, sword and dagger — mine the rapier set King Henri had given me, the gilded hilts and scabbards wrapped in leather.

Lark had a bulky sack. 'Essentials, Johnnie!' I didn't waste time, just tied it to her saddle and tossed her up. She nodded bravely down to me, lit up with excitement. 'A fine laddie, that's me!'

Was the lane clear? Yes. But just as we rode out and turned left up towards the street, there was a thundering on our front door, and shouts of 'Open in the king's name!' Without a word we turned and headed right, away by the back lane. Another minute and we'd have been caught.

As soon as we were out of earshot of the guards we spurred on, leaving a satisfactory trail of angry memories behind us to the St Denis Gate. I'd wondered if the guards there would have been warned, but they let us through without paying any attention. I had to knock over a handcart before they noticed us, and then I shouted, 'Come on, Lark!' and we galloped ostentatiously down the road, cloaks and clods flying, clearly laying a false trail. I hoped . . .

When we paused to rest the horses, dad asked me quietly, 'Lad, how far do you trust that man o' yours?'

I shrugged. 'He's loyal, dad, but he'd not put his head on the block for us. I'm sure he'll say nothing the first time they ask, but if he's threatened with imprisonment, say, he'll answer them.'

'Then why tell him we're goin' to Loyes?' I grinned. 'Ah, another false trail? So where are we headin'? What other estates have you?'

'Well. There's one near Lyons, two at Orleans, one by Aix. But I've also got one the cardinal gave me, a small one that not many know about, near Rheims. So tonight, we'll break off the road here and head east.'

Lark joined in. 'We can stay there till the hunt dies down.'

I grinned. 'No, lass. A clever wee man, our Chicot. He'll know about it, all right. We'll make sure we leave enough trace for him to think we've turned off to Rheims, trying to hide our trail. But we'll not go there.'

'What?' Dad puffed in exasperation. 'If it's no Loyes, as Pierre will tell them, an' it's no Nantes, where Guy's leading them, an' it's no Rheims, that you're layin' a false trail to — where the blazes is it?'

'Well.' It was very satisfying, to impress dad. 'Chicot knows they're all possible. We could sail out from Nantes; we could lie low in Rheims; we could wait

221

at Loyes to join Queen Marie. But what Pierre won't tell them, unless they ask specially and I don't think they'll think of it, is that Montgomery told Lark he'd be in Calais for her any day now. So — I paused to enjoy the effect — 'we'll just quietly head for Loyes after all.'

They stared, and burst into laughter. I grinned. 'We'll go roundabout, in disguise, as soon as the false track's laid. Loyes is but ten miles from Calais. We'll put a lad down to the port to bring us all the news, while we have a pleasant day or two helping with the hay, and let Chicot chase round Nantes and Rheims till he runs up his own backside. When Montgomery comes, we'll all sail with him, and make our own way up to Scotland. Or if Marie's ready to sail first, Nicola'll smuggle us aboard, and we'll leave word for Montgomery to follow and collect Lark when he can. What d'you think, dad?'

He eyed me sideways. 'I mind you once told Nicola she had a corkscrew mind. I'm thinkin' if she was but taller she'd be just the right wife for you. You're a pair!' Praise could go no further. 'But are you sure he'll be the one followin' us? Will he find all these false trails you're layin'?'

'I underestimated him once,' I said grimly. 'I ended up wedded. I'll not do it twice. And aye, he's after us. He'd let no-one else do for me.'

We stopped at an inn that evening for a meal. When we left after dinner, we tipped the ostler far too well, so that he stayed out in the yard to watch us ride off west. A hundred yards on we turned right, off the road. We were clearly silhouetted against the setting sun; anyone watching must have seen us, but thought we didn't know it.

To make sure, four miles east, we led our tired horses into a farmyard and slept the night in a barn, warm and comfortable, to be found in the morning by the farmer. I overpaid him with a silver denier, and we rode out east again, the farmer watching. He'd remember us.

After another few miles we passed another farm, carefully keeping out of sight of the house — but not of the lad herding pigs in the nearby wood.

Right. Enough misleading 'hiding' — our pursuers would just think we'd got better at it if they didn't hear of us from now on. We headed north-west again, avoiding houses, across the woods, healthland and marshes.

Since Amboise, all my horses were unremarkable. With sleeping rough, our plain clothes were soon crumpled and dusty, and we looked like country folk. Lark's sack held a brown skirt, and she changed from a boy to a girl and back again. We bought two more sacks, and often Lark would perch behind me or dad like a peasant girl or boy while the third horse rested, carrying only the sacks stuffed with grass. We moved slowly and quietly, sometimes walking and leading the horses, sometimes split up in two and one instead of a threesome, wary of robbers. Not a soul noticed us.

It took us five days to reach Loyes. Under an ancient oak by the road a shepherd lad was playing a pipe. I wondered why he didn't rise to greet us; then I remembered our disguises. I must be more used to being a lord than I'd thought!

I cleared my throat of dust and called, 'Hey, lad!' He rose slowly, ambled over and patted my horse's neck. 'Are there any strangers about?'

He took ages to think. 'Eh? Strangers? Folks I don't know? Oah. Aye.'

'Who?' God's wounds, was Chicot here ahead of us?

'Oah. There's you.'

Lark, behind me and clinging round my waist, started to giggle. I elbowed her in the ribs.

Jacques, the young steward, welcomed us warmly. We wanted it kept quiet that we were here? Certainly. A watch on the road, and horses always to be kept saddled? Of course. News from Calais? No problem.

There were cheeses and geese to go to market anyway, and the lad could stay on in the town.

We didn't act like the lord and lady of the manor. Lark bought a country girl's Sunday gown of embroidered creamy linen, and kept her eye in with the local lads. Dad and I helped on the farms as I'd planned. The hay-making was finished, but we learned there was more to herding geese than we'd thought. The horses were well rested, and so were we. We were just waiting for the word to move.

It all seemed too easy. It was. Because the word didn't come.

And the longer we waited, the longer Chicot had to track us down. Half-way to Nantes, back to Paris, off to Rheims, then back-tracking to Loyes; he could be here any time . . . It was hard to hide my worry from Lark.

At last, after ten eternal days, a lad came running late one afternoon. Lark and I let the geese look after themselves on the pond behind the house while we heard the news. 'The Scottish queen's there, my lord! With hundreds of servants! I spoke to the dwarf, Nicola, for you, sir. She'll get you a place on board. Queen Marie's got a great white galley, and some little ships for the lords going with her. But they don't know when they'll be leaving. The Queen of England still won't give her a safe-conduct!'

'Are there no English ships?' Lark asked anxiously. She held forgotten in her hand a sweet posy which one of her admirers had given her.

'Aye, my lady!' The lad was eager. 'There's four, just outside the port. And this morning, there was a man came round the taverns seeking word of you. Montgomery, his name was. I spoke to him!' He was justly proud of himself. 'He'll bring a boat in for you tomorrow, he said!'

Lark tossed the flowers high, dancing to scare the geese, singing at the top of her voice for joy. The lad was grinning as he watched her, but then he bit his lip and looked at me gravely. 'My lord, they're saying that the English aren't looking for your sister. That's just an excuse. They're waiting to attack the queen, when she leaves.' God's wounds, what next?

Lark danced back. On the pond some goslings bobbed by, balls of yellow fluff cheeping happily. 'I'm a gosling, John!' she sang.

'Getting fattened for Christmas?' I teased her.

'Paddling away from the shore. Oh, I'm so happy! Nothing can go wrong now!'

Lark

Next morning, we set out early. When we reached the coast, dawn was edging silver above the trees. We decided it was best not to take Lark to Scotland with us, on Queen Marie's ships. 'Even if we could get you aboard, lass, it'd make it that much harder for Montgomery to come an' take you off our hands,' dad said. Lark stuck her tongue out at him.

'And we'd best not try to take you out from Calais itself, when the English ships are here to try to intercept the queen,' I added.

Lark didn't understand, and was shocked when I explained. If Marie was carried off to England, Queen Elizabeth would be publicly horrified, but privately delighted. She'd be in a very strong position to insist on the signing of the Treaty of Edinburgh, and maybe other agreements, before her most dear cousin, so lovingly entertained and guarded, would be allowed to go on to Scotland. 'Gabriel wouldn't do that!' she protested. 'Not when she helped save him!'

'Maybe no. But he's an officer o' Queen Elizabeth now, remember. He's no his own master. No, it'd be

226

— tactless, eh? — to row out from Calais. Or wait for him, in a town full o' Queen Marie's men, all annoyed at the English.' Dad chuckled. 'Quieter just to slip you away first.'

So we turned aside before entering the town, across the fields to a huddle of fishermen's shacks above the low cliffs, where a dark man, weatherbeaten almost black, was baiting lobster pots with rotten fish.

'Good day, man!' dad called. 'How's life with you?'

'E-ech.' He spat, with a surly stare. 'Too many damned foreigners.'

My temper started to rise at the insolence, but Lark shook her head at me. She was wearing her embroidered linen gown, and looked very pretty in her excitement. 'Sir,' she said, 'of your kindness, do you know where we might hire a boat to go out to a ship?' He gazed up at her. She smiled at him. Learned a lot, my wee sister had, with the Flying Squadron. In less than a minute, he was bargaining.

He was unsurprised at our wanting a boat, but it soon was clear he thought we were Huguenot refugees. We didn't bother to explain the truth.

We finally got lobsters roasted for our breakfast — we were starving — and his aid to row out to the English ships, for five testons. It was probably more than the man made in a year from his fishing. But we had to go, and he knew it. It was worth it.

While the fisherman's wife made our breakfast, we gossiped. 'Has the safe-conduct from England arrived yet?' I asked.

The fisherman spat. 'E-ech, no! But the Scots queen sails today anyway, safe-conduct, English ships or not! E-ech, so!' He was delighted to know more than we did. 'Had a row with her uncles. She'd come to France in spite of all old King Henry could do to catch her, she said, and she'd go home in spite of Henry's daughter. Off on the noon tide. E-ech, so!'

Dad and I exchanged glances. What? We'd not known there was such a rush. Six hours, or we'd be left behind. 'Can we get out to the ships and back in time to reach the harbour by then?'

'E-ech, so!' he grinned hideously. 'Time aplenty! It's no more than half an hour's row from here to the port!'

We tethered the horses to graze outside, and thoroughly enjoyed the roasted lobsters. In spite of the stink of rotten fish, when the man and his wife were both occupied, I took the bank papers for Lark's dowry from my saddlebags, slipped into the hut and hid the bags safely deep in under the pile of dry seaweed that was the bed. Dad grinned like a slice of melon.

Carrying the oars, which the man said were always kept in the hut for fear of thieves, we scrambled down the steep white rocks to the beach. There was a thick white mist lying across the water. I hoped the fisherman knew which way to row. We baled out three inches of water from the boat while he sneered at such finicky ways, helped Lark in first, shoved it down the sand, splashed out beside it and scrambled in.

As the fisherman rowed out into the mist, I grew very unhappy. It wasn't logical, the way the boat jiggled about beneath our feet. I'd often been boating before, but only in good weather, on a quiet river or lake where if you sit still the boat keeps still too. Waves were new to me, and I could easily do without them. Lark and I soon lost our lobster.

Dad was sympathetic. The fisherman wasn't. 'E-ech, landsmen! Be quiet now, and let me listen!' Suddenly he shouted, 'Aho! English! Aho!'

In the mist ahead of us a ship's side loomed up, and shouts. Shouts in English, I realised. A boathook was lowered from the deck above, and a rope to tie the boat to. A strong, hearty voice shouted, 'Hey, it's a lass! Give her a hand, then, you clumsy lubbers!' Arms were stretched down to lift Lark up to the deck, and dad and I struggled up after her.

They laid her on a roll of canvas, and I sat beside her, while dad spoke to the captain. The motion wasn't much easier on the larger vessel. I still felt I was dying. After a while there were shouts, men ran about pulling on ropes and shoving us out of their way. I felt too ill to object. Dad came back to us. 'Now, lass, you've no to be discouraged!' he said, smiling kindly. 'This isn't the *Martha*, that Montgomery's on. But she's no far off. Captain Tregannon here's sendin' a boat for him, and he'll come for you in just a wee while, eh?'

It worked like magic on her. She sat up, a touch of colour coming back to her face. 'Gabriel? He'll be here soon? Oh, dad, I must look a fright!'

The sailors laughed. They were rough men, but kindly enough disposed, and the captain called his servant to show her down to his cabin, fetch her hot water, give her his comb. He was dressed richly, his beard trimmed, his shoes high-heeled, of fine leather; the commander, rather than the sailing-master. Lark smiled and thanked him graciously as she left; another man under her spell, I could see. But when he asked where our baggage was, and dad said that we were returning to the shore, the atmosphere changed.

'Are you not coming to England with us, sir?' Tregannon asked coldly.

Dad bristled slightly. 'My daughter is, sir,' he replied, equally coldly. 'My son an' I are in the service o' Queen Marie o' Scotland.'

'Indeed?' There was instant, stiff suspicion in the captain's tone, and the sailors round us started to mutter. 'Then why board an English ship, at this moment? Are you spies?'

Dad was turning red, just about to open his mouth and jump right into it. I staggered to my feet and grasped his arm, apparently to stay upright — and not far wrong, either. 'Captain Tregannon, there's no state of war between England and France, is there? Or between England and Scotland? Then why should we not board an English ship?' He frowned, but keeping up the appearance of legality, he nodded acceptance. 'And as a gentleman, captain, you'll take our word as gentlemen that we came aboard your ship simply to escort my sister to the safe-keeping of her betrothed. We had and have no intention of spying.'

He considered, stroking his short beard. 'Two points, sirs. The lass is converted to the Reformed Faith, I'm told. But you're not? Is it reasonable, think you, that a man of one faith should be so lax as to help his child change to another?'

'Sir,' dad said steadily, 'my wife was of your faith. She was murdered by Catholics. I hold by my own beliefs, but should I act as they did, an' slay my daughter as well? God commanded Abraham no to kill his son as a sacrifice; I'll no do what God has forbidden. I trust that by His mercy all folk o' good heart may come in the end to His love, whatever their creed.'

The sailors muttered round us. The captain eyed dad in disgust. 'You advocate tolerance? Freedom for every man to choose what he will believe and what he will not? But —'

'Sir, I'm no here to argue doctrine,' dad interrupted. 'You have my answer to your first question, whether you like it or not. What's the second?'

The captain was taken rather aback, and his lips worked tightly together as he controlled his annoyance. 'Very well, sir. Montgomery has told us about his betrothed. Her father and brother, he says, are in the French Guard of Scots Archers, and her brother one of the Bodyguard, even. You say that you are now in the service of Queen Mary Stewart. It's a possible change of loyalty. But in either case, sir,' he turned a distrustful eye on me, 'there seems no reason why people of such wealth and rank should be dressed like farmers — and poor ones at that!'

Tell the truth and shame the devil. 'Sir, until two weeks ago I was indeed an Archer of the Garde Ecossaise, and my father Homme d'armes of the First Company of that regiment. However, my sister and I had the misfortune to offend Queen Catherine, who has ordered our arrest. We — frankly, sir, we have had to disguise ourselves, in order to escape.'

He looked me up and down. 'Escape from the Serpent Queen? Young man, after what she did at Amboise, there's no surer way to my heart!' Smiling broadly, he clasped me in his arms and clapped me heartily on the back till I near threw up on his chest. That would fair have changed his opinion!

The sailors got on with their work, my innards gradually settled into something approaching calm, and dad told Captain Tregannon a bit about Lark's adventure at Amboise, which had him beaming at her when she reappeared, bright and pretty again. He complimented her, she blushed, he assured her that Montgomery wouldn't be long.

Then Lark asked innocently, 'Sir, I understand why Gabriel has come. But I'm told there are several English ships here. What are you doing?'

He paused before answering. I was about to intervene. He couldn't admit the truth before dad and me. It would help no-one to embarrass him. But Lark went on sweetly, in the tone we'd learned by long experience to recognise as leading to trouble. 'Are you sent to escort Queen Marie on her journey to Scotland?'

He seized on it as an escape. 'Aye, mistress. Our queen wishes to do her cousin every honour.'

Lark smiled. Dad was tense beside me. My guts

churned up again. God's wounds, what was she going to land me in this time?

'Oh, isn't it a pity you've missed her!' she exclaimed. 'For she sailed last night.'

In the instant before Captain Tregannon's eye swept round to us, dad's mouth fell open to match mine. Whatever I'd expected Lark to say, it wasn't that. I was dumbfoundered. The captain's face filled again with suspicion.

But Lark didn't stop talking. 'Oh, dad!' she cried in anguished apology. 'I'm sorry! I wasn't to mention it! Oh, I'm sorry!' She turned to the captain. 'Sir, I'm sure I was mistaken. She's still there! I swear it! Of course she is!' She babbled more and more desperately, and her lip trembled. I tried to bring my face back under control. She was watching me, and dad, and the captain, tensely, her slim hands folded tight as if in prayer. 'Johnnie, tell the captain! Please!' she begged me.

Suddenly two thoughts balanced in my mind. One was of the magician Nostradamus, telling me that Lark would affect three kingdoms, and that when she called on me, I must help her. The other was the glorious realisation of just what Lark had done, by saying that Marie had already gone, and then denying it. We owed Marie our lives, and Montgomery's. We could repay her now, if we could make Tregannon believe Lark. He'd leave, with his ships, and the queen's way home would be clear. And the final perfection was that we didn't need to lie; just tell the truth. But so unconvincingly that we'd not be believed.

I cleared my throat. 'No, no, captain. The galley's still there, I swear.' I had no difficulty in making my voice stiff and stilted.

Dad agreed, vigorously. He didn't know what was going on, but he knew the truth. 'The lass is talkin' nonsense. Lark, speak sense or speak seldom.' His natural bark made him sound over-eager. Personally, I'd not have credited a word either of us said.

Tregannon didn't, either. He stared at Lark, humming and hawing, pulling his beard. Was it a real mistake? Or was she lying? Or were we? How could he check?

Peering above the layer of mist that was gradually thinning over the sea, the masthead lookout confirmed that he could see the masts; the big galley was still in port. The mate admitted nervously that several vessels had passed out during the night, or at dawn; just small fishing boats, though.

The fisherman was produced, alarmed by the rough hands shoving him along. Tregannon held out a silver coin. 'For you, for the truth!' he said. 'Where's the Scots queen? Mary of Scotland?'

'Marie? Calais.' Tregannon puffed with satisfaction and tossed him the coin. 'Merci, capitaine!' He smiled horribly, and destroyed the captain's relief, explaining as if to an infant, 'Ship Calais, Marie Calais.'

Tregannon scowled. 'Could she — Mary — have gone in a fishing boat?'

'Marie? Go in boat? E-ech, no!' The fisherman shook his head, waving his hands to show the fast motion. My stomach heaved in sympathy.

'Oh, Queen Marie's a good sailor,' Lark assured us enthusiastically. She looked at dad's frown, and gulped. 'But she'd only go in her own ship. With her maids, and everything.'

The captain considered. He must decide, surely, that Lark in silly innocence had given away a vital secret. He must decide!

He decided that he wasn't sure. 'Hell's teeth! Mistress!' Lark turned her big brown eyes on him, but he didn't melt this time. 'Can you prove who you are?' God's wounds, what was he after? 'It's well known Montgomery's here to fetch his bride. And that this isn't his ship. It's in my mind you're an impostor, sent with a false tale to lure me away. I've no way of knowing that you're truly this lass he's to meet.'

'You've no as much sense as a cow can hold in her clenched fist!' dad protested. 'Montgomery's comin' for her. How could we get away with it?'

'How should I know? Maybe Montgomery's a spy himself!' His antagonism was growing, and the insult didn't help. 'Prove who you are now, here, this minute. Or I'll have all three of you in irons, and him as well, and we'll let Queen Elizabeth's justices in Dover untangle the knot.'

God's wounds! Suspicious ass! 'Ridiculous!' I protested. 'Don't be a fool, captain!' After years handling Francois, I should have known better.

'Fool? Ridiculous?' His moustache bristled. He'd never back down now. 'Prove it! Prove it!' He'd got an idea in his head, and however daft, he'd not have it budged. And time was passing. We'd miss the galley . . .

Lark stepped forward. 'Captain, I think I may satisfy you.' One or two of the sailors smiled in response to her smile, but Tregannon glowered. 'Gabriel has spoken to you about his betrothed? Long ago, maybe, before anyone knew he'd be here today, or you, or the queen? What has he told you about her?'

The man glowered again. 'He says she sang for the King of France.'

She sighed in relief. 'Well, then. A spy, an impostor, who can sing so well could scarcely be found at short notice. If I sing well enough for you, well enough for a king, will you believe I am indeed who I say I am, only Alice Russell, come to find my future husband?'

Tregannon considered. Dad protested. 'You can't, lass! Not without music, out of doors! You've no practised for weeks! An' you're tired, an' seasick!'

234

She smiled. 'All the more proof if I can, dad!'

The captain agreed. 'Aye. You sing, well enough for a king's court, an' I'll believe you. But if not, it's off to Dover jail with the lot of you!'

The sailors were all round dad and me. They'd grab us before we could draw sword. We were helpless, in Lark's hands.

Moving aside a pace to the shelter of the poopdeck, she sang a couple of scales under her breath, to ease her throat. The captain's frown grew. His whole crew clustered round, perching on the bulwarks, climbing the rigging above us, excited by the strange challenge, pressing close and craning like children to watch and listen. She tossed back her head, and smiled at him and them and us, and suddenly her glorious voice soared around us.

She sang in English; a version of the Magnificat. 'O all ye works of the Lord, bless ye the Lord; praise Him and magnify Him forever.' The creaking and bumping of the ship, the muttering of the sailors, even the gulls and waves seemed to fall silent in reverence of the richness and purity of her tone. 'O ye waters that be above the firmament . . . O ye winds of God, bless ye the Lord.' From the long psalm she sang the verses that had to do with the sea and ships, so that they nodded approval, and Tregannon's hard frown softened.

Then she laughed out loud, and changed key and style. She sang a love-song that the captain must know, 'Greensleeves', written by King Henry of England himself for the mother of Queen Elizabeth. 'Alas, my love, you do me wrong, To use me thus discourteously.' She smiled at Tregannon with a quizzical twinkle in her eye that caught every man's humour.

As she finished, and curtseyed deeply and gracefully, the sailors applauded her, and the captain sighed, shaking his head, deeply affected. 'Aye, mistress,' he said quietly. 'I do believe you, that you've sung for the King of France. Your voice would please God himself.'

And at that moment Montgomery himself climbed over the bulwark, taller and more golden than ever, and she held out her hands to him, radiant, and he took the three steps to lift her in his arms and kiss her.

At the captain's insistence, Montgomery questioned her, 'Alice, I must ask you. As you love me, where in truth is the Queen of Scots?'

Dad, who had by now realised what she was doing, held his breath; but he needn't have feared. Lark looked down, then up; a child, almost, bravely facing scolding adults. 'Gabriel, when you are my husband I must answer you. But that is not yet. I may not tell you.' It was her softest, sweetest voice. 'And if you cast me aside for denying you, my love, then I would not blame you.' Aye; and the moon's made of green cheese. I was hard put to it not to laugh. He'd soon learn what that tone meant!

They honoured her, of course, for her loyalty to her queen; and therefore believed her. They were urgent to be away, now, and dad and I were rushed, rather than ushered, over the side, with no proper exchange of news with Montgomery. But I took time to make sure he knew her dowry was in the papers in her bag. She was no draggle-tail slut lifted in charity from the dykeside, even if her wooing and wedding were unconventional.

I kissed her, and wished her good fortune. Dad just kissed her.

As we climbed down into the little boat, my heart sinking, my belly heaving, she leant over and whispered, 'Johnnie ... At least I'll get you in no more trouble, eh?'

'Thank God!' I told her. 'Fare well, my dear!' We parted smiling.

Before our oars were well into the rowlocks, the

master was calling orders. Sails were set, the anchor raised, and in seconds the English ship, with a little white figure waving on her deck, was moving to gather her mates and race off to try to catch Queen Marie; who was in Calais.

Farewell

Dad gave the fisherman a hand to row — as soon as we stepped into the boat I was beyond it — and for some reason to do with the tide we returned to shore faster, thank God, than we'd gone out. They ran the boat up the sand, picked up the oars and headed for the path. Feeling better at every step on solid ground, I staggered up to the hut after them.

'How are you, son? Better? It's a nasty thing, the sea-sickness.'

'I could just about beat Guy at pat-a-cake,' I grunted.

Dad laughed. 'Sit on the bench there, then, while we saddle up.' The man's wife brought me a drink of rough cider, and I recovered gradually, leaning back on the oars which they'd stood up against the eaves of the shack.

I got out my saddlebags with our money from the seaweed, under the woman's rather peeved stare — if only she'd known! We paid the fisherman, and thanked him, and saddled up. I checked that the bags were buckled tight behind my saddle, and we prepared to mount.

'What about the other horse, dad? Lark's one?' I asked.

'Take it with us, and give them all to a priest at the harbour?' dad suggested. 'He can sell them and give the money to the poor.'

'Especially to dwarves!' As we laughed I turned to mount, and over my horse's neck saw a patch of bright colours between us and the road. 'Dad.'

He stiffened, alert at my tone, and looked round. 'Hell's teeth!'

I couldn't have put it better myself.

Swiss Guards. At least forty of them. Heading towards Calais, they must have seen the horses by the hut, and turned aside to investigate. And out in front, triumphant, was a small orange figure on a big black horse.

Chicot had caught us.

Shrilly shouting, he gestured with a pistol, enormous in his small hand. Most of his men spread out among the huts, cutting us off. Chicot rode slightly forward, to stop about thirty yards away, in front of the rest. A short bowshot, but out of accurate pistol range; and we hadn't a long gun or bow. But they had, and the Switzers were dismounting for better aim.

'De Rouxelle! Surrender yourself! And your sister! Your father can go free!' he called. 'I wish him no harm!'

Dad snorted cynically. 'Aye, when the devil's found dead in a ditch.' He looked at me; I looked at him. 'Well, son? What are we waitin' for? An invitation to dance?'

We checked that our swords were loose in their scabbards, and our pistols primed and ready in their holsters King Henri's sword would be drawn on King Henri's son's men this day. The fisherman and his wife grabbed their baby and fled. Dad set a hand on my shoulder. 'Just to let you know, son. I'm glad to have fathered you!'

'I'm not unhappy about it myself, dad!' I agreed, smiling. God's wounds, Montgomery would have loved this!

We mounted, taking our time. We could still be coming out to surrender; no harm in making sure our girths

were tight, our seats firm. It was like that tournament
. . . The tournament . . .

I felt the spring of a vast glee surging up in me. 'Dad!'
I muttered urgently, a crazy grin spreading over my face
in spite of the danger — or because of it. 'Dad, keep
behind me. Don't argue, or try to be a hero! Just do it!'
He nodded, puzzled, wondering what I had in mind.

I reached over, picked up one of the twelve-foot oars
leaning against the hut, and weighed it in my hand.
Heavy; no point; no balance; no proper handgrip; no
fine silver pennon. But honest, solid wood, with no
tactful knots hidden under the paint, either.

Dad snorted beside me, suddenly understanding what
I had in mind. 'Hah! Go on, you daft dollop! Give him
a bone to pick that'll push his teeth out his bum!'

No room to pick up speed. I spurred hard, to drive my
charger straight into a full gallop. There were bangs, as
arquebuses and dad's pistols fired. Behind me, I vaguely
heard him roaring joyfully, 'Scotland forever!' My whole
mind was concentrated on the small black-bearded man
on the tall horse fifteen paces in front of me.

Chicot fired, dropped his pistol and hauled on the
reins to flee. Something burned my bridle arm, but I
paid no heed. His horse spun round and jumped, like
a sensible animal, to get out of my way, but too late. I
swerved my own horse to follow, and was on him.

I aimed right for his back. The unbalanced oar,
waving, missed, but not by much. Its flat end bounced
off Chicot's saddle, slid below his backside and caught
in his trunks. The plump saddlebags strapped bulging
behind me held me steady like a cantle. I gripped tight
and heaved, and the sheer speed of my charge scooped
him like a pea on a pin up out of his saddle, to perch
for a second on the oar, screaming and waving, arms,
legs and cloak flying.

It was the funniest trick I'd ever seen him do.

I laughed; but I'd no leisure to sit and enjoy it.

The oar slung him yelling on top of the soldier behind him, and slammed into the pair of them. I let go just before it broke my wrist, and still laughing snatched for my sword.

For over a year I'd spent at least two hours daily, training my charger for war, to turn fast, rear, kick, bite and generally create havoc around him. Ten miles this morning had scarcely worked the itches out of his legs, he'd had four hours' rest, a painful jab with my spurs had stirred up his temper, and he was just starting to warm up. He spun at the twitch of the rein and the shift of my weight, and I charged back into the Switzers. Dad had already downed two men. My horse trampled a third on foot and kicked a fourth. I parried a sword thrust from one Switzer, got a slash through an epaulette from another, ran a third through the shoulder, they were all round me, I was in trouble, but their horses suddenly shied violently away; there was Guy, standing at the side, throwing sharp flints at the Switzers' mounts! I reached a hand and he scrambled up behind me, grinning and yelling.

Right. Enough was enough. The dismounted Switzers were racing towards us, waving swords. Withdraw! Get out while we could!

Dad, who enjoyed a good fight, had other ideas, but I pricked his horse's rump and drove him swearing up the track. A few Switzers remounted and chased us. At the Calais road I pulled out a pistol, turned and fired past Guy. I hit one of them, a lucky shot at speed, and when I drew my other pistol they reined in.

The queen's ship was due to sail. We mustn't miss it! We'd no time to sit about and congratulate ourselves. But we cheered as we galloped down the road, for we'd be away by the time Chicot could organise his men to come after us again. If he was fit to ride, of course! Dad enjoyed the story of Chicot's upfall so much he near fell off his horse laughing.

While we rode, Guy shouted explanations. 'I did my best, sir! Got past Angers before they caught us,' he boasted proudly. 'And I didn't tell them anything, however hard they beat me! But the dwarf, he wouldn't let me go. Brought me with him, back to Paris. Pierre tried to keep quiet, too, but when they threatened Annette he said you were coming here. Chicot didn't believe it. Too easy, he said, sir.' Dad grinned at me; I'd been right. 'He hunted till he found where you'd turned off. But he rode hard, sir. And as soon as he found you weren't at Rheims, he turned straight for Loyes. He just laughed, sir, and said you'd learned from him.' I nodded. It was true. I had. 'And the steward — he told him you'd gone to Calais, for a teston, just!' Dad spat; my fine, loyal young man!

Then we raced into the town. Down to the harbour. There was the ship!

And the crowd.

Half the Court was here to escort Queen Marie and bid her farewell; and the trains of six dukes and a cardinal are large. And all the folk from ten miles round had come as well. The jam was near as bad as her wedding.

However, this time I had assistance in getting through. I passed Guy over to dad, and set my charger into his extremely showy exercises. Folk looked round, saw my foaming, cavorting beast bearing down on them, mostly on two legs, and nobody stood their ground to argue. Dad and Guy followed me at their ease, laughing fit to split, down to the less crowded quayside.

There were enough pages about to fill a book. I called a couple and told them to hold my horses. They sniffed at my shabby doublet with the stuffing leaking from the slashed epaulette, but no wee whippersnappers in fancy satin were fit to stop me this day. I snarled through my scars; they deflated and meekly reached for the reins. I patted my charger's sweating neck; he'd saved my life today, and I was sorry to lose him. But I couldn't take him with me. I turned away after dad and marched along to the gangplank.

The Duc de Guise's guard, officious in red and white, wouldn't let us aboard. Not without permission from their commander, or the duke. Halberds poised, they threatened to throw us into the water if we tried to pass.

Where was the captain? Seeing to the cannon that would fire a salute when the galley left. The duke? Aboard the galley.

God's wounds, this was important! Send in a message!

What, disturb Her Majesty's farewell to her family? Ridiculous!

The crowd was laughing at us. My temper was rising rapidly. Dad snorted in frustration. The guards' faces under their shining helmets and halberds were as determined as my own. I was going to end up in the harbour if something wasn't done.

At the stern of the ship, a small figure appeared.

Corkscrew thinking? To blazes with corkscrew thinking! I took a deep breath and yelled, 'Nicola! Nicola la Jardinière! Come and get us on board there! It's vital!' Guy crimsoned. Dad choked, and coughed to hide a laugh.

Amid glares from furious guards and embarrassed servants, cheers from the crowd, Nicola came running. We were summoned aboard and led to the stern gallery to push our way through the glittering throng and kneel to a frankly laughing queen.

'De Rouxelle!' she scolded me, giving me a hand to kiss. 'Is this the way to enter the royal presence? Bellowing like a bull? And in tatters?' Her uncles eyed us in astonishment. 'Your doublet! It has more holes than a Gruyere cheese!' She took my sleeve between finger and thumb. 'Bullet holes! And is that blood?' It must have been Chicot's pistol. I'd scarcely noticed the nick. 'And you stink of fish!' I'd noticed that, all right. 'Jean, what on earth have you been doing?'

'Your Grace, it's a long story. Perhaps later?' The eye of the Duc de Guise was icy. 'I apologise for thrusting myself into your company so unseemly. But I have vital news. Your Grace is aware of the English ships?'

Her head tossed. 'Indeed, sir! But I intend to set sail despite them.' Smiling, she nodded to the cardinal. 'My uncle has suggested that I should leave my jewels here in safety. But if I may hazard myself among the dangers of the sea, surely I may risk my valuables also!' Having no courage himself, he reacted to her teasing with mixed affection and irritation.

'I can't be absolutely sure, madame, but if Your Grace set sail immediately, I think you would find the ships no longer there.'

Her eyes were bright as the crystals on her white gown. 'Your doing?'

'My sister's quick wits more than mine, Your Grace. She felt that she owed Your Grace a great deal, and wished to repay the debt.'

Marie gazed absently at me for a second, no doubt remembering a room at Amboise . . . Then she was alert again. 'Very well, Jean. We shall act on your advice. Captain! Pray order the smaller ships to set sail at once. Uncles . . .' A scurry of lords and attendants vanished to their vessels.

The sailors were already casting off ropes as, after the last farewell kisses, the Guises turned to the gangplank. I knelt to catch the attention of the Cardinal of Lorraine. He looked down at me coldly. 'Well?'

'May I beg Your Eminence's favour to sell our mounts there and their harness, and use the money for the benefit of the cripples of the town?'

A gift for the Church? That earned me a smile, even. He nodded agreement and passed on.

As I rose I grinned to dad, standing by the bulwarks. But dad wasn't smiling. His face was rigid. Guy was staring, puzzled.

A horrible intuition gripped me. I glanced down.

Dad's hands were empty. And Guy's.

I looked across the quay. Behind the crowd of nobles, our horses were still held by the pages. My charger, alarmed by a flag flapping near his eyes, reared. And there, bouncing on its saddle, I could just see the saddle-bags which held every denier I owned ... not fifty feet away on my horse ... which I'd just asked the cardinal to sell, with its harness ...

The ship pushed out from the quay and began to ease us away from the waving, cheering crowd.

There was not one single thing I could do.

Guy tapped my shoulder. 'Sir — your father's told me. I still have these, sir ...' He held out to me the five gold ecus I'd given him ten days before.

At the back of the quay there was a disturbance. Someone was trying to force through, on horseback. I could just make out an orange blur. Chicot. Too late, but he'd not give up. He flung himself from his saddle. As we drew off, he wriggled through the legs of the people, avoiding the guards, pointing, tugging for attention at the robes of the Duc de Guise, until the soldiers swooped on him. They'd had to let one intruder through; the next wasn't going to get away with it! A screech, a swoop of orange, and a splash; as the galley swung away and drove for the open sea, Master Chicot landed spluttering in the dirty water of the harbour, treading water, screaming in rage, spitting in finally frustrated hatred.

I beckoned Nicola desperately. 'Nicola, for God's sake, find me a quiet spot before I burst!' Blinking, she led us down to her cramped, tiny corner of a cabin. There I fell onto her bed and laughed myself silly. I laughed as dad apologised, and hugged him, and hugged Nicola as she gasped in horrified comprehension when Guy told her what had happened. I laughed till my sides ached, till I rolled helpless off the bed to the decking, till my throat and jaws were on fire. And at last, as they saw that I wasn't acting, they started to laugh with me.

Ten minutes later, we were almost sober, with just an occasional hiccup of mirth. Nicola produced two bottles of wine, and since she had no glasses we passed them round among us. 'God's wounds, Nicola, I love you!' I said, sighing with relief and happiness. 'Dad, shut up, for God's sake! The less gear, the less care! I forgot too! Look, Guy, go and find us somewhere to sleep.' I turned to dad. 'Drink up, man! It's not just my money that's gone — it's yours too. That house up in Strathmore — you'll have to wait for it till I've made us another fortune!'

'Maybe not, sir.' Nicola's voice was quiet and calm. 'I've something here that belongs to you.'

'What?' In the dim light I peered at the little bag she was holding out. 'What is it?'

She opened the bag, took my hand and spilled into it a flood of gleaming gold and green. 'It's the necklace Queen Marie gave you.'

I sat up, my smiles vanishing, and dropped it to glow on her skirt. 'But that's yours, Nicola. Your dowry.'

'And therefore yours, sir, as my husband. You were kind to let me keep it, but it's never really been mine.'

I argued I'd given it to her, and I didn't take back gifts. 'Then I'll give it to the church, sir, as you did with your horses.' She chuckled. 'When could I ever wear such a jewel, and not look ridiculous? Or what need have I of it, that have a post with a kind and generous queen? But if that was all, sir, I'd keep it, as you urge.' She took my hand gently between her own small fingers. 'Sir, you've always been my friend. You've treated me like a normal woman, not a freak. I owe you more for that than any necklace could pay, though it was

246

worth the whole treasury of France! I cannot keep it, while you go without even a decent suit to your back. For look at that one!' She smiled, her eyes shining in the candlelight. 'It's a disgrace! I'm surprised the queen didn't have you thrown off the ship for coming before her like a scarecrow!'

She was trying to turn the subject. 'I'm not going to take it, Nicola, and that's flat!' I told her.

'You are, sir, and that's flatter!' she declared firmly. 'Am I your friend? Then you'll take it in friendship, as it is offered. Or am I your enemy, to be slighted and hurt for the sake of your pride?' She paused. 'Jean, it will make me happy if you take it, and unhappy if you don't.'

How could I refuse, after that? She poured the king's ransom of gems back into its bag, and gave it to me. I shrugged helplessly, stowed it away inside my shirt, and kissed her. 'Nicola — what can I say?'

'Say thank you kindly, sir. And then do me the favour to forget it.'

I laughed. 'Thank you kindly, sir! But I'll never forget it.'

Dad grinned, but Nicola didn't. She took a deep breath. 'And now that's settled, I have something else for you.' It was a parchment; and even as I unrolled it, I knew with a sudden chill what it was.

The annulment of our marriage.

I lifted my eyes to her. She was smiling, but her eyes were glistening with tears. 'Yes, sir. At last. You're legally free of it.'

I sat with it on my lap for a full minute. Then I raised my head. 'But I don't want to be free, Nicola.' Dad, silent and still beside us, stiffened, and his breath hissed. I ignored him. 'You remember what I said, when the king said we were to be wed? I wanted to shame him, so I said that you were the finest lady I knew. I didn't know then how true it was. You outdo every one of them, in every way, except one, that you can't help. After all, it's not that you're too small; it's just your lack of height that makes you seem that way!' She didn't smile at the childish joke, but I somehow felt that she was softening. She leaned towards me as I spoke. 'And if you wore high pattens, nobody would know —'

She sat up as if I had slapped her. I'd hurt her. I didn't know how. I reached for her hand, but she leapt to her feet, speaking to dad, not to me. 'Sir, will you see that he understands? I can't — I can't — She gave a huge strangled sob and ran for the ladder up to the deck.

I was going to go after her, but dad stopped me. 'Leave her be, son,' he said gruffly. 'She's right. This marriage is wrong for you, and for her. She's a fine wee woman, an' generous, an' a sight wiser than you. But she's no the right wife for you. An' you're no the right man for her. For you'd grow ashamed of her, an' that'd destroy you both.'

Deep down in my heart, I knew he was right.

I was ashamed of myself, now. That didn't change the facts, though I tried to argue. 'But she loves me. I know it. And I love her.'

'Aye, son. But no enough. Or you'd never have mentioned pattens.'

There was a long silence. 'I feel sick.'

'Maybe it's the sea-sickness again.' But it wasn't the sea's motion that made me queasy, and we both knew it. It was disgust at myself.

I took out the bag with the necklace she'd thrust on me. 'And still she does this for me ... How can I face her?'

'You must, son. You owe her too much not to. But nobody's perfect. And she's a grand woman. She'll forgive you.'

At last, I stood up. 'I'm going on deck.' I didn't

look at dad. Behind me I heard the crackle of the parchment as he folded it and tucked it away in his shirt. I could have torn it up ... But I hadn't. And I wouldn't.

Reluctantly I climbed the ladder. Far ahead of us three English ships, paying the great galley no heed, were chasing hopefully after the ship they thought bore Queen Marie of Scotland. I'd better start thinking of her in English, I thought; Mary, Queen of Scots. Everyone was crowding the rails, looking back, many weeping. The mist was almost clear. The white cliffs of Calais lay well behind us, a bright ribbon of white.

Nicola was standing very straight, by the bulwarks just below the break of the poop. She also was staring back towards France, her homeland, which she was leaving forever. Maybe that was why tears were trickling steadily down her face.

I forced myself to go to her side. She glanced up for an instant, silent. I could feel her embarrassment, her fear that I'd make a scene, draw attention to her private feelings that she usually hid so brightly.

Gently, I put a hand over hers on the polished wood. She sniffed, and her hand twitched; then it lay still under mine. After a while, she sighed deeply, glanced up again, and her lips moved in the faintest of smiles. Marriage, it seemed, was beyond possibility for us; but friendship we could maintain.

Above us there was a stir of white silk. A clear voice, muffled by hard-held tears, whispered, 'Goodbye, France! Goodbye, dear France!' Marie sobbed, once. 'I fear I shall never see you again.'

There was a long, long pause. We didn't dare move, in case she realised we could hear her almost-silent, shuddering breaths. Then the queen sniffed hard, and roused herself to her usual gallant gaiety. 'Livingstone! Fleming!' she called. 'Why are we all so mournful? We're

249

going home! Cheer up! Blow your nose, Fleming! Smile! That's better! Seton, Nicola took off Master Russell somewhere. Send a page to find her and tell her to bring him here. The man has a story to tell us, about his sister Lark!'

GLOSSARY

auld — old
aye — yes, always

bairn — child

château — castle, palace [French]
coucher — royal ceremony of going to bed [French]

de — of [French]
denier — small silver coin [French]

écu — gold coin [French]

Garde Ecossaise — Scots Guard [French]

hussy — girl

levée — royal ceremony of getting up in morning [French]
lettre de cachet — letter of authority, ordering someone's
    arrest and imprisonment without trial until the letter was
    cancelled [French]
lickmadowpin — toadying

merci — thank you [French]
Mon Dieu! — My God! [French]

no — not

patten — platform shoe, sometimes three feet tall
points — laces to tie breeches onto shirt.

sou — penny, small copper coin [French]
soutane — priest's gown

teston — large silver coin [French]
tisane — herbal tea

wee — small

Other Kelpies by
Frances Mary Hendry

Quest for a Kelpie

It is a crucial moment in Britain's history: Prince Charles Edward Stuart's attempt to regain his grandfather's crown from the Hanoverian King George is in the balance.

Jeannie Main is warned that she will make a king and break a king. But how could a wee fisher lass do such a thing?

What will bring her four times into the shadow of the gibbet? And why should she risk her life by riding the Kelpie, the most dangerous monster in all Scotland?

This fast-moving tale won the first BBC Scotland/SLA "A Quest for a Kelpie" competition in 1986.

"...a remarkably accomplished first novel.... the packed, realistic story of a girl from a fisher family caught up in the '45 rising." *The Guardian*

ISBN 0 86241 136 X   £2.95

Quest for a Maid
Frances Mary Hendry

With the Scots King murdered, the path to the throne is now clear for the ambitious Lady de Brus and her son Robert. But there is a rightful heir to the throne -- an eight year old princess -- the Maid of Norway. As powerful forces of witchcraft, sorcery and wealth plot her destruction Meg and her loyal friends, Peem and Davie, risk their lives for her safe rescue. Their crucial mission is dogged with danger but the fragile young princess's life is in their hands -- and with that they hold the key to the peace and destiny of a nation!

"... a terrific novel, wholly engrossing... fast-paced, exciting and great fun." *The Sunday Times*

"I ended this novel with a rare sense of disappointment that there was not more to come! A truly remarkable novel." *Junior Bookshelf*

ISBN 0 86241 315 X   £2.25